PRAISE FOR MARGOT EARLY'S PREVIOUS BOOK,
THE TRUTH ABOUT COWBOYS:

"Honest feelings abound. Emotions go deep into the heart
and soul. A story you will remember."
—*Rendezvous*

"Beautifully honest. Ms Early writes straight from the
heart.... *The Truth About Cowboys* [is] totally
believable, engrossing and absorbing."
—*Under the Covers Book Reviews*

"In this splendidly different kind of cowboy tale,
Margot Early's distinct voice illuminates the lives of her richly
textured characters in unique and memorable ways."
—*Romantic Times*

"Margot Early has created a vivid, sprawling tale peopled
by full-fleshed characters... Her writing is gritty and
poignant, an homage to a dying breed: the true cowboy.
The Truth About Cowboys packs an emotional wallop.
Bravo, Ms Early!"
—*Calico Trails*

"Truly endearing. Truly engaging. Emotional intensity
and poignant honesty flow from every page...
Full of irresistible passages you'll want to read out loud,
The Truth About Cowboys is a book to be remembered
and read again and again."
—Laura DeVries, aka Laura Gordon, author of
contemporary and historical romance

"*The Truth About Cowboys* continues her rise to stardom in
the field. The truth about Margot Early is that she is a
brilliant and diverse writer."
—*Affaire de Coeur*

ABOUT THE AUTHOR

Margot Early's first Superromance novel, *The Third Christmas,* was published in1994 and was a RITA Award finalist for Best First Book. *The Keeper,* her second novel, was a finalist for the 1996 Janet Dailey Award. She is profiled in the *Romance Writer's Sourcebook,* published by Writer's Digest Books. *Who's Afraid of the Mistletoe?* is Margot's seventh Superromance title. Next year, watch for her miniseries, The Midwives, which will be published from September through November. Margot will also appear in an anthology, *For My Daughter* (May 1998).

When not wandering the fictional realms of her stories, Margot lives in Colorado—within sight of the San Juan Mountains—with her husband and son.

Margot enjoys receiving letters from her readers. You can write to her at: P.O. Box 611, Montrose, CO 81402-0611.

Books by Margot Early

HARLEQUIN SUPERROMANCE

WHO'S AFRAID
OF THE MISTLETOE?
Margot Early

Harlequin Books

TORONTO • NEW YORK • LONDON
AMSTERDAM • PARIS • SYDNEY • HAMBURG
STOCKHOLM • ATHENS • TOKYO • MILAN
MADRID • WARSAW • BUDAPEST • AUCKLAND

ISBN 0-373-70766-5

WHO'S AFRAID OF THE MISTLETOE?

Acknowledgments

People often ask me how I research the sometimes unusual professions and avocations of the characters in my books. Most often, the answer is that I speak at length to someone in that line of work or someone who practices that hobby— and consequently gain new understanding and appreciation for an unfamiliar art.

That was certainly true with *Who's Afraid of the Mistletoe?* For several years, our home has been filled with dishes, tumblers and mugs made by potter Bill Wilson (and on numerous days, his harmonica has wailed Robert Johnson and Muddy Waters tunes from our backyard during jam sessions with my husband, who plays blues guitar). One of the great pleasures of working on this book was learning more about the fascinating and very technical art of pottery from Bill—and gaining an even greater appreciation for the beautiful stoneware in our home. Also, Bill and his wife, Nancy, used to race sled dogs. Their dog stories and Nancy's suggestion of an additional research source were invaluable in helping me write this book. To Bill and Nancy—for all of this, my heartfelt thanks.

Finally, many thanks to my son for providing information on reindeer and to both my husband and son for their daily love and support.

All technical errors in this fictional work are mine.

Wild-grazing reindeer of the hills between the rivers
are surely strong enough to draw me and my sweetheart.
They're strong enough surely to draw two in a sled.
Wild-grazing reindeer of the hills between the rivers
are strong enough surely to draw me and my sweetheart.

—a *yoik* recorded in 1673
by Johannes Schefferus,
translated into Swedish
by Björn Collinder and
from Swedish to English
by Israel Ruong

PROLOGUE

Tarra Valley, Sweden
In the age of snowmobiles and the month of November

TAGE SKIED AHEAD of the *rajd,* the reindeer caravan, while
the snow blew at his face and clung to his five-day-old
beard. In the wind, he could barely hear the bells on the
härks pulling the sleds or even the sound of eight thousand
reindeer ankles clicking as the herd crossed the plain. He
knew this cold well. Worse than January in Minnesota,
more like sudden bone-freezing Alaskan blizzards, this
Lapland cold was the arctic cold of his youth, the cold that
had formed him. The cold he loved.

Now, it had sucked all the fat from his bones, from all
their bones. Even the dogs looked like skeletons. Behind
him, the boy was lagging. Against the white, his legs appeared as sticks, while his sister was just a small dark
bundle in the sled.

Tage's stepfather, Nils-Isak, had been right. This jour-
ney was not for children.

A selfish flame inside him ignited, and he doused it
again. The race...

Anyone would have been horrified if they knew his
thoughts. Anyone who had never run the race.

It was Tage who had said they could come on *this* trip,
though at first he had spoken as though there was only
Lars, only the boy to consider. *He has just lost his parents.*
And this archaic migration, with its perils, was their re-

quiem. A requiem for a Saami shaman, Tage's brother, Peter. Peter and Marit were both dead, killed in a car crash.

Lars was an orphan.

Hearing the boy's plea, to accompany the reindeer on their annual migration to the lowlands for the winter, Tage had remembered his own hunger to go on migration when he was twelve. Remembered that—and forgotten what autumn migration was like. That it was like...the race. Yesterday, they'd had to carry their skis, while the snow gusted off the rocky fields and into their faces. The Farewell Burn all over again.

But Tage had told his stepfather, *Lars should be allowed to come. The girl, too. We are doing things this way for Peter, for his memory.*

Doing everything right for Peter.

Nils-Isak had shrugged. *You are their guardian.*

Guardian of Peter's son. And of the six-year-old Tibetan girl Peter and Marit had adopted two months before their death.

The guardianship had been a shock as numbing as Peter's death. Worse, in some ways. The total disruption of life...of important plans.

Cool it Tage. Cool it. Try to be like other people. Try to fit in.

He wasn't sure how he ever would. He could only face the flying snow and ice that carried his brother's soul, while Snutte, his brother's dog, charged after a reindeer that threatened to stray.

He halted the *härks* and petted a velvety antler while he waited for Lars. As the boy poled closer, Tage called over the wind, "Get on the sled." Holding the lead line, he skied back to the child. His own blue eyes gazed back at him from under Lars's Saami hat with its four-pointed tail. Ice had frozen on the boy's cheeks and clumped in his eyebrows. And in the blond hair that was also like Tage's own.

There were things more important than the race.

Much more important.

In the sled, the girl waited, alert and curious. She seemed unaffected by the cold, both trusting and invincible. Her family in Tibet had been nomads. She'd lived two years in a Chinese orphanage before Peter and Marit had adopted her. Her name was Lobsang—"kind heart."

Trembling, seeming vulnerable in his new and spindly adolescence, Lars stepped out of his skis. As he tied them on the sled, he slipped on the snow in his reindeer fur boots. Tage lent a hand, settling him beneath some skins behind his sister, whom Lars immediately hugged as though she were a doll, immediately tucked in more securely. "Don't sleep," Tage ordered in Swedish.

The boy wouldn't lower his face from the wind. He gave Tage no chance to turn away. "Will we live in the United States with you?"

No, because I'm going to leave you with your grandparents or other relatives here in Lapland. People you know. I'm going to do things the way your father and mother should have arranged them.

And race...

It wasn't what came out of his mouth. "Do you want to live with me?"

The wind had gusted snow over the skins, too, and the herd was getting too far ahead. Tage heard one of the bells through the static cry of the weather. It was too cold to stand and talk. Or listen.

Lars's frozen lips vibrated, succumbing to cold, and Tage watched them, transfixed. Thinking of other lips that trembled, of someone far away and out of his life, he wondered if every family had secrets.

"Were you married to my mother once?"

"Before you were born. For a very short time. Don't sleep, and don't let Lobsang sleep." Tage headed for the front of the caravan to follow the herd, now just a film of gray in the white. Snutte was circling back to join the sleds, his black tail waving. A good dog. Tage knew many.

He missed them, missed his team.

He went mad for a moment. The race...

"*Coecci.*"

Tage stopped. Of course, Lars would speak Saami, as well as Swedish. His father, the shaman, would have insisted on that. And now, Lars had used the Saami word for a paternal uncle younger than one's father.

It was a title of respect, and the sentiment was mutual. It couldn't be otherwise in this wind, a week after Peter and Marit had died, when he'd watched their reedy son carrying his skis over icy rocks, never uttering a word of complaint.

Their son.

"I want us to go with you," said Lars. "I could help you train dogs."

"Ah." Tage nodded, meaning only that he had heard, that he acknowledged his nephew's wishes. "Don't sleep." He skied away, skied hard till the lead *härk* lowered its head, antlers jutting forward, and began to pull.

I want us to go with you.

The request was lead inside him. Heaviness and...fear.

It was what he'd been afraid Lars would say. Because now that he'd said it, Tage could not say no.

Winter Twilight

CHAPTER ONE

Thanksgiving
Manitou, Minnesota

SHE CALLED THE FIRST night they were home, on the house phone, not the business line for Good Dog Kennels. Although, it turned out, she was calling about a dog.

"Tage?"

He recognized the rough boyish timbre, the way she spoke the two syllables of his name. *Taag-uh.*

It surprised him that she'd used the phone. Until now, she had never, never once, called him. Letters or e-mail... Or visits. Always he had gone to her, except one March in Alaska, the last time they were together. She'd seen him off in Anchorage, had hugged him at the Iditarod checkpoint when he held the silver halfway trophy brimming with three thousand dollars' worth of silver ingots. In Nome—two Nomes ago—he'd had a ring for her, and she was gone, like a deer through the trees.

She said his eyes were like the fjords.

She stuttered severely.

He hadn't forgiven her for Nome.

Lars was out of earshot in the kitchen, Lobsang upstairs, asleep after a bowl of cereal. Tage and the boy had been speaking English—good practice for Lars; his school English had suddenly become useful. Tage had been telling him about Craftsman houses and how this particular Craftsman home had come to be his. As much as possible, he had avoided discussing dogs, except Snutte, the dog they'd brought home. Craftsman houses, not dogs or races. How odd that Sarah had called in the midst of that conversation. About the house.

He spoke into the receiver. "Hello." Frozen snowflakes made a white glaze on the panes of the three casements in the alcove; each held eighteen panes. Beyond them, a field of white dots descended against the security lights near the kennels—the long stone building and the otherworldly concrete dome guarded by the trees of his woods. He listened for singing, canine voices.... He heard it, as always.

At the pace of molasses pouring from a jar, Sarah said, "I need your help. I have a...dog. It's a w-w—"

He waited, his mind on the children, Lars especially. But Lobsang, too. She'd lost her birth parents on a pilgrimage when she was four. It was a mix-up that Peter and Marit had adopted her; they'd planned on a two-year-old. Now the Tibetan girl had lost them, too, before she'd even learned their language.

In days, a couple of weeks, he'd learned to care.

"W-w-wooolf. Hybrid."

Tage snapped alert. "What?"

The silence dragged through a minute, imprisoning both listener and speaker. At last, he knew she wasn't going to talk, so he did. "Mostly dog. Right?"

"N-n-n-noooo."

Anyone who owned a dog should master the word "no."

He cocked an ear for sounds from the back of the house. All was silent there, though the wind beat the maples outside. Though he could always hear the dogs.

"I ask you to train him."

I ask... She'd substituted words, avoiding difficult sounds. No speech therapist recommended the technique—or trying to hide a stutter.

She hadn't stuttered now. She'd asked a favor.

Tage sank down at the cherrywood table he used for a desk. A stack of file folders sat before him, illuminated by the orange glow of an isinglass lamp, one of those he'd inherited with the house. Out of habit, he checked the television screen in the corner of the alcove, against the walnut frieze. Closed-circuit TV monitors in the alcove, the kitchen and his bedroom allowed him to monitor all the kennel buildings from the house. The only dogs he couldn't see were his own—outdoors in the sled dog compound. Sometimes he slept with them. Many nights, he'd slept with them. "You want to come here?"

"Yes. Unless you've—"

A block. While she struggled to say the next sound, he waited, his chest and stomach muscles rigid. His reflection, that of a blond man in a bright blue wool shirt—a colorful shirt with handwoven red braid at the cuffs and neck, the Saami shirt he'd worn home on the airplane with Lars—made a broken and watery image in the windowpanes.

"M-m-m-*maaarried* someone and it's awkward."

"No." As fast as he could say it, the race forgotten.

"I could—"

Tage's own breath slowed, relaxed, as though by relaxing his vocal folds he could relax hers. He heard her sudden inhalation. No speech came. *Don't hang up, Sarah. It's okay.*

"S-s-s-stay in the studio. If it's still there."

The studio? Why would she offer to stay there, out by the lake, where... "The cabin needs some work." She shouldn't come. Lars was here. And Lobsang.

It couldn't be helped. He didn't owe Sarah, but he owed the memory of a man who had cared about Sarah. Who would have wanted Tage to give her what she needed. to help her in this predicament. Sarah had never asked for anything before. But now that she had, it was the same as when Lars had said he wanted to come to Minnesota to live. Tage couldn't say "no." Just, "You don't train wolves. They train you." Like his point dogs Wa and Tu-kin, bought from a musher in the Yukon. Like Molinka, a stray bitch who'd wandered into his campsite one winter night and started a dog riot. Gazing past you with slanted eyes the color of lemons, they did as they pleased.

It was some time before he noticed the silence. She'd never responded. He asked, "What do you call him?"

It took her a full minute to begin the first sound. "M-M-Mooooses."

She'd named her pet for a stammerer. *They will not believe me nor hearken unto my voice.... I am not eloquent, neither heretofore, nor since Thou hast spoken to Thy servant, but I am slow of speech and slow of tongue.*

So was Sarah. And she had trouble with *M.* "Does he know his name?"

An indecisive sound.

"If not, you should change it to something easier to say. Something with two syllables that starts with a vowel. Like my dog Anna." He'd come home to find Anna, his lead dog, in heat, confined to the isolation kennel by his assistants. *Anna.* He wouldn't let go of Anna. Couldn't. "Where are you, Sarah?"

"Colorado."

He knew the word was a substitution, easier to say than Sneffels. Sneffels was an old mining town in Colorado's San Juan Mountains. During winter, it practically shut down, dangerous because of avalanches and stubborn ice on the sidewalks. That was perfect for Sarah, who spent her days skiing the back country or hunkered over her wheel in the nineteenth-century carriage house she used for a studio. He'd stood in the snow with her on winter nights while the kiln glowed and shot flames through the brick, while her pieces fired.

The studio at his place sat in a remodeled cabin on the lake. Sarah had used it summers during college, years before Tage came to the U.S. She'd looked after things whenever the property's former owner was away, visiting the Arctic.

The first owner. At the funeral, when she and Tage had seen each other for the first time in nine years, Sarah had called the property's owner "the once and future king." With her stutter, it was hard to tell if she was being ironic.

After an interminable silence, she spoke, saying another one of those mystifying things that should have made him wonder just what Arthur had done. Tage was incurious. "It's a pity I can't name him after Arthur."

THEY HUNG UP MINUTES later. She promised to e-mail to say when she was leaving Colorado. She would drive, bringing all the bricks for her reduction kiln. The studio already had a raku kiln and a salt kiln. Would Sarah *use* the salt kiln? The thought had him tensing. But firing ceramics had inherent dangers, with any kiln. *Forget about it; you can talk to her when she gets here.*

"Training" Sarah's wolf could take...years. Tage hadn't said that. Just, *It will take time.*

She had responded like a woman who'd never run away.

He hadn't mentioned Lars and Lobsang.

Or Nome.

Or all the Nomes to come.

Standing, he listened again before he headed through the living room and the hall and past the door to the cellar and around the corner to the kitchen.

Lars was crying.

You didn't intrude. You stepped back into the narrow passage with the pantry shelves and listened to a boy quietly sobbing for his parents. You didn't go to him, because his dog was there, and dogs knew what to do.

But Lars must have sensed his presence. The muffled sounds stopped.

Still, Tage didn't go in, but slipped through the dining room to the library. From the bottom shelf in the wall of books, he plucked one of Arthur Tennyson's texts about the Saami. It was Arthur who had owned the Craftsman before Tage, who had left it to Tage in his will. Arthur had been Sarah's stepfather, one of several. Nearly everyone close to Sarah, Arthur included, had married many times.

Tage would show Arthur's book to Lars, then go out to the kennels, check on the dogs and exercise Anna. Light exercise... Get her used to the difference. And focus on the other dogs, clients' dogs. His assistants had run the kennel and school beautifully while he was in Lapland.

When Tage returned to the kitchen, Lars was forking chicken into his mouth. His eyes and nose were red in a thin face at that stage of awkwardness when hormones were beginning to explode and bones had far to grow. He had lost three fingernails from the cold on the migration, but they would grow back. And now that it was over, Tage knew it was right that Lars and Lobsang had come.

"Here's a book Arthur Tennyson wrote," he said. "You'll recognize people in the photos, and we're all in the acknowledgments, including your father." Though not Marit, Lars's mother; Marit hadn't joined the family yet, during those years Arthur had lived with them off and on. The anthropologist had died suddenly when Lars was seven months old—died and left his house and land to Tage. At that time, more than a year had passed since Marit said she loved Peter. Since Tage had said, *Okay. Okay, I see that,* and had let them have their happiness. And Lars.

"Why did he give you the house?" asked Lars.

"Didn't he have children, do you mean? He did." Children and stepchildren, like Sarah. "But if he gave it to all of them jointly, they would have sold it. To give it to one of them—" Sarah, for instance "—would have shown preference." Instead, Arthur had divided his life insurance among his family, and Sarah had given her portion to the others. There was only one thing she'd wanted, and Tage had let her have it.

"But why *you?*"

Why not my father? Lars was asking.

You didn't mention infidelity or disloyalty. You didn't dishonor a father before his son. *He's Peter's son, Tage. Remember that.*

"When I was your age, I used to ask Arthur about the house. He told me about Gustav Stickley and the Arts and Crafts movement. He said that the house had been designed for simplicity and utility, yet that if I saw it, I would perceive it as a castle." Lars and Lobsang had seen it the same way. They'd gaped at the fieldstone-and-shingle exterior, at the casement windows with all their panes reflecting the snow on the maples. "You might say he indoctrinated me to Stickley's way of thinking about space. That the space in a home should feel open, with few barriers between common rooms, so that families will be together. That elaborate ornament is a distraction from simple pleasures. From community—from being together."

"But you have no family." The moment Lars had spoken, he looked down and became absorbed in his food, almost as though no one had said those words.

Peter's boy had nice manners.

Peter's boy.

Tage thought of his dogs and didn't say he'd never needed a family. "Not till now."

The child was too polite to argue, to say that this awkward arrangement was not the same as a family.

Taking his seat, Tage realized they were eating off

Sarah's dishes, the ones she'd made for Arthur. The salt glaze gave the pieces an orange peel texture; the pattern on each tumbler and plate represented the leaves and berries of the mountain ash. She'd fired them in the salt kiln in the studio. Every night Tage ate off her plates, drank from her tumblers and never thought about it. Not lately.

He made himself explain to Lars that the woman who had made the dishes was coming to stay, to train a wolf. She would have her own cabin, out by the lake, and shouldn't be in their way.

Then, having introduced Sarah, he could make Lars see why Arthur Tennyson had settled his estate as he had. "Arthur was once married to Sarah's mother, when Sarah was a little girl. They weren't married long, but he always treated Sarah as a daughter, till he died. He brought her to Lapland one winter when she was a teenager, and she fell through the ice, and I pulled her out."

"Ah," said Lars. Even a boy could understand—that it might be a reason to give a man a Craftsman house and four hundred acres touching the Superior National Forest.

Tage made himself say, to Sarah's salt and pepper shakers, "If you ever need to talk, Lars, about your feelings, I will listen. My father died when I was eight. It can make a person...angry."

Lars didn't answer, which was how Tage had known it would be.

Sneffels, Colorado

THE STUDIO IN THE carriage house was cold. The woodstove heated it well, but tonight the cold stole through gaps in the floorboards and in the walls. It didn't matter. Sarah wasn't working, except on disaster relief. Moses had overturned a tower of metal shelves holding 120 bisque-fired tumblers and mugs. Her Christmas order for a gallery in nearby Telluride. A week's work.

Now the wolf dog, who had urinated and defecated in fear at the crash of breaking pottery, lay under the wedging table, tearing into a plastic bag of commercially pugged clay. His thick white coat and slanted amber eyes said "Ellesmere Island, Greenland"—arctic places. His intelligence startled, awed and sometimes frightened her.

Sarah grabbed her shop broom to sweep up a powdered glaze formula, weighed out for the Telluride pieces; it had sat in a five-gallon pail with the lid off. At least Moses wasn't eating the glaze.

Tage's voice was still with her—the distinctive accent she knew as different from other Swedish accents, because his first language was a Saami dialect and his second Norwegian. Or maybe just because he'd come from above the Arctic Circle; his blood was different, and so was he.

In Sweden, his family were still reindeer herders. Lapps, though Arthur had told her not to use that word. *A Lapp is a patch on your clothes. It implies they all wear patched clothes, that they're disreputable. They're not Lapps. They are Saami.* She'd learned the word at fourteen, on the plane to Sweden, to Lapland—which *was* all right to say, though Lapp was not. Arthur had plucked her from her grandmother's Victorian in Sneffels, the same house where Sarah now lived, and had given her adventure. Fairy-tale magic and winter twilight.

Lapland had been a storybook come to life, with a sixteen-year-old named Tage Nikkinen on every page. Since he'd come to the U.S., they'd filled more pages together. But there were chapters that Tage hadn't read.

Sarah dumped the ruined glaze in a large plastic trash can. With one eye on Moses, she used a trowel to scoop up his mess and drop it in a plastic bag. She wouldn't punish him for his mistake. After all, he was in the habit of throwing himself at her when he greeted her, and she'd gotten used to bracing herself against a wall and being licked all over the face. She'd just braced herself against the wrong thing, and when she stepped aside...

The urine was harder to deal with than the rest. It wasn't just the puddle on the floor, where Moses had peed in fear. A yellow streak ran down the side of her electric kiln and adorned a two-foot lamp base she'd made on special order. One hand against her forehead, pushing strands of light brown hair back toward her ponytail, Sarah toed through the broken unglazed shards turning to pink dust on the concrete floor and snatched a towel from a hook.

He'd done it again—there, on that box, packed with tumblers and toothbrush holders to ship to a bed-and-breakfast in Taos.

Unlike the broken pottery, Moses's peeing wasn't an accident. Puppy accidents happened on the floor.

Wolves scent-marked.

Moses had been with her for almost five months now. For fun, Sarah had begun keeping a list: Things My Wolf Dog Has Destroyed.

It wasn't fun any more.

When she looked up he was gone, and she whirled, expecting to find the door open and no Moses. He knew how to turn doorknobs, even open certain locks. Once he'd gone missing for a week. She'd barely slept and had spent every day hanging flyers and combing the mountain trails on a hopeless search. Miles of wilderness.... But no, this time he'd moved only a few feet, to lie beside the stacked pails of feldspar and other glaze materials that had missed the crash.

He was chewing on her notebook.

Sarah flew toward him, though she knew better. You didn't take things from Moses. Once he stole them, they were his.

But this wasn't her wallet or the twenty-dollar bill she'd left on the counter or her hiking boots or a pair of wooden snowshoes or receipts for income tax or any of the other things the wolf dog had devoured. That notebook was her life. It contained fifteen years of glaze formulas recorded nowhere else, except—in the case of the two most frequently used—in her mind.

His growl had her jumping back, her breath stuck in her throat.

His gums seemed almost bloody against his teeth, his ears stood forward, and there was no dog in the shape of the long white body guarding her notebook. Saliva had already smeared the ink on the pages, but if she could only get it back from him...

She opened her mouth. *Moses, come.* The words lodged in her brain, and she tried to say them, tried to get her lips firmly around the first syllable of his name. *Moses, come.* When she was small, she used to jump up and down to try to make the words come out. Now her mind seemed empty. Panic filled the void. *Moses come.* "*M-M-M-Mooooses,* come."

He ate the formulas for cobalt blues.

There was nothing to do. Nothing except start working from memory, getting out her book on glazes and trying to remember percentages of feldspar and flint.

She couldn't think at all. She was still hearing Tage's voice and seeing his face in her mind. Tage...

Asking him for help was better than approaching a different dog trainer. It was better than letting a stranger see and hear her stutter.

But instead Tage would see her that way, at her worst as she tried to give commands to Moses, tried to say "sit" and "come." Making ghoulish faces, turning red, all in front of Tage, who was a model of physical perfection, confident bearing and total coordination. A man with the strength and endurance and tenacity to have run the Iditarod five years in a row.

It's all right, Sarah. You can pull it off.

She knew tricks to avoid stuttering. She was less sure how to deal with the emotions of returning to Minnesota, to Manitou, to Arthur's lakes and Arthur's woods. There the cycle of the seasons was eternal, though she'd half expected everything to die when Arthur had. That place, his place, was her Avalon and her Thebes. With eyes open or shut, she could see the climax maples shading the Craftsman. Could see the cedars, the spruce and the white ladies of the birch forest. The cabin and the water where the loons flew low. Whispering Wind Lake would be frozen now, a white field like the lakes in Sweden. Sarah hoped that would help; it hadn't last time. He'd died in winter.

And she had avoided visiting Arthur's place since his funeral. Since that weekend she'd first made love with Tage.

WHEN LARS WAS IN BED, Tage went out to check on the dogs, to make sure they were set for the night. He visited Anna in the isolation kennel behind the house, took her for a brief run in the snow, the kind of exercise that could only leave her grumpy and puzzled, then toured the long stone building nearest the Craftsman, refilling water, finding lost chew toys for his clients' dogs.

The stone building housed twenty-four runs on one side and a kitchen and grooming area on the other. Each kennel had a pophole connecting it to an outdoor run sheltered by an overhang and floor-to-ceiling sides to prevent fencefighting. Tage had built those runs himself, converting the old stone building. The dome had come years later.

A hundred-and-five feet in diameter, it stood at the far end of the stone building, flagged with aspen and birch, its entrance angled toward the parking area. The dome contained forty more indoor runs and the kennel office, and its back door opened onto the training field.

He would never have built it if he had run the Iditarod first.

He would have made his entire life sled dogs—real dogs. Instead, his life was divided, and he was divided.

And he was about to lose the half of himself he preferred.

He paused outside the chain-link fence, outside the place where his dogs lived. He'd seen them two hours earlier, but they went mad again when they saw him, mad from having missed him and wanting to run. Jo gobbled up snow, tried to climb the fence. Boots, his best wheel dog, wagged his tail. Dickens—who'd saved a now-deceased dog from an earlier death on the Iditarod—stood very still, as though sensing something amiss. All sixty-four—missing Anna—lived in this labyrinth of snowy runs circling part of the dome's exterior. Tage had raised most from puppies, had indulged them and delighted in their nature. Others, like Comet, the lead dog who'd brought him the halfway trophy, he'd adopted from the animal shelter. Several more he'd bought from other mushers. And Molinka had come from the woods. All of them lived by different rules than the dogs he trained for clients. Respect for humans was the only law here, except those the dogs made themselves.

And in the end, respect for humans always came second to a taut tug line. To how heartily they would pull a sled.

He refilled their water bowls, adding beef broth to make sure they drank before the water could freeze. The radio, wired to speakers indoors and out, played Christmas carols, and when they'd lapped up their water some of the dogs sang along. Others licked and gnawed the skulls of beaver carcasses bought from trappers and moose bones donated by a neighbor. Tage's youngest dog, Jedi, watched him anxiously, as though worried that he'd go away again.

Tage tried to ignore it, all the small things. Tried to ignore the dogs and knew at the same time that he was putting it off, putting off what he had to do. What he had to do because of a boy who looked like him and a girl who didn't. What he had to do because people needed him. Children.

Things would be different now.

WHEN HE CAME BACK INSIDE, he did what he knew he must. He called another musher, a man in Ely, an hour away.

His friend said he'd rustle up some help and come right then—no problem.

And while he waited, he avoided drinking but just returned to the sled dogs' compound, to choose friends. To say goodbye to fifty of them—the number he had arbitrarily chosen to let the musher in Ely take. That would leave fifteen, including Anna. Plenty for recreational mushing, even local sprint races if these distance dogs could learn to sprint. Not nearly enough for the Iditarod.

It was right for him and right for the dogs who would go, most of them his best dogs. His friend from Ely would treat them as they deserved. Some of them, Tage was sure, would run from Anchorage to Nome this spring.

Anna would stay... Letting himself in the compound, he called out his other lead dogs—Comet and Molinka—and moved them to runs on the end. Molinka was ten years old. Comet, well—you didn't give away someone who had saved your life, someone you loved that much. In darkness, while Christmas carols still played, he chose the others he would keep. Unsentimental choices now. He wouldn't trust any big dog alone with a child as small as Lobsang, but he kept the most gentle dogs.

Not Dickens, who drew blood every time Tage put him on the tug line. Not Tukin, with his wolf eyes always watching for weakness in the leader, whether the leader had two legs or four.

Tage wondered how he could love dogs like that so intensely.

When he'd sorted through them, he got the other dogs ready to move, then went into the dome to wait. Killing time with clients' dogs, whistling along with carols.

It was time to hang lights and trimmings around the kennels for Christmas. Even at the height of training, the season always made him miss Sweden, miss his family, miss the winter twilight, even the weeks of darkness.

It would be a nightmare for Lars, with his parents dead.

Peter and Marit. Lars would always be their son.

The past trapped him, stayed with him there until he couldn't stand it, till he forced himself to think deliberately of other things. Sarah. Wolf hybrids.

He headed for the house, and Snutte met him at the door. He'd gotten out of the boy's bedroom.

Lars had said, *Snutte can sleep in my room.*

He's your dog, isn't he? But you're responsible for him, too. And no dogs on beds. He'd said that not from concern about the beds but because Lobsang was so small; Snutte was going to have to learn to take commands—obedience commands. If you wanted that, you had to show him every minute who was the leader. Subordinates did not sleep on beds.

"Hello, Snutte."

The black herding dog, the Saami dog, followed him into the living room.

In the alcove, Tage switched on his computer, and while it booted up he fed the fire. You couldn't go among dog trainers without hearing opinions about wolf dogs. Mushers had opinions, too. Tage had owned many dogs with wolf eyes, with wolf ways. What was more, he had seen the work of wolves who came across Finland from Russia in the winters. No, wolves were not what people thought. Neither were wolf dogs.

They weren't good house pets. He didn't know how he was going to get that across to Sarah or what they could do about it now. While the computer worked and the modem linked him to the web site for the International Wolf Center in Ely, he squelched dreams of changing his mind. Telling his friend to go home.

Sending two children back to Sweden, to live with his married sister—or with his parents.

Running the Iditarod.

Impossible.

The wolf center's web page referred him to sites of wolf hybrid enthusiasts and of wolf hybrid rescue facilities. Tage tried to imagine a musher sending a dog to such a place and couldn't; there was always another musher willing to try a dog—or fifty. But the refuges were crowded.

He printed some articles, carried them into the living room and sat on one of the cushioned benches in the inglenook, his back against the oak. Snutte began playing near the alcove, tugging on a rubber kong toy Tage had given him and pouncing on it when it bounced away.

Trying to read, Tage saw Sarah Calder instead of words.

He dropped the sheets on the bench and got up, headed into the library as though there were answers there, among Arthur's furniture and books or in the two ceramic pieces sitting atop the panels that flagged the entrance to the room. Arthur had made those abstract vases fired with brilliant raku glazes. It was Arthur who had first put clay in Sarah's hands.

After more than a decade, Tage was still a stranger here. The Craftsman remained Arthur's place—especially this library with its walnut roof beams and row of tall casements, each with a smaller stained glass panel above. A window seat stretched beneath them for the length of the room, blending with the wainscot. Hanging lanterns and a floor lamp with a stained glass shade cast an orange-gold light on the room, on a rare Frank Lloyd Wright cantilevered couch.

Yes, the house mocked Gustav Stickley's vision. Even Lars had seen why. No family had ever sprawled itself comfortably through these rooms, not for decades anyhow. This Craftsman was a relic and a showpiece—not a home.

Tage had known homes. His earliest memories were of being inside the *lavvo*, a cloth tent arranged around a frame of stout birch poles. After his father died and his family had moved from Norway to Sweden, winters were spent in a small frame house on the outskirts of Jokkmokk. Summers, they had lived in a *goattieh*, a traditional Saami hut. He and Marit had lived the same way when they were married.

It's nighttime, Tage. The darkness makes you feel like this.

But he sat through the play again, the play of old recollections replete with detail and feeling. Marit and Peter and their new baby, Lars. Leaving Sweden when Arthur died.

You couldn't agree to be guardian to a child and stay distant. It wasn't right...to withhold love.

Again he let go of the race. March. Just months away.

Tage thought of Sarah, as though Sarah was a refuge.

False. Sarah was thin ice. She admitted it herself, with an honesty that *wasn't* thin ice but was as hard and certain as permafrost. She'd admitted it three years ago at the Iditarod checkpoint, beside his fire, with his dog team sleeping nearby.

I don't stay. I'm not a staying person. Don't count on me.

He had said, *I want to count on you. Come on, Sarah.*

In her potter's studio, she conjured colorful vessels from earth, water, fire and air. He found her magical and untouchable. She'd said once that she found him the same way, but she'd meant something different. She'd felt infatuation, not enchantment. Her favorite childhood book was *Snipp, Snapp, Snurr and the Reindeer;* she'd shown him the battered hardback.

He'd laughed. *If I had any reindeer now, I would name one of them Prince, for you.* Like the reindeer in the book. And before leaving Nome where she'd never shown her face, he had bought a new sled dog puppy and named him Sampo, like the dog in the book. Sampo turned out to be slow, and Tage had sold him and never sought Sarah's company again.

He distrusted magicians. His brother, Peter, had been magic, a shaman. Peter... Sarah... And one other.

There had been a perfect, mutual enchantment between Sarah and Arthur, her once and future king.

THE HALL CLOCK tolled 11:00 p.m. Outside, tires crushed snow and gravel. Tage dragged himself to his feet.

DURING THE NIGHT, the mercury dropped below zero. When he awoke, Lars Nikkinen knew it by the quality of the icicles on the eaves outside his bedroom, by the texture of the snow frozen on the branches of a maple in front of his window. He knew because he was Saami and his father had taught him such things and had taught him all the words for snow. This snow was *vacca,* track snow, new snow fallen on old snow. His uncle's Saami boots left their imprint as he crossed to the kennels below in only sweatpants and a T-shirt.

Through the icy panes and a frustrating web of tree branches, Lars watched him let a husky-type dog, one of the sled dogs, into the big maze of chain-link beside the dome.

You can call me Tage, he had told Lars days before. *"Uncle" makes me feel old.*

And he *wasn't* old. Tage was younger and taller than Lars's father was—*had been*—and he had the kind of body Lars wanted, the sooner the better. When Tage wore no sweater, you could see he was all muscle, no fat, like a movie star or something.

Lars touched the cold window with a finger missing a nail and saw his fingerprint left there. It *was* better to be here than back in Jokkmokk in school, just as it had been better to be on migration than left at home to wish he was dead. At least Tage realized he was a man now, even though he didn't want to be, simply because the most terrible thing that could happen had happened to him.

The window and the bars of tree branches grew even more watery looking, and Lars stopped his tears, didn't let himself cry. His father hadn't raised him to be this way. His father had taught him that death was no evil, that one mustn't be sad for those who died. He had taught Lars to feel the souls of the trees and the snow and all the animals.

The thought made him turn, blinking past the sight of his father's troll drum, his shaman's drum, on the bureau. Where was Snutte?

The bedroom door was open. Had Snutte opened it? He was a smart dog. Tage had said Snutte might be bored with no reindeer to herd, that Lars must train him, give him work to do.

In his pajamas and bare feet, knowing that his parents were dead and he would never see them again, never feel his mother touch his hair or his father hug him, Lars went out into the strange hallway in the house of hardwood, his uncle's house, and whistled for his dog.

Another door opened, and Lobsang stood there in blue pajamas.

In Swedish, Lars asked her if she'd seen Snutte. As usual, she said nothing. He'd never heard her say a word, except when his father had tried to talk to her in Tibetan, using a Tibetan phrasebook. Well, now Lobsang was going to have to learn English. He would talk to her, would help her.

After he found Snutte. What if Snutte had done something in the house? Chewed on the nice furniture or peed on things? What would Tage do?

Lars hurried down the stairs, over the cold smooth wood, and heard Lobsang following. She was very small. He'd laughed when he'd first seen her and learned she was six.

The front door was opening.

Tage came in and saw Lars. "There you are. Good morning, Lobsang. Snutte, come." He led the black herding dog into the house, and Snutte wagged his curled-up tail and leaped toward Lars, then Lobsang.

Tage had found Snutte! Or maybe he'd taken Snutte outside himself. The dog was on a lead, a lead attached to a nylon collar that looked like it was made from climbing rope. As Lars crouched to pet him and hold him back from Lobsang, Tage said, "He let himself out of your room. Now that we know he can open doors, we'll have to be careful he doesn't run away. How did you sleep?"

The language was a little difficult for Lars, but he managed to come up with the answer. "Good." Going to sleep was always better than waking up and remembering about his parents.

"Lobsang?"

As she shrugged, Lars said, "She doesn't talk."

Tage smiled. "Ah, but she just did, and we understood her." The hall clock tolled 7:00 a.m. "If the two of you help me with the morning work, we can take the dogsled out later.''

"Okay.'' At least it wasn't boring here. And when Lars had helped feed the dogs yesterday afternoon, he'd actually stopped thinking about his parents for a few minutes.

But somehow that was even worse.

AFTER BREAKFAST, all three went out to the kennels, Lars leading Snutte. "We'll put him in with the sled dogs,'' Tage explained, as though he hadn't lost fifty dogs in the middle of the night.

Lars noticed their absence. "Hey, where are all the dogs? You had more.''

"A friend is taking them. He's training for the Iditarod.''

"Oh.''

While Lars let Snutte into a run where Boots and Jedi waited, Tage greeted Comet and let him lick his face. *It's going to be fine. I'll be fine.*

Lars and Lobsang would be fine, too.

He studied the girl, to see her response to the boisterous dogs and the chaos of barking and howling. She was small enough that he would have to padlock the sled dogs' run, and he told Lars so. Lobsang seemed to be listening. But not shaken. Peaceful.

Perhaps she wouldn't need much from him beyond food and shelter.

Right, Tage. Dogs needed more than that. A little girl who didn't speak English and a twelve-year-old boy—not just any boy but *Lars*—now depended on him. As the thought settled, it was like dozing off in the cold; needing to act yet being unable to move.

Take care of the dogs.

Both of his assistants were gone for the weekend—they'd worked extra hours while he was gone—so he'd have to clean all the runs himself. His system used water brooms, and the pens were squeegeed afterward. Hot water piped beneath the concrete, indoors and out, provided heat, and the floors always dried immediately. Ultraviolet lamps throughout the kennels were an additional precaution against infection.

He found ways both children could help him with the chores. Lars helped move dogs to exercise runs, and Tage guided Lobsang through a similar task with the toy breeds. Then Lars manned the water broom while Tage started Lobsang mopping the ceramic tile in the reception room in the stone building. After that, he would teach her how to measure dog food into bowls. She was bright and seemed happy to play with the water.

When the kennels were clean, Tage brought boxes out of storage in the dome and carried them to the entryway. "Christmas lights," he explained. "Do you think you can hang them around the eaves of the stone kennels, Lars? The hooks are already up, and I use this ladder." It was small, practically a stool. He would string lights in the trees later.

As Lobsang touched one of the colored bulbs, Tage watched Lars. Would this first sign of Christmas bring him new pain?

Lars just lifted the box, ready to take it outside.

I don't know him, Tage reflected. As he'd never troubled to know what Peter and Marit's life together was like. Besides seeing him when he was an infant, a couple of visits to Sweden had constituted Tage's sole contact with Lars—before this. On those visits, Tage had avoided him, as he had the first time he'd seen him, the day after his birth.

Hold him, Tage. It's all right, Peter had said.

No, thank you.

While the boy hung the lights and looked after Lobsang,

Tage swept the fieldstone steps of fresh snow, shoveled a path to the kennels, then cleared the road with the tractor and blade. When he returned, the children were building a snowman. Tage found sticks for the arms, then went into the dome and brought out the harnesses and lines. So different this time. Seeing the gear, the sled dogs sounded a cacophony and raced about their runs.

Lobsang followed him in her reindeer fur Saami boots, boots Tage's mother or sister must have made, while he laid out the gang line and anchored the sled with a single prong snow hook. He sorted out the three dogs he wanted and tethered them by chain leads to stakes behind the stone building.

Lars crouched beside the sled. It wasn't the toboggan sled Tage had used for the Iditarod. This was a touring sled. Tage had split and bent the white oak, laced the rawhide. The boy glanced at him, as though to ask if he could touch it. But before Tage could give an encouraging nod, Lars caught sight of the team. "Only three dogs?"

"They're very strong. I thought we'd tire them some, then give you a chance to drive. Yes?"

Lars's eyes showed a spark of pleasure, grief forgotten for an instant. It was a small triumph.

Over what? Do you want him to forget his parents?

"For now," Tage said, "you can help harness them."

It took far longer than it would have taken Tage alone, but Lars seemed interested, eager to learn. When the dogs were ready, standing with gang line tight, Tage stepped on the runners of the wooden sled and nodded to Lars to climb in the basket with Lobsang. "Hang on to her, Lars." He freed the hook from the stout birch he'd chosen as an anchor and whistled sharply to the dogs.

The sled was off, the runners whispering and clattering in the snow, the cold biting his face. Slow... So different with two passengers. These two. The path was ungroomed, but the sled flexed with the turns. On each corner, Tage shifted, spreading the runners slightly, pulling the weight of the sled into each turn, keeping out of the trees. He did it automatically, unconsciously.

He tried not to think or feel too much about the days and weeks and years to come. Running behind the sled on a climb, he tried to ignore the fear. He was thirty-six and used to living alone with his dogs. He'd almost forgotten to have Lobsang brush her teeth that morning; then, he'd had to do it for her. Neither child had bathed since they'd left Sweden.

And Lars... *Death.* Suddenly no mother and no father. The grief had only begun.

They entered the national forest and joined an unplowed road leading north over low hills, through balsam fir and white and black spruce. Twelve miles north lay the Boundary Waters Canoe Area Wilderness. The fire-colored berries of the mountain ash defied winter; nuthatches flitted among the shrubs, taking their fruit.

"Whoa!"

The three dogs, dogs he'd never expected to be running in quite this way, eventually slowed and stopped.

Twisting in the basket, sprinkled with snow thrown free from the runners, both children squinted up at Tage, who was anchoring the sled. Tage, who was again reliving the decision not to hold an infant Lars.

Tage smiled then. "Your turn, Lars."

IT WAS 10:00 P.M. when he checked his e-mail.

The day should have turned his hair white; it had been that kind of day. He'd gotten Lobsang to take a bath and Lars to shower. He'd washed their clothes but left their boxes of belongings untouched.

He could use another pair of hands, and another pair

was coming. But Sarah Calder needed *his* hands—with her wolf.

One e-mail message was from his stepfather, Nils-Isak, welcoming him home. The other was from Sarah.

Tage,
I'm leaving tonight because the weather is good. See you sometime Sunday. Won't stop much because of Moses. Thanks for your help.

Sarah

Tage composed a return e-mail, explaining about his brother's children. But the post contained a subtle lie of omission, a lie he didn't want to tell Sarah. A lie about Lars.

He deleted her message and his reply.

In the kitchen, he drank wine from one of her mountain ash goblets and dreaded Monday morning, when he would enroll both children in school and leave Lobsang in a world where no one spoke her language. Lars was going somewhere worse—junior high.

He'd turned the heat down some and brought Comet inside. There was no reason not to acclimate him to nights indoors now. No reason...

At the trestle table, with Comet at his feet, Tage turned the goblet in his hands and pictured Lars and Lobsang as they'd sat in the sled that day. Especially, he saw Lars, with his winter eyes and his Saami hat, and he knew a father's fear—he would not teach his children well. That a boy would grow up wrong or take a fatal misstep because no one cared enough—because of death and abandonment and all their sudden consequences.

Tage saw Lars and saw himself in his face.

Counting the features they shared had become another ritual of night.

CHAPTER TWO

Sunday

HE HAD FORGOTTEN about the wolf.

When Sarah opened the tailgate of her twenty-year-old Jeep Wagoneer, the crate was there, facing sideways among glaze pails, clay, skis and snowshoes, a CD player, soft pale gold kiln bricks. Her luggage must be under the tarp on the roof.

Falling flakes dropped a curtain around the vehicle. The sled dogs were baying and howling and racing in their runs, but Tage didn't even glance their way. Lars and Lobsang were in the dome training Snutte. The herding dog had begun chasing wildlife, and basic obedience and tracking were better outlets for his energy. A dog that intelligent needed work to do, a sense of mission.

Sarah pulled the crate across the tailgate, turning it around. Snow gathered in her straight, light brown hair, ending in clumps of white halfway down her back. So far, she had spoken one word. *Hi.*

He hadn't said much, either. He'd forgotten the golden and blond lights in her hair. Forgotten her skin. Forgotten that her beauty was a cold and intense sensuality—brown eyes and a mouth that could be almost sulky at rest but that drew his gaze, drew everyone's gaze. A curse for a stutterer. Sarah hated her mouth, and he loved it.

"The roof leaks," he said, "on the cabin." The place by the lake had originally been a one-room cabin built by the French in the eighteenth century. After World War II, Arthur's predecessor had constructed the addition, two rooms sided in mint green clapboard with a glassed-in porch. Arthur had bought the place the year he'd both married and divorced Poloma Calder, Sarah's mother. Sarah was seven. "You don't have to stay out there. There's room in the house."

"It's okay."

He could only trust her judgment. It was twelve years, after all, since Arthur had died out there. "I'll try to do something about the roof tomorrow. The propane is coming, too." For the kilns. Tage's voice trailed off. From the depths of the crate, topaz eyes watched him.

The creature cowered, ears flattened, lips retracted. He extruded his tongue and whined softly, and when Tage briefly met his gaze, the wolf dog snapped his teeth. He'd already soiled the crate. *Fear.*

A wolf. It was really a wolf, not a wolflike dog as Tage had hoped.

Sarah opened the crate door.

"Don't take him—" Tage began.

Moses lunged at her, knocking her backward into Tage. Tage caught her and held her upright while the huge white animal, hind legs now on the snow, forepaws on Sarah's chest, washed her face with his tongue. The yellow eyes were sweet as innocence, and Tage knew he could not train Moses—probably not even to pull a sled. The wolf would train them instead.

Not a pet.

He eyed the massive paws near his hands. "If I let you go and he knocks you down, he might regard you as prey."

"Down," said Sarah.

"Off. Down means 'lie down.'" *Lie down with me, Sarah.*

"This takes a while. For him to get down."

It was snowing on them. He could smell her shampoo.

Tage released her and she stepped back, and the wolf seemed to have had enough and got down.

As Tage grabbed his collar, Moses lowered his hindquarters, head and ears. He whined, then snapped his teeth again. Sarah bent down to clip on a lead.

Backing away, out of biting range, Tage tried to detach himself from what she'd done. From the fact that she'd adopted what looked to him like a wolf. An arctic wolf. Long legs, sprawling paws and a tail that hung down long and straight instead of curving like a sickle or curling up over the back like a domestic dog's.

No, Moses wasn't a pet.

And Tage thought of Lobsang.

Moses was beautiful, and his eyes were not a dog's. His brain was larger than a dog's. Wherever he'd come from, he carried the charisma of his ancestors, and Tage was not immune.

"Come," he told Sarah, nodding toward the stone building. Number 24 was the pen at the end, with the outside run big enough for a great Dane. But not for a wolf.

"I can take him out to the cabin."

Even when fluent, she spoke more slowly than anyone else Tage knew, and her lips quivered.

"No. If he gets loose…" He imagined explaining to the forest rangers in Tofte.

The glass doors on the dome's vestibule opened, and the children came out into the snow. Lars and Lobsang wore Saami dress, which was much of the clothing they owned. Most Saami saved native dress, *gakti*, for formal occasions. But Peter had worn his blue-and-red tunic and four-pointed hat every day, proclaiming his cultural identity. Even in the U.S., Tage wore his frequently. It was good for business. Americans were fascinated by "Lapps."

Sarah's lips parted as her dark eyes tracked the figures.

"The boy is Lars, my brother Peter's son. Lobsang is his sister. She was adopted from Tibet three months ago. She doesn't speak English, but Lars does. Peter and Marit were killed in a car wreck earlier this month. They appointed me guardian of their children." Tage squatted on his heels, keeping his body turned sideways to Moses, and the wolf dog took a tentative step toward him, then lowered his body, licking his tongue toward Tage. "Hello, Moses. Yes, you're quite a wolf, aren't you?"

Time slowed while Moses sniffed him, then backed off, then came closer, then fled. Sarah's nose and lips had grown numb before Tage's hands touched the wolf dog, gently rubbed his throat. Dazed, she watched the children approach.

Children. Tage had children, now.

That meant he must not be training for the Iditarod this year. Any year.

Oh, Tage. Hard. Very hard for him to give that up.

But he'd be a responsible guardian, Sarah knew. Like her grandmother had been. She had lived with her grandmother from the time she was two until Grandmother died when Sarah was nineteen.

She should lure Moses back inside his crate and get out of here.

Relax, Sarah. There was nothing for her in Sneffels. Learning that his pieces would be late, the Telluride gallery owner had canceled his order. Her other orders had been filled and shipped. She'd unplugged her answering machine, happy to disappear. Tage's situation had nothing to do with her. She would be living in the cabin, with her hands in clay. But would he stay away from the studio?

Tage had never stayed away, not until this last couple of years. Before that, he'd visited as often as he could stand being apart from his dogs. They'd made love intensely. Outside in the snow, in the heat and light from her kiln in Sneffels. In her grandmother's house. In Anchorage, Alaska.

And in the Craftsman, sixty yards away.

"I'm sorry," she said. "About—" His brother's name lodged in her mouth. "P-P-P—"

Tage didn't say the word for her. He never finished her sentences the way everyone else, even Arthur, always had.

"P-P-Peeeeter and his wife."

"Me, too."

The children reached them. In the wet, heavy flakes, against fieldstone and birch bark, the miles of intricate braid on their costumes was festive as the bright Christmas lights on the eaves. Once, Sarah had e-mailed Tage, *I could marry you for the clothes.*

He'd answered, *I would marry you for no clothes.*

All jokes. She could not marry him.

"A wolf," said the boy, in an accent like Tage's. His pale eyes narrowed on Moses.

Snow collected on the wolf dog's creamy coat, turning it lighter. In the kennels, dogs howled, and Moses lifted his head to answer. The haunting song shivered over the ice and seemed to make snow drop from the trees.

"Lars. Lobsang. This is Sarah Calder."

Sarah smiled tensely, wanting the shelter of the cabin by the lake, wet clay on her hands, a kiln's transforming fire. Solitude. What did you say to children?

It's S-S-S-Sarah. Do you want to jump rope, S-S-S-S-Sarah?

She'd never been good with children, even when she was one.

Moses made for the woods and was stopped by the leash in Tage's hand. Still, he tried to go, fleeing the din of the kennels. Ignoring the resistance, Tage walked toward the training field. After a second's hesitation, Moses followed, keeping his distance, looking toward the woods. When they'd gone twenty feet, Tage turned. His tracks began to etch a large triangle in the snow. The wolf's path, each foot falling directly in front of the other, crossed his, then crossed back as Moses explored the range of his leash.

After a dozen turns, his boredom showed. After two dozen, still spacing himself from Tage, he lowered his head and allowed himself to be led to the kennels. The sled dogs howled and barked. With a nervous glance at the children, Sarah turned to get the crate. She should clean it, but where?

It was eleven years since she'd been here—twelve in February. The only things unchanged were the house and the forest. Snow had candy coated the window ledges and roof of the Craftsman and dressed the leafless maples nearby.

She looked for a white-haired man with Alec Guinness eyes and the beaked nose of an eagle smiling at her from the porch. No Arthur, but his ghost would always be here, and she would always see it. Like Heathcliff, she *wanted* to see it.

Briefly her eyes lingered on a snow-draped shape outside the garage. Though she'd never seen it before, she knew what it was. An automobile chassis built into a rig for training the dogs in warm weather. A musher's chariot. A vehicle that moved by dog power and steered by human speech.

She swallowed, looked away.

Okay, the stone building had been here before, and obviously Tage had kennels in there now. Maybe she could hose out the crate inside? Awkwardly, she eased it down to the snow. If she carried it past Tage, maybe he'd show her where she could clean it.

Behind her, the boy kicked the fresh powder. The girl

stood staring into the Wagoneer, apparently enthralled by the contents.

At least the Tibetan child didn't expect conversation. It was restful to know that someone didn't understand English and that you didn't have to talk to her.

Lifting one end of the crate, Sarah dragged it through the cold flying flakes as Tage secured the gate of Moses's new kennel. Footsteps crunched behind her. What was with these kids, that they were following her like she was the Pied Piper? It had happened with men before, but never with children.

Tage stepped past her, took the crate.

"Th-thanks." As she began to block, she turned the word to a whisper and looked away, through the birch and aspen toward the monolithic dome, the new and most obvious change to the grounds. It was science-fiction modern, and Arthur would either have loved it or hated it.

"Lars, get the door." Tage waited for his nephew to open the door to the stone building. They all followed him in, and Sarah's eyes swept the kennel runs to her left as their residents began barking. Tage set down the crate near the grooming area. Leashes and collars hung on numbered pegs from the wall. The ceramic tile floor was broken by six-inch drains.

As Tage cleaned the crate, Lars asked Sarah, "What are you going to do with the wolf?"

Sarah shrugged. As she hunted for words she knew she could say, her face grew hot and she couldn't think at all. *It's happening, it's happening...* The mortification took over, built on itself like a snowball growing as it barreled down a hill.

"You can't train a wolf," said Lars. "They're wild. The people up north, they cross them with dogs and teach them to pull sleds, but they keep them on chains and beat them. You have to."

"Thank you for sharing your wolf-training philosophy, Lars."

At Tage's words, Lars raised his head with a start, then said something in Saami and walked out of the building.

The door swung slowly shut behind him.

Sarah looked to Tage.

"That was the Saami way of saying, 'Excuse me for living.' Not your fault."

"I didn't think it was."

He'd finished with the crate. Noticing the tiny Tibetan girl in her Saami dress and reindeer fur boots, he picked her up and carried her toward the runs and began talking to her about the dogs as though she could understand his every word.

He was just a man with a child in his arms. He was just Tage, gorgeous Tage, holding a pretty little girl from Tibet.

But it seemed as though the friend of Sarah's youth had suddenly stepped away from her, joined the ranks of married with children, passed into some realm she couldn't enter. They were a family—Tage and a moody twelve-year-old and a little girl he could still carry.

Leaving them, leaving the crate, Sarah found her way to the old oak door and let herself out into the snow and wind that had become a real storm. She didn't know why she suddenly felt like crying.

DON'T LET HER STAY.

In his room, Lars directed the unspoken plea to his parents, as though they were in a position to change things. The wish was something he would never voice to Tage. *I can't stop him from having a girlfriend.*

And Tage had never once said that Sarah Calder *was* his girlfriend.

He hadn't mentioned that she was beautiful, either.

But she was, and Lars knew how the story ended. The

man-to-man companionship he'd known with his uncle was gone.

Lars wanted more mushing, more advice about training Snutte. Tage thought Snutte could earn a Schutzhund title. Tage had promised to take Lars to a dogsled race. He'd mentioned ice fishing and hockey on the lake. But anyone could see that a beautiful woman who showed up with a wolf, showed up to *stay*, was going to wreck the only things that made life tolerable.

So what? Did you really expect things would be great here?

Lars had. Ever since his uncle had said he and Lobsang could go on autumn migration. He trusted Tage. Or had until now, till Tage had turned sarcastic about the wolf.

He missed his father. His father had never been sarcastic. Annoying sometimes, like when he'd decided they should adopt a girl none of them had ever met. In any case, Lars had never had to worry about some stuck-up woman who looked like a model showing up and his father not loving him any more.

Now... Well, things had never been worse. His parents were really stupid to die in a car wreck and leave him and Lobsang to have to live with other people. They were really stupid.

And he missed them so much he didn't see how he could go on.

SHE WAS OUTSIDE Moses's run when Tage carried Lobsang from the building. Snow covered Sarah's Scandinavian sweater and clumped in her hair. "Where's your hat?" he asked.

The wolf dog huddled in the darkest recess of the run, eyes watchful.

Sarah shrugged.

Tage resisted desire. He could make her warm and

needy. But he'd grown away from using Sarah's powerful infatuation with him. When a woman had a shaking desire, you could get almost anything from her. But he hadn't been able to get what he wanted from Sarah, not with any dignity.

The child in his arms seemed unable to stop looking at her. No wonder. Sarah was very pretty. Tage smiled at Lobsang and kissed her cheek. She grinned, missing teeth. How quickly she trusted. How quickly she accepted that the people who had brought her from Tibet were gone, that she had a new home and a new caregiver.

What made a child that way? It could have been bad things, but more likely it was something good. Maybe the way nomads treated their babies. *If only Lars could adjust as easily as you.*

The Christmas lights on the eaves cut through the gathering darkness, the growing storm of white. Perhaps they could ignore Christmas, he and Lobsang and Lars.

He had to speak over the wind, which was now banging a loose gutter above their heads as the temperature fell, cut through clothes to flesh and bone. "The studio is unlocked. I left the key on the wheel." A potter's wheel like the one he'd seen her use in Sneffels when he'd come to visit. Her hands that knew how to shape mugs and bowls knew how to touch a man, too. "Lars and I stocked the woodpile and cleaned the chimneys." Her life's work was playing with fire. But he said, "You won't use the salt kiln without telling me."

Her sorceress smile was no smile—just darkness. Introducing sodium chloride to a firing kiln released chlorine gas. The salt kiln had killed Arthur. "I'll tell you."

"You can stay in the house." She could stay in his bed, if she wanted.

"It's *all right*, Tage."

Remembering Nome, he stopped pressing Sarah and adjusted Lobsang's bonnet. She handled cold like a Saami, but she was still just a child and he should get her inside. "I'll drive out there behind you and light the woodstove."

"It's not necessary." In fact, it would be worse, Sarah decided. She should be alone returning to the lake. She hadn't seen the studio since she was twenty-three, on the morning after Arthur's funeral, when she'd crept out of bed before Tage and skied down to the frozen lake.

"It's necessary," Tage said. It was three quarters of a mile to the cabin, through the woods on an unplowed road. This was a storm blowing her snow-laden hair. "Let me tell Lars we're going."

TREES JOINED THEIR LONG limbs over the road, and occasionally snow showered from the branches, onto her windshield. Sarah was glad for the Toyota 4Runner behind her as the Wagoneer pressed through the heavy veil.

The little girl must have stayed behind with Lars, because Tage had come out to the garage beside the Craftsman alone. He seemed like a natural father, even looked like he could be Lars's father. In the irony of life, Lars looked more like Tage than like Tage's dark-haired brother, Peter.

When they'd driven for some time and Sarah at last made out the shape of the cabin ahead, she couldn't see the lake beyond. Snowing too hard. It didn't stop her knowing where she was. Once, Arthur had said all this would be hers. Months before he died, he'd reneged. *I'm leaving it to Tage. You'll see—that will be best.* As if he'd known he was going to die soon—and had planned that she and Tage would end up together.

She parked near the three-sided lean-to that sheltered the kilns, where Arthur had been found. When she left the Wagoneer, the wind almost blew her into the trees. She'd forgotten about the wind off the lake, how much it could snow on this shore.

She remembered sunsets on water. Mosquitoes.

Another car door slammed, and Tage came toward her, his skin that shade of raw honey, his dark eyebrows like Japanese brush strokes on his face. Her heart lurched hard, saying that he held the key to some internal safe she'd never opened. At fourteen, she'd believed in destiny. He'd rescued her, after all, from ice and paralyzing cold. He had flattened himself on the ice and lifted her out as though her water-soaked clothes weighed nothing. In seconds, he'd stripped her of her wet things and dressed her in reindeer fur while she trembled and fell in love as only a fourteen-year-old could love.

Twenty years had passed. Things had happened.

The teenager become a man caught her shoulder, steered her toward the cabin, the old part. When he opened the door, it banged against the log wall. Inside was chill and dead, and drafts licked Sarah's skin.

Clean, though. A wool blanket from Sweden, one of Arthur's, was stretched tight over the mattress on the lodge pole bed. Red numbers glowed the time on a clock radio on the nightstand.

No mosquitoes. No humid heat.

The snow was actually visible through the broken, bowed roof. It wouldn't leak, thought Sarah, till the cabin warmed up. An aluminum milk pail stood beneath the gap in the timbers and tar paper. The cabin tried to be the same place it had been many summers before and failed. At being the place of Arthur's death, it had more success.

She was incomparably sad and knew it didn't show. The last time she'd needed to share sadness, she'd been a child.

A bag of clay blocked open the door to the studio addition. The one-room cabin had a small stove, but the larger stove in the studio had always provided better heat.

Sarah wandered through the door, onto the speckled linoleum. Behind the windows was the glassed-in porch; beyond that, the white lake. Here was Arthur's wedging table, Arthur's wheel. The door to the old kitchen was open.
Metal shelves held things he'd fired in the raku kiln. Arthur
had left the studio clean. He'd been firing just the one
piece.

Tage opened the door of the big stove. He'd built the
fire already, but he lit it now, and it caught at once, growing fast. He always did things like that very well, she
thought. On the first try, as though his life depended on it.

Sarah sat at the wheel, pressed the foot pedal. The wheel
spun.

When she lifted her foot, Tage had shut the door of the
stove and stood beside it, watching her. His eyes told her
nothing of him. Affection and curiosity had made her and
Tage friends; desire had made them lovers.

But they were strangers by design.

"I'd forgotten how beautiful you are."

That was how he talked, in his sexy accent, and Sarah
had to believe him. He wouldn't lie. Lies came from cowardice or kindness; Tage feared nothing and knew better
ways to be polite.

His perfect simplicity reminded her of Arthur's house,
the Craftsman. The thought made her laugh.

"What is it?"

His boots were suddenly beside the wheel. They were
reindeer fur, too, like the children's. She knew he wore
them without socks, that he stuffed them with sedge grass
brought back from Sweden.

"It occurred to me that Arthur thought you would be
the perfect ornament for his house."

After she'd spoken, she glanced up.

Tage knew that trait. She talked to some other point,
then looked at the person she'd been addressing. But never

looked him in the eye. It was more of a quick check, as though to see if the listener was still there.

"You," he said, "were Arthur's idea of the perfect ornament."

She reddened.

He shouldn't have said it. He knew she hated the suggestion that Arthur's loyalty to her could have sprung from anything but a stepfather's love and compassion. Usually, Tage was careful never to make it—more careful than he wanted to be. "I meant only that he loved you."

Her color intensified. She was in agony, and he had done it to her. While she recovered, he studied the top of her head. There were silver-white hairs there, blending with the shades of blond and light brown. He had them, too.

He forgave her for Nome.

"Sarah." He crouched beside her and slowly spun her stool to face him. Her eyes fastened on him with a cold stare he ignored. "Do you really want to spend life alone?"

No reaction or response.

"You're going gray," he said. "So am I. Are you ever lonely?"

She shook her head, once. She was a lake in January, when there were no thaws unless you made them. Sarah had always claimed she didn't want another man. *There's no one else, Tage, all right?* She claimed she wasn't fit for the long haul, that she would drop out and go away. He'd always suspected that was a lie.

Her intense blush was too recent to forget.

Give up, Tage. She just said "no."

Tage stood and wandered back into the cabin. The timbers were creaking and the roof had begun to drip. Water pinged into the metal bucket. Opening the door of the smaller stove, he lit another match. As the fire caught, she came in, and he asked, "Did you think to buy groceries?"

"Yes."

A woman who wanted him would have forgotten.

"I'll help you bring in your things."

A half hour later, he left her to her solitude, hating her the way he had when he'd come home from Nome. And vividly jealous of something he couldn't see.

SHERYL CROW COMPETED with the wind whistling in the chimneys and with the creaking of the old cabin next door. *At least, I thought to bring music.*

Her fingers shaped an ornamental tea bowl. She was building it from hand, in traditional style. For years, she'd missed the raku kiln and the dazzling glaze effects it had made possible, but she had resisted building one in Sneffels. No salt kiln, either. Now, for as long as she was here, she would make raku pottery, moving pieces from the heat with tongs, feeling closer to the blaze than she did with any other sort of firing.

She swallowed, biting her lips together hard. It was past midnight. Arthur came and went from her thoughts. Increasingly, Tage stayed.

You're going gray. So am I.

As though neither of them had other options. Like the world was short of women or women didn't like Tage.

Or like they were meant for each other, and he was just waiting.

No should have been enough a long time ago. She'd never said it.

She'd said *yes*. In her bed in the Victorian in Sneffels, trying to ignore her grandmother's memory. It would always be her grandmother's house, and Grandmother wouldn't have approved of a blond man naked in front of the living-room hearth with Sarah or out in the snow by the kiln. They'd had Christmas without clothes, feeding each other glasses of *glögg*, until she'd grown indiscreet and briefly fluent.

She'd known all the time that he was falling in love and that she wouldn't—not in a way that needed him.

Relationships were either like theirs—dignified—or they were broken, like all of her mother's and all of Arthur's. Poloma, her mother, had been married so many times Sarah literally had to stop and count husbands if someone asked the number. And her father—well, Joel Calder was married now, but Sarah knew what that marriage was. A story for the television, for his constituents. A U.S. senator should be happily married, should have a family.

Should ignore the stutterer his first wife had borne.

Why, Sarah wondered, couldn't she have inherited her father's gift for eloquence in public speaking? Instead, she'd become a stutterer like Poloma. Poloma, who covered with a Marilyn Monroe whisper and thought life was a European spa.

You didn't even show up in Bath, Mom. But when had her mother ever kept an appointment with her? Never.

Sarah's fingers caved in the side of the bowl. It was after midnight, and her hands had grown uncooperative.

Something rustled in the corner, and she peered at the shadows. A rodent of some kind. They always got in. Squirrels, chipmunks, mice. She'd have to find the holes, block them the best she could.

Once, she and Arthur had rescued a chipmunk together. It had died.

She shivered and let her mind wander.

It returned to her parents.

Christmas was coming. She never heard from her father any more. Maybe he'd gotten tired of her not answering the phone. Her mother's call would come either the day after Christmas or days later. Actually, once in a while she managed to remember Sarah on Christmas Day, but those occasions were rare. Gifts arrived in June.

You're going gray. So am I.

What did Tage think? That she wanted to settle down and have kids? She'd told him "no." She didn't even like children. And now he had some.

Guilty, she contemplated Moses in Tage's kennel. It was a relief to work without him destroying everything in sight. Each day, her aggravation toward Moses warred with her pleasure at being loved unconditionally, the way no one in her life had ever loved her. The wolf dog shared her bed at night, sprawled beside her. Sometimes she woke in the morning with things in her room chewed up, but an animal's companionship was straightforward. No judgment.

Giving up on the tea bowl, she cleaned up and switched out the lights in the studio. A rectangle of orange glowed around the door of the stove.

Are you ever lonely?

She'd been lonely in his arms.

She had brought flannel pajamas to sleep in, but the bed was cold, even under the Swedish blanket and a down quilt. Arthur had loved down. Feather pillows and fine linen.

Arthur...

This was the place to think of it, alone.

She got up, opened her duffel bag and dug through her clothing in darkness until she felt the cold shape with its platelike surface interrupted by carefully molded ridges in some places, warped by overfiring in others. The pits from the salt glaze were smooth beneath her fingers.

She could barely make out the expression of the mask, a bearded man releasing a scream of anguish. It had been left in the kiln too long; besides the warping, the glazes had run. Arthur had been dead three hours when he was found.

The wooden walls shivered and creaked. The metal of the stovepipe expanded with a pop.

She lay down, holding the mask.

Tage had no imagination, or he would have guessed. Or else he didn't care... She liked to think him shallow and unfeeling. Round up the usual suspects; any excuse would do. Tage wasn't good enough or strong enough or smart enough for her.

And she forced away the disturbing reality of those two children in Saami costume, a twelve-year-old who had lost his parents and a little girl who couldn't speak English. Tage had carried the little girl in his arms.... As Sarah neared sleep it seemed to her that Tage was moving away from her, a child on each side of him.

The cabin creaked again, and her bed shifted in the night.

She was thinking of Arthur and holding the mask when the roof collapsed, burying the bed in snow.

CHAPTER THREE

COMET HEARD THE SOUND on the porch before Tage. As Tage opened his eyes to darkness, the dog whined at the bedroom door and wagged his tail, ready to greet an intruder the only way he knew, with universal love.

Downstairs, someone was knocking.

It had to be Sarah. Which meant something was wrong. The wind still scraped tree branches against his window.

He hurried. When he opened the door a minute later, snow blew in with a white-covered figure. Comet whipped her with his tail and spun in circles round her knees.

"Sarah." As she slipped on the hardwood in the vestibule, Tage caught her, then shut the door. Snow showered off her pumpkin-colored guide parka.

Sarah's knees wobbled—not from the work at the cabin, trying to save furniture, putting out the fire in the woodstoves, tucking away the mask. Not from skiing through the night because her car wouldn't start. Just from knowing Tage held her in case she should fall.

Here she was. In Arthur's house again.

She straightened.

The hanging lamps in the hall painted warmth on the wood. Words came with difficulty. She pressed on the floor with her foot as a familiar husky cross sniffed her. Comet, Tage's lead dog. A reminder of Nome. "The c-c-cabin c-c-c-collapsed. I s-s-s-saved what I could and shut the door to the addition. I think everything's all right."

"Except you. Are you hurt?"

"No."

She could have died, Tage knew—and he would have found her in the morning.

"Come in by the fire. Better yet, let's get you up to the bath. I'll find you something to put on."

While the blue-eyed dog parked at her feet, Sarah sat on the bottom step to unlace her ski boots. Tage knelt and untied them for her. The lamp caught the white-and-gold lights in his sleep-tousled hair, and the sight of his shoulders in a worn Norwegian sweater soothed Sarah for no reason.

In a shivering daze, she let him remove her boots and rub her feet through her wool socks. Suddenly, his head lifted, and he looked past her.

Sarah twisted to peer up the stairwell.

The Tibetan girl's pajamas were pale blue.

Tage said, "Hello, Lobsang."

Reaching the foot of the stairs, Lobsang sat down beside Sarah and stared at her.

"Hi," Sarah whispered, shaking as warmth flooded her veins.

Lobsang said, "Hi."

Tage sat back on his heels with Sarah's feet against his thighs. Lobsang had spoken. To Sarah. *She thinks you're beautiful, Sarah. That's why she looks at you, why she likes you.*

"Sarah was staying in the cabin by the lake, Lobsang. It collapsed." He demonstrated with his hands, and her eyes examined each motion.

He rubbed the firm muscles of Sarah's calves. The only women he knew who skied faster or harder than her lived in Lapland. "Should I go out to the cabin tonight?"

She shook her head, riveted by the child. He'd seen Sarah cold and wet before but never so affected by it. The accident had done this. "Were you inside?"

"Yes."

She must have been buried in snow and debris....
"Come, Lobsang. Let's take Sarah upstairs and find her
some dry clothes."

Lobsang trailed after them while Tage guided Sarah to
the second floor, his arm around her shoulders.

Once, for no reason he could see, she shuddered and
gave a small jump backward, as though she'd seen a ghost.
Her hair whipped his face as she searched out his eyes.
"M-M-Moses. Can he come inside?"

No, your wolf dog cannot come in my house. "Not tonight."

In the bathroom, Tage filled the massive claw-foot tub.
Saami art and the art of other arctic cultures adorned the
walls. All of it was contemporary. Arthur had never collected artifacts. And Tage had altered little in the Craftsman.

"Lobsang, would you like a snack?" he asked. "Something to eat? I'll be back, Sarah. Are you all right?"

She nodded and sank down on the lid of the toilet. Her
eyes reflected the water running into the tub.

She was sitting there minutes later when he returned,
after leaving Lobsang to the fascination of the closed-
circuit TV monitor in the kitchen showing the dogs in their
runs.

Sarah had shut off the water.

He closed the bathroom door and locked it, and when
she came to him he helped her out of her wet parka, then
lifted off her sweater. Drawing her to his chest, his fingers
touching the wet cotton of her turtleneck, he measured her
heartbeat. Fast. Racing. So was his.

"I need help," he said. "With Lars and Lobsang."
There was no reason to tell her about Lars. He'd never
told a soul. Earlier, it would have been indulgence. Now,
it was too late.

Tage bent his head over Sarah's, and she kissed him right away. Shaking.

"I can't help," she said, lips trembling. "I'll end up leaving."

"No, you won't. It works like this." He kissed her again, and she pressed into his thigh. "You lean on me a little, Sarah, and I lean on you a little. We begin to trust each other. We already do—some."

"No, we don't."

He lifted his eyebrows and bypassed her words. "I want to marry you. I wanted to in Nome, and nothing has changed. I won't leave. You won't leave. You're not your mother."

She pulled back. "I know who I am. You don't."

She'd spent twelve years running away, and Tage knew exactly who she was. He hated her again, and he asked her what he never had. He formed words for the ghastly. "Did you sleep with Arthur?" As soon as he'd said it, he wished he hadn't.

Her answer was a hiss. "Yes. As a consenting adult."

The room shifted for Tage, became bright and intense and moving, all the fixtures glinting like crystal, like evil and magic. Like Arthur, who had gone ahead and done what he wanted.

Sarah... Sarah couldn't have wanted it.

He met her eyes and knew she had.

SARAH WATCHED THE movement of the old-fashioned handle as the door clicked behind him. Shaking, she stripped off her clothes. The heat leached into her feet and calves, then the rest of her body as she lowered herself into the water and shut her eyes, held her hand against her face.

The aching rhythm in her chest matched another sensation rising along her spine. The shut door was the final curtain on childhood dreams of the friend who'd pulled her out of the screaming cold, who'd taken her into his tent and dressed her in reindeer fur and fed her reindeer meat.

And married a Saami like himself.

Sarah had seen the postcard from Nils-Isak Nikkinen, Tage's stepfather, to Arthur. Reading that Tage was married, she should have felt little. At the time, she hadn't seen him for more than seven years. But she'd been raised on fairy tales, and the postcard had jarred her. *Oh, this is real life. He wasn't the prince, after all.*

In real life, the prince could be as old and wise as Merlin. As Arthur.

I want to tell you something, Arthur had said after the fact. After what had happened between them. *You must put this somewhere, and it shouldn't be in the cupboard of shame. We have never shared a home. You were never my ward. At various times, when you were a child, your family entrusted you to my care, and I never betrayed that trust in thought or action.*

She believed him, simply because he'd always smiled upon her and Tage, always encouraged letters and friendship, always encouraged her teenage crush.

When she'd turned to Arthur on that June night, it was as an adult. She had never considered him a father. Only a friend. But Arthur had known what her mind would have to bear afterward and that all she could do was replay his words.

There are stories older than this life. There are common threads in mankind that explain what happened here. Don't succumb to shame.

It haunted her. Had *Arthur* succumbed?

Shame was thick in the air now, like perfume. The scent was disillusionment. Tage's. *What did you expect, Sarah?*

She'd expected this.

Twenty years ago, when Tage had rescued her from the

ice, he had averted his eyes from her naked body while helping her dress. In fact, it was nearly an hour before he was able to look at her. Then he'd said, *You are very beautiful. Are you hungry?* While they ate, he'd told her that in the old days, when a Saami man wanted to marry a woman he would lead his reindeer caravan three times around her tent. If she came out and unhitched his reindeer, that meant she wanted to marry him.

His family's religion was Laestadian Christianity, named for the man who had converted the Saami. The Laestadians frowned on premarital sex and birth control. The faith was strong in revivalist feeling, in the ecstasy of the spirit—perhaps what had first caught the attention of the Saami, who so revered nature. When she visited Lapland, Sarah had accompanied Arthur to a rare church service, and Arthur had told her that the Saami preacher was telling ghost stories. Nearly all the Saami Sarah had met spoke more often of troll drums and *yoik*ing—the singing of Saami poetry—than they did of their Christian faith. Tage never went to church any more.

But all cultures loathed certain things. In all cultures, certain things carried a vast burden of shame. Why else did the masks of the Greeks sometimes weep?

Sarah sank deeper in the hot water.

Well, Tage wouldn't ask her to marry him again. At least she wouldn't have to worry about that.

The thought shouldn't have made her cry.

ACROSS THE HALL, Lars Nikkinen sat by his window in the dark. The night was so stormy he couldn't make out the colors of the Christmas lights on the kennels, couldn't make out the shape of the dome. Of course, he never could see them that well anyhow, because of the tree; in the summer, with leaves on it, it would hide his whole view.

Who cares? Summer was a million years away. And

right now, tonight, Sarah was in the house. He'd heard
Tage speaking to her in the hall, speaking to Lobsang
about her. Everyone was awake, and for some reason his
uncle's girlfriend was in the house.

It changed everything.

Since his parents had died, he'd known Lobsang needed
him.

But she didn't now. She had Tage and Sarah. He
couldn't do anything for her that they couldn't or wouldn't
do.

A warm tongue swept across his hand, and Lars reached
his fingers into Snutte's thick black fur. The dog's black
paws thumped on his knees, and Snutte licked his face. It
made Lars cry, and he didn't even care that he was crying.

Death wasn't bad for the person who died, but it was
awful for everyone else. If his parents expected him to be
happy for them, they expected too much. He wanted to be
with them. He didn't want to wake up another morning
and have no parents.

The herding dog tried to climb up in the chair with him
and sit in his lap, tried to put his forepaws on Lars's shoulders. In Saami, Lars told him to cut it out. Snutte was a
smart dog. He wriggled into a sitting position beside Lars
and sat calmly, watching Lars's face.

Lars cried harder, hugging Snutte, and Snutte licked his
face and ears. The one person who understood was a dog.

IT WAS ONE OF THE RARE times in his life that Tage had
found it difficult to speak. The others were after Marit had
said she loved Peter and after he'd first seen Lars and after
an Iditarod checker had handed him Sarah's note in Nome.

It was important, he knew, to speak to Lobsang, so that
she would learn English. In fact, he'd already begun trying
to teach her words, using a Dr. Seuss dictionary and a
Richard Scarry book. She'd finished her cereal, but right

now he could only show her how to rinse her bowl, then how to open the dishwasher and where to put the bowl. One of Sarah's bowls.

The power of language would undoubtedly return when he saw Sarah again. He'd promised her dry clothes....

He filled a glass with water and made Lobsang drink it, a bad but expedient substitute for brushing her teeth again. "To bed," he finally said, trying to smile.

Speaking the language of all children who have been loved, she lifted her arms. Tage picked her up, hugging her close. Odd how, in some way, it already felt as though this child had never been anyone's but his.

And how the other, Lars, would never be anyone's son but Peter's.

HE KNOCKED.

Sarah opened the bathroom door, wrapped in a towel, and stared past him, through him, like a blind woman. Or a stutterer.

He handed her a pair of his sweatpants, a long-sleeved T-shirt and a sweater, and said what he'd planned. "You can use the sleeping porch. The windows are on it now, and I've built a fire. If you need more blankets, you know where to find them."

Sarah searched his face. *If you need more blankets, you know where to find them.* Was that a barb? She didn't think so.

"If you're too cold out there, we can switch rooms. But I think you'll be comfortable." This way, Tage reasoned, Lars and Lobsang wouldn't get the wrong idea, wouldn't perceive her as more than a temporary guest. If he gave her his room, they might think she'd come to stay for good. "I'll let you dress."

A backward step into the dark hall removed him from her space. Across the stairwell, beyond the banisters supported by square spindles, the door to the sleeping porch stood open. A faint orange glow from the fire he'd lit brightened the opening. Tage followed the railing around the stairwell and past the window seat in the spacious upstairs hall and entered the enclosed porch. Flickering firelight reflected on the windows. There were no blinds except the red maples outside, obscuring the isolation kennel where his lead dog, Anna, slept. He wished he could run her with the other dogs; dogs who were gone. He wished he could do it right now, tonight, and not return for days.

A Mission-style double bed was the focal point of the room. Tage slept in here in the summers, when the glass was off the windows, when the humid Minnesota heat came through the screens and the mosquitoes buzzed outside, landing on the barrier.

Sometimes, even in summer, he used the fireplace with its copper hood. Like the matching piece on the downstairs hearth, it was engraved with a Craftsman legend: *The lyf so short, the craft so long to lerne.*

Although he'd never seen Arthur in his house, it was easy to picture him standing by the hearth, trim and elegant and rugged.

Had it happened in here?

Unlikely. There had been no bed here when Arthur died.

No... It would have happened across the hall.

It could have happened anywhere. In Sneffels even, where he'd made love with Sarah himself.

You're not really surprised, Tage. You're horrified but not surprised. He lived in recollection for a moment. After the funeral, in bed, kissing. *Have you had a lover, Sarah?* She was shy, very shy. And he'd had just one—Marit, his wife, who had fallen for Peter.

Sarah had said, *Yes.* She'd had a lover.

She hadn't looked him in the eye, not till they were

making love. When he'd asked her to look, when she had, the shadow was there, touching him. Things out of kilter.

Oh. Oh, God, something is black here.

He jumped as Sarah entered the room.

"Thank you," she said. "It's fine here."

No. It hadn't happened here. Because then it wouldn't be fine.

Again, he imagined the man by the hearth, blue eyes reaching into his own with some older wisdom that Tage suddenly saw was a lie. He couldn't forgive either of them.

He only nodded to Sarah by way of good-night, and in the hall he shut the door behind him, feeling that he was locking up an attic of shame, of secrets.

Sleep was not an option. He raided Arthur's cellar and chose the wine he knew to be the finest, because Arthur had told him almost as much about wine as he had about Gustav Stickley and Craftsman houses.

The warm clothes were in the closet by the front door. He laced on boots with lug soles for traction instead of Saami boots. He wanted to see the wolf. He didn't know how Sarah would ever be able to live with Moses. If anyone had the answer to that, it was Moses. Moses was who he must ask.

The wind had stopped. The snow had not. Moses was the only animal, except the sled dogs, that he'd left outside. The outdoor runs were sheltered from the wind, but Tage preferred his clients' dogs to exercise under supervision. Outside, the chances of escape and injury were higher.

If any of his clients could have seen the sled dogs now, their tails wrapped over their noses, a layer of snow collecting on their fur, there would have been questions. Sometimes people asked anyhow, and he answered, *Mushing is a different discipline.* From obedience. He didn't say that most of his dogs would not come when called and that he liked them that way and so he never called them.

Moses begged different treatment.

He begged more room.

Tage shone a flashlight toward the wall of the run, not wanting to frighten him. Eyes glittered in the night, reflecting the beam. Even when Tage let himself in the gate and set down the bottle of wine, the wolf kept his distance.

Tage addressed him in Saami, asking if he liked Minnesota. An outdoor speaker, to keep the sled dogs company, broadcast the public radio station. Now that the wind had died, Tage could hear a selection from George Winston's *December*. He'd taken Sarah to hear the pianist one winter when he visited Sneffels. They'd driven up to Telluride for the performance.

Since Arthur's death, Tage had spent perhaps fifty nights in Sarah's bed. She'd refused invitations to come to Minnesota, even if he bought the plane tickets. Coming to Alaska for the Iditarod had been her idea and her expense. She'd been here just once since Arthur died. For the funeral. They'd made love in the center bedroom, and he'd never guessed.

The wolf reminded him to stay alert. This wasn't an animal with whom you could let down your guard.

Moses licked his tongue at him but held his ground.

Checking the water dish and refilling it, Tage felt every movement Moses made. All that moved was the wolf's head and his eyes and sometimes his ears.

It took patience to gain a fearful animal's trust. He had patience tonight because his thoughts were so many and so deep, like the snow collecting beneath the trees, coating the woods in white.

Had she liked it?

The white shape in the corner rose to its feet, then lowered its body. Moses slunk toward Tage in the darkness, tongue licking.

Tage fixed his eyes past Moses. You didn't meet the

eyes of a wolf. And Moses was far more wolf than dog. He should ask Sarah what she knew about him... Another day. His eyes told him Moses was wild-shy and would never be tamed. But if turned loose in the wilderness, Moses could not fend for himself. He must learn to live with humans.

Humans must learn to live with him.

The creature licked Tage's face, a wolf greeting of respect to a leader. Unearned, Tage thought. Moses was playing at submission and maybe hoping for a meal. It was kennel policy to start feeding the day after the animal's arrival. Better for appetite, better for digestion, better for control.

"What does she feed you?" He stroked Moses's throat and glimpsed his eyes. The thrill in his own veins was a thrill beyond dog fancy. He loved the wolflike northern breeds, with their intelligence and independence.

I know why Sarah wanted you, Moses.

The horror he'd felt when she called and told him she had a wolf hybrid was gone. Something both more pleasant and more dangerous had replaced it.

Maybe this is what Sarah felt with Arthur. She knew it was wrong and wanted it anyway.

He could pretend the thought of her with an old man was disgusting.

Or he could recognize that some men never aged but only died.

No, he wasn't disgusted, and his shock was fraud, the fraud of those who had again and again muted the unspeakable question to which the answer was Sarah's hissing and unretractable *Yes.* Yes.

He was angry. And violently jealous in the way he'd never been jealous of Peter's sleeping with Marit.

The comparison brought life speeding back to the present, flying to the corner bedroom where a blond twelve-year-old boy slept, or tried to sleep, his parents dead.

About Lars and Peter, he could be jealous, too.

Not wanting compassion from the wolf, not expecting it, he bade Moses good-night, collected the wine and left to go into the dome, to find a coffee mug Sarah hadn't made, to find something to drink from that had nothing to do with her.

And he opened the bottle in the toy breeds' section, taking a minute to play with a despondent Kerry terrier. Then he took the wine and a cheap coffee mug out onto the training field and stood in the snow and toasted Arthur in obscene terms and thought of Lars.

If he'd held him when he was a baby, everything might have been different.

CHAPTER FOUR

Early Monday

THE SLEEPING PORCH held a cold and frightening solitude. It wasn't the first night she'd lost sleep over what had happened with Arthur. She'd left Minnesota the next morning, but still, for weeks afterward, she had pondered the moments. Second-by-second replays. Breaths and skin and pulse. Then it had slipped away, faded—an experience she and Arthur had shared, one she couldn't explain to anyone. After his death had come another wakeful week; it ended in Tage's arms.

Tage must have known. At least, he'd suspected.

Awful secrets seeped through the pores to rub off on a lover's skin. Maybe Tage hadn't recognized the scent, but he had smelled it. Tonight, finally, he'd asked.

Until she answered and saw the answer penetrate, Sarah had imagined the matter unimportant and escapable. But Tage's face was the clearest mirror she'd ever seen. It was her first glimpse of herself, and she was a monster.

The storm played with the roof, and her mind found ways to recall profound moments. She relived them, relived first sex, which had been with Arthur Tennyson. She longed to turn her body inside out and scrape herself, her substance, away.

She had meant to try to tell Poloma in England. Back in April, she had gone to England to meet her mother, and this time they were supposed to spend two weeks together.

And this time, like the previous time, Poloma had not come. She'd sent a fax to the hotel. She'd met someone, in Greece. She was going to his home. Was Sarah enjoying Bath?

No. Bath was a nightmare. Travel was a nightmare when you couldn't give directions or ask them. When you handed a piece of paper to a cab driver to say where you wanted to go.

So many things she couldn't say.

I slept with your fourth husband.

Night faded toward day. Beside the windows, in the star shade of winter morning, a snowy owl stared against the gray bark of a maple. His flame-colored eyes welcomed Sarah awake. Owls portended death.

Deaths occurred to her. Her own was one of them.

Wishing for it, she sat up. She and Arthur had worked together in this room checking over the manuscript for his last book. It had been her way of repaying him for letting her use the studio. But even her work for him was a debt she couldn't repay. He'd done her another favor, teaching her about editing. It was a useful skill, he'd said. It was one she'd never used.

In summer, the air had been thick and fragrant. Now, double panes stretched around the room on three sides. The ashes in the fireplace were gray, cold and dead.

She should leave today. Tage wouldn't want her here now. She would leave—and leave Moses, too. What else was there to do? Tage would take care of the wolf for life.

She dragged herself from the bed. She'd slept in Tage's long-sleeved T-shirt, and when she cinched the tie on his sweatpants, they still hung low, too long, too big. The owl remained in the tree, even as she left the room. The hall was dark, the bedroom doors all shut. Tage's room was in the center; a child slept on each side, dependent on him.

"Shit," she whispered on the stairs. She wanted to take

back what she'd said the night before, wanted it unspoken, unacknowledged. Suspicions were intangible. She wasn't relieved at having said it out loud. How it all had ended hadn't occurred to Tage and never would. He didn't know enough about salt kilns.

She could have turned at the base of the stairs, passed through the little hall to the pantry and kitchen. Instead, she stepped into the library, to see the blue-white world outside the row of casements. To step into the dining room.

The built-in china cabinets on each side of the dining-room casements held her pottery, pieces she'd made for Arthur in the days before it ever occurred to her that she would make love with him. Back then, he was just a special friend with a rare sense of culture and an aura of the otherworldly. A friend. He had always called her his friend—*my friend Sarah*. She'd felt those words acutely. Sarah had been proud to know him, proud that he found her remarkable. Proud that he considered her at least a friend, even though he and her mother had divorced so fast.

She manufactured excuses like widgets. They were weak, slumping things. *Are we the best you can come up with?*

She realized Tage used her dishes. Would he still?

The pantry next. Tage had taped a gold-bordered copy of the Twenty-second Psalm to a cabinet door. Sarah paused and read it.

Be not far from me, for I am in distress;
be near, for I have no one to help me....
Indeed, many dogs surround me;
a pack of evildoers closes in upon me....

Tage must have put it up because of the reference to dogs. It made sense to Sarah only because she knew him, because she'd visited his camp that night in Iditarod. His sled dogs were not the evildoers. But clients' dogs, dogs who lived for anything but the joy of running, might seem that way to a man who would prefer to live in the wild among his own pack.

She could only read aloud by whispering or singing, and she whispered, "'O my help, hasten to aid me. Rescue my soul from the sword, my loneliness from the grip of the dog.'"

Like a sleepwalker, she found her way into the next room. She had just removed a bag of coffee beans from the freezer and discovered the coffee grinder when Comet raced into the kitchen. Tail wagging, he sniffed Sarah's hands and the sweatpants she wore.

Tage came next. Leaning against the counter in his pajama bottoms, he pressed his thumb and forefinger to the bridge of his nose and squinted at the monitor that showed the dogs in the kennels. She tried not to notice his golden skin or that he was sinewy, hard from work and running behind a dog sled. She didn't want the feelings, but they were there—attraction and familiarity. The rough stubble on his jaw in the mornings had never been just that. It was Tage's warm and fine skin against her skin, the relief that he did *not* grow a beard, and that he was a young man and not confusing to her.

Too late, Sarah.

All she could do now was ask if he'd keep Moses for her. Then she could go, get out of his sight.

Forget she'd ever heard him say, *I want to marry you... I won't leave. You won't leave.*

As she replayed the words, something inside her shook. *I won't leave. You won't leave.*

Tage was right. She wasn't her mother. She wasn't her father.

Sarah Calder did not abandon living things.

"W-w-w-will you still train M-M—" *Moses?* She tried to get the word out. Her lungs were bursting, her breath as trapped as the word. "M-M-*Mooooses?*"

Tage straightened slowly, hungover. He hadn't expected to find her in the kitchen. He'd expected to find her gone.

His eyes left the monitor. "Yes." Taking the coffee bag from her, he opened the top of the grinder and poured in the beans.

"I w-w-will pay you. R-r-r-rent, too."

He shook his head. Preoccupied, he nonetheless asked, "Where did you get Moses? Tell me everything."

Sarah stirred behind him, filling the decanter, and he half turned to glance at her. The sunlight streaming through the kitchen window caught the palest shades in her hair. Arthur... Arthur...

"On the highway. I—"

The coffeemaker gurgled.

Tage waited for her next word. And the next. Using substitutions yet still blocking often, she told him she'd bought Moses from a man with a pick-up truck on the shoulder of the road to Telluride. She'd paid a thousand dollars—a discounted price because Moses was already several months old, the last of the litter. The breeder had been moving back to Canada. He'd insisted on cash, and Sarah had driven all the way back to the bank in Sneffels to get it. The breeder claimed Moses was "ninety-eight percent wolf."

Tage rolled his eyes over the quoted "percentage." But the breeder's single piece of advice had been sound, if not useful. *Never hit a wolf.* Tage would have said, *Never hit.*

He asked the one thing that continued to puzzle him. "Sarah, why did you do it? Why did you buy him?"

"Impulse."

If it was impulse, some change must have preceded it. Sarah was careful to avoid responsibility for others. It wasn't the kind of thing she would have done on sheer impulse.

She shrugged. She couldn't imagine ever explaining it to Tage. The bottom line was, she'd been lonely and just couldn't stand it anymore. This was the year she'd accepted that her mother really didn't care about her. And Tage, of course, hadn't called or written since Nome. The future had looked empty. And the idea of a wolf— Somehow, she thought Moses might turn out to be *like* her, and he was, but she hadn't counted on that being a problem. That he was so shy and loved to run away, even from her.

Tage's breath was concession; it meant he wasn't going to probe any more—on that issue. "What have you been feeding him?"

"S-S-S-Science Diet. And r-r-r-road kill."

"Bad idea—unless you're the one who hit the animal. He needs some bones and fur, but there are better ways to take care of that." Beavers from the trappers. "In the meantime, use the meat in the walk-in in the dome." *I'll deal with all this later.*

Lars and Lobsang would start school today. He must awaken them soon and take them to their different schools to register them. Critter and Lisa, his assistants, would be here by eight to clean the kennels and feed the dogs. Critter worked part-time at the Manitou Animal Shelter. Lisa was completing an apprenticeship with him. He could use more help. Since Lars was so interested in training Snutte, maybe he'd want to earn some pocket money.

Tage poured himself some coffee in one of Sarah's mugs. *Arthur's mugs—she made them for Arthur...* "I have things to do this morning. You can feed Moses and exercise him, but don't let him off lead. And don't give him any commands he won't obey. When we start training, we want him to know that he has to do every single thing you ask him to do."

Sarah laughed ruefully. "I ask little."

Because of her stutter.

They'd never discussed her stutter. Sarah could not have reached the age of thirty-four without speech therapy. Clearly, she coped as she could. He knew about stuttering because he'd made it a point to know—trying to find out why she ran away. Why she'd refused to be his. Now he knew.

Wanting to blame someone besides her, besides Arthur, he asked, "How is your mother?"

Sarah gave a secretive shrug.

There *were* no secrets. A mother who loved her wouldn't have let her go to Lapland with Arthur. Never in his acquaintance with Sarah had Tage seen evidence that her mother cared about her.

Sarah made it a point not to need or be needed. Moses was an exception.

"We should change his name," he said. Too close to her, he caught her scent, the scent of Sarah in the morning. Her breasts and nipples formed soft contours beneath the worn T-shirt he'd lent her. It covered her slender hips, and she'd had to roll up the legs of his sweatpants, huge on her.

She never noticed him looking.

He felt like a lecher. Had Arthur been this way with her?

Of course, Tage.

He filled the coffeemaker and switched it on. Sarah reached past him to the cupboard. It was filled with her mugs. Her hand was bare. She never wore jewelry, had never pierced her ears.

"I like his name," she said.

Moses. Tage liked it, too.

He wanted her, and Arthur was there in the kitchen with them, would always be with them. It eclipsed sudden guardianship, his brother's death and the end of his Iditarod dreams. How did you treat her, how did you pretend you could train her wolf, how did you start two orphans in school, when you cared about nothing except one fact—that last night you'd kissed her and asked her to marry you and she'd told you she'd slept with your friend, her stepfather? *As a consenting adult.*

A black nose sniffed Sarah, and a black tail swatted Tage. Comet and Snutte danced around each other, roughhousing, then chasing into the other room, and Lars flattened himself in the doorway, getting out of the way. His cool eyes swept from Sarah to Tage before his gaze hit the floor and he turned his back and left the room.

Abruptly, Tage cared about something besides Sarah.

LARS WAS IN THE vestibule, pulling on his boots. The bench, whose seat lifted to store snowshoes and hockey sticks, was long enough for three or four people. Tage left plenty of space between him and Lars.

Ice blue eyes stared at his. In a dog, it meant dominance.

It meant the same thing in a twelve-year-old boy, but Tage remembered being angry about death, being sad and helpless.

Lars looked away. *"Vad?"*

"There is school today. Be ready at seven. We'll take you first, then Lobsang. After this, you can ride the bus together."

Lars nodded.

"The cabin where Sarah was staying collapsed last night. She's staying here now, in the sleeping porch off the upstairs hall."

A quick glance from Lars said many things. That it was the best place to sleep, with so many windows and so many trees. That a woman as beautiful as Sarah could get anything she wanted.

It was the most cynical look Tage had ever seen on the face of a child.

Lars said, "Why don't you just sleep with her? It's not like we're going to care."

It was a good time to wait for his eyes. To look at him until he looked away and jumped up. Snutte was waiting at the door, and the boy went out with him, and Tage sat quietly.

So Lars didn't like Sarah.

After Nome, after what she'd revealed about Arthur, it should have been the last straw.

But she was complicated, and she'd done something new. She had a pet, and she was hanging on to it, wasn't abandoning it.

He thought about the word "deflower." It didn't mean to make love.

He felt the magnitude of what she'd told him and knew her secret bound him to her.

It was very hard for Sarah to say anything out loud.

LARS STUDIED THE reflection in the tall oval mirror in the corner bedroom. Beside an unfamiliar bed and all the boxes he'd brought from Jokkmokk stood a blond person in jeans, a red-trimmed blue wool Saami tunic and a four-pointed Saami hat. The costume represented the region where his father and Tage had been born, in Finnmark, Norway. Lars's grandfather, Nils-Isak, wore a different costume, from northern Sweden.

Maybe he was a jerk to go to his new school in his *gakti,* but Lars didn't care. His father had taught him to be proud of being Saami. Some Saami only wore native dress for church holidays, that kind of thing. But his mom and dad had worn theirs every day.

It seemed loyal and right to do the same. Especially because Tage had become such a pain. Lars didn't like to think about Tage being married to his mother. To Marit. It was easier to picture him with the stupid girlfriend who had a wolf for a pet. Wolves were bad; some Saami said the devil made them. A wolf had killed Lars's favorite reindeer when Lars was seven.

Since he was dressed and he'd already fed Snutte and put him in with the sled dogs, Lars picked up his father's troll drum and the *arpa,* the brass ring, which he set on top. Figures and symbols were painted on the oval surface of reindeer skin. When Lars beat the drum with the hammer made from a forked reindeer antler, the *arpa* jumped around. Wherever it landed would show a hunter what to hunt.

For fun, Lars set the *arpa* on the center of the skin and beat the drum. When he stopped, the *arpa* rested on the figure of a woman.

Sarah.

Ah, that was the message. Get Sarah to leave. Sarah and her wolf. The idea seemed to have come not just from his father's drum but from his father, as though his father was answering his plea. *We can't make Sarah leave, but you can, Lars.*

Someone knocked.

"*Ja?*"

His uncle came in. Lobsang was with him, wearing jeans and a pink sweatshirt and her parka. Eyeing the position of the *arpa,* Tage winked at Lars. "Ah. Girls. Good hunting. Just don't forget to study."

Lobsang squatted and beat on the drum.

Lars took the antler from her, confused. His uncle had surprised him. Tage thought the girls at his new school would like him. He had joked about it, man to man. This was the uncle who had taken him on autumn migration.

Yes, the problem was Sarah.

Thoughtful, Lars picked up the drum.

The *arpa* had stopped on a woman again.

MOSES WANTED TO WALK behind the house. Sarah dragged him in the other direction, along the road to the studio, wishing she was wearing snowshoes instead of skis. Damn it, he was going to pull her over.

She yanked on the lead again, hard, and a hundred pounds of wolf dog argued with her, and she lost a ski trying to stay up. Whatever was behind the house, he probably wanted to eat it. Nothing doing. With difficulty, she got her ski back on and coaxed him on down the road. Finally, when they were deep in the trees, he stopped fighting and trotted ahead of her.

She relaxed, held her balance and let him pull.

At least, she was out of Tage's hair now. He'd said he had things to do. He probably had to take the children to school. Had they only just arrived in Minnesota? Before she left for the studio, she'd vacuumed the upper hall— the place was thick with dog hair—and the little girl had come out of her room. The room was full of boxes with airline stickers on them, as though there had been no time to unpack.

Nothing to do with me.

She breathed raggedly in the cold. Her toes were numb, and so was her face. In the studio, she'd get the stove going and see if she could do anything about the cabin.

It appeared ahead of her, the fallen structure against the pale green clapboard siding of the studio. Today, the lake was a glistening plain. From here, she could see that what was left of the old cabin had filled with snow during the night. Moses trotted toward it, his wolf head sweeping from side to side. He saw the lake, too, the wild, and Sarah felt the change in him, the awareness of open spaces. The desire to explore them.

She held tight to the lead and said, "Wh-wh-whoooaa."

No effect. It was always this way. The trick was to stop without falling or breaking a leg.

But Moses paused at the cabin, to scent-mark.

The ruin was filled with snow—just history now. One of those places that strangers saw without knowing the things that had happened inside. But she knew, and now Tage knew, too. Their relationship had spent twelve years creeping toward this moment.

This was his chance to leave her.

THEY WERE BRAVE, Tage thought. Both of them. Not even Lobsang had cried. At the junior high, Lars had taken in his surroundings like a general preparing to conquer new territory. Tage had spent most of the morning in Lobsang's class, where half the children were out with chicken pox and those who were present seemed to have colds.

When he left the elementary school, Tage drove in to Manitou in freezing rain. He had a larger collection of books on dogs and wolves than the local library, but it couldn't hurt to see if the library had anything he lacked.

Sarah's stutter was going to be a problem in training Moses. Perhaps Moses could be taught to respond to hand signals and body language. But that wouldn't be a cure-all. Alpha wolves growled at subordinates; mother wolves growled at cubs.

And Sarah could never count on saying what she set out to say.

Downtown Manitou was two gas pumps, a market, a diner, a Swedish Lutheran church and three canoe outfitters. Four banners at the town's small center celebrated the holidays.

It was time to find gifts for his family and mail them to Sweden. Lars and Lobsang, too—he needed to find out what they wanted for Christmas. And he dreaded asking something that could seem so trivial, particularly of a twelve-year-old whose respect for him was dwindling.

I'm failing with Lars.

It had been the same between Peter and Nils-Isak. Peter hadn't been much older than Lars was now when their father died. Peter had rebelled against their stepfather...always. Even the peace they'd achieved in order to herd reindeer together had been fractious. Tage had been peacemaker till he left.

Then, two months after he'd gone, the nuclear reactor at Chernobyl had caught fire and winds had scattered radioactive substances throughout Lapland, contaminating everything, including reindeer lichen. All the herds had to be destroyed. Tage should have felt lucky to have slaughtered his reindeer before the disaster—to have been paid for the meat, to have known one last good season.

He had never felt anything but guilty.

He parked outside the library building, an old clapboard house. A flimsy wooden kiosk decked in red tinsel advertised Saturday dogsled races near Lake Gegoka. Tage noted the registration time. Lars wanted to race. Already, Tage had begun thinking in bribes. He wished he could resurrect the dead for Lars. He would have taken the pain on himself if he could.

The library was closed—open only Tuesday, Thursday and Saturday. As he left the steps, a woman emerged from a building two doors down, the vet clinic. Long gray hair spilled from beneath her navy stocking cap and she rushed along the sidewalk, hurrying toward an old Buick station wagon he should have noticed earlier.

"Critter!"

His assistant trainer started, then strode toward him, her wire-rimmed glasses fogged in the cold. "I'm sorry, Tage. I know I'm late. We had an emergency at the shelter this morning."

"That's fine. I need to tell you, a friend of mine is staying at the house."

Critter blinked. "With the kids?" She'd met Lars and Lobsang on Thanksgiving, the day he'd brought them home.

"Her name is Sarah Calder. She's brought a wolf."

Critter's face changed suddenly.

"His name is Moses. She says he's a wolf hybrid, but he looks like a wolf."

On the snowy sidewalk, Critter shifted, made an impatient movement as though she wanted to get in her car. Her glance darted back to Tage, and her mouth opened, then shut. When she said, "Anyhow, I'm glad I saw you. Let me tell you what just happened," he knew it wasn't what she'd been about to say.

"The sheriff busted a roadside zoo this morning. A lion escaped and walked into a lady's backyard."

Tage knew which zoo. He'd stopped there once, parking outside but not paying admission. Without going in, he'd seen enough to make him sick. "Dizzy G's?" He knew what Critter wanted.

"Yes."

"How are the reindeer?"

"Skinny. Will you take them, Tage? We'll construct the corral and pay for feed, if you'll keep them on your land. The humane society doesn't have facilities for reindeer."

"All right."

She kicked at the snow. The kiosk absorbed her. "Is this the same Sarah who ditched you in Nome? Arthur's stepdaughter?"

Critter and Arthur had been skiing buddies—and maybe more. It was Critter who'd found Arthur and shut off the burners. Five years later, she'd agreed to work for Tage.

"It's the same Sarah," was all he said.

And Critter kept her thoughts to herself.

WHEN HE GOT HOME, he went to Anna. She was waiting at the gate when he entered the isolation kennel. If things were different, he would have kept her in the outdoor run, in the snow and the cold. But with so many strange—and sometimes aggressive—dogs on the property, indoors was better. So he'd turned down the heat to make it comfortable for her.

She scampered around him as though looking for a harness and something to pull. Her mother had been a red Siberian, her father a large Nordic-type mutt. Her fur was mottled, her face masked, her eyes blue like Comet's.

They ran in the woods behind the house, where the maples gave way to mature cedar and spruce. Even in season, Anna wanted to pull. Her fawn-colored tail plumed behind her, and his own boots kept up on the trail.

He never confused his dogs with idle chatter. But minds could talk, too, and a man learned by listening.

What lesson will you teach me today, Anna?

She ran ahead, unimpeded by deeper snow. She did not complain. She gave everything. Always.

SMOKE CURLED FROM the chimney of the studio, and Christmas music—pipes and a tin whistle and vocals—played behind the ice-glazed windows. As Sarah had said, the cabin had collapsed on itself. Stepping out of his skis, Tage studied the wolf tracks he'd followed from the kennels. They fell in a straight line instead of zigzagging like a dog's.

She'd asked yesterday if she could bring Moses out to the cabin, and he'd said "no." But today he'd told her to exercise him, and she'd ignored the rest.

With his glove, he touched a wet and weathered board. Beyond the pale green clapboard building with its pale golden lights in the window, snow fell. The field of polka dots misted away the trees on the far side of the lake. It was one o'clock, and Sarah hadn't returned to the house to eat. The cabin's wood-burning cookstove was a white-draped shape in the timbers, its chimney jutting upward like a periscope. She must have moved the small refrigerator into the studio to get it out of the weather.

Tage skied around to the lake side of the studio and left his skis on the glassed-in porch. She didn't open the door, so he went in.

No wolf. Just heat and a choir singing carols.

Sarah was on the wheel, her head down as she shaped a vase. Her hair hung in a messy ponytail, and the wet clay traced up her arms. It had splattered her jeans and her faded long undershirt.

He noticed white fur beyond the kitchen door, near some bags of clay and pails of glazes. *There you are, Moses.*

The choir sang, *"Il est né, le divin enfant..."*

Sarah sang with them, in perfectly enunciated French, her voice a husky alto. Foreign languages had always been easier for her; he'd taught her some Swedish and some Saami when they were teenagers, when she'd visited with Arthur. Singing, she never stuttered.

They'd sung many Christmas carols together.

He sang with her now, and her hands left the clay with practiced care. She stopped the wheel, and wisps of hair hung before her flushed face.

"I brought you lunch."

Moses never moved, never showed himself, even when Tage opened his pack and brought out a Thermos of Japanese green tea, her favorite, a Tupperware container filled with soup and a small tub of yogurt. Tage's wolfiest sled dogs had never behaved like Moses. They'd been bossy and smart but not shy.

"Let me...deal with this." Sarah cut the vase from the bat and placed it beside some bowls on a high shelf. At the sink, in the kitchen, she soaped her hands and arms, then her face.

Burying her face in a towel, Sarah drew some deep breaths. Why had Tage come? Was the food a peace offering? *It won't give me peace, Tage.*

As she reentered the main room, she turned down the music. He'd settled in a folding metal chair and was drinking coffee from his Thermos. He wore a wool Saami tunic. He owned so many *gakti* because his mother and sister made Saami handicrafts to sell at fairs. He got new clothes every Christmas.

Tage made things, too. Figurines and knives carved from antlers. Sarah's collection was in Sneffels, a reminder that she was *visiting* Minnesota, not moving here.

He had left her the overstuffed chair with the torn cushions. Sitting down, she tucked her feet in wool socks beneath her. "Thanks. For the food."

Words deserted Tage. He still couldn't talk to her about Arthur, didn't know if he'd ever be able to. He just wanted to forget it. That seemed possible until he imagined making love with her again.

Arthur had touched her, maybe caressed her with his mouth. Tage had pictured it all with genius. Now—out here—he pictured more. Sarah and Arthur had spent many hours together in this building.

He drank more coffee. Behind the glaze pails, the white tail shifted. "He's being good."

Her laugh turned his head.

"He's afraid."

"Shy, anyhow. What's his mischief like?" He wondered why he bothered to ask. No one told the truth about a dog where the dog could hear. Dogs had gone for his throat while their owners were in the midst of saying, *I'd trust him with a baby!* A malamute could be humping his leg, and the owner would say, *Sexual mounting? Oh, he never does anything like that....*

Like this, you mean?

"D-d-d—"

Sarah gave up on speaking, set down the soup container she'd never opened, and stood. She rustled in a backpack, over by the sink, and returned with a spiral notebook, which she flipped open and handed to him.

Tage read, *Things My Wolf Dog Has Destroyed.*

"Ah. Your wallet. Your driver's license. Your grandmother's quilt. Money..." He read the rest of the list silently and handed the notebook back to her. It would be nice to know what she'd written on earlier pages. It would be nice to know if she ever wrote things about him.

She used to. He'd read her diary in Sweden when they were teenagers. It was *all* about him. He eyed her curiously.

She slammed the notebook shut, her eyes darting away, then back to his. Her flush and his answering grin changed in a second—changed with a single shared thought.

"Where did it happen?"

Her head tilted toward the shut door that led to the original building, the fallen cabin. Her lips bit shut. She opened the soup container and picked up the spoon he'd brought.

A soprano sang, "O Holy Night."

The roof had fallen. Under the weight of snow, thought Tage, or the weight of secrecy. The cabin was gone.

No peace came. She'd slept with Arthur. Kissed him...

As a consenting adult.

Arthur had died right outside.

"M—" Tage was the one who couldn't speak this time. "Moses—" He didn't know what he meant to say. Just something. To try to return to a time when his knowledge had been unformed and imprecise, a heaviness never put into words or thoughts. When it had still been unthinkable.

The carol's refrain of hope filled the studio, marched Christmas Eve through the pink dust, made human tragedies momentarily redeemable.

"Lars is my son. My biological son." He drank more coffee, found things to look at. The pots she'd made that hadn't been fired. The wheel. Moses's tail.

Sarah.

She blew on the tea in the Thermos cup.

"Marit told me she loved Peter. It turned out she was pregnant. She still wanted a divorce." Wanted Peter. "I said, 'Okay, you'll be good parents.' It was insane."

"Or generous."

He shook his head, drank coffee. It was still hot enough. "I didn't want visitation—or her child. It's obscene to fall out of love so fast."

"My m-m—"

Tage kept one eye on the second hand on the ticking wall clock, an old 1950s piece, probably the original clock in the two-room addition. Two minutes passed before she said her second word.

"M-m-mother always does. Fast."

Fall out of love.

It had been easy to fall out of love with someone who preferred his brother to him. And easy to see how it had happened. Peter was, well, Peter. The shaman with the glowing eyes.

Sarah sipped tea, drank soup.

The CD ended.

Snow fell outside the window, so fast it seemed to be bouncing in the air.

"I'll never tell Lars. Peter is his father. It's too late."

Sarah burned her lips with the tea. Why was Tage telling her this?

For twelve years, he'd kept it secret.

Karma didn't happen over lifetimes. It happened in seconds, and people said, *What goes around comes around.*

"It has to hurt," she said. "The Iditarod." She blocked, dazzled in blankness, her mouth hugging a word. "We-w-wwwwere you going to…" The question was too difficult, and she gave it up and looked at him to let him know she was done.

"I'm surprised it hurts so little."

So was Sarah, and she had the feeling again of him walking away, with a child on each side of him.

He wasn't thinking of the race.

"I want to know what happened between you two," said Tage. "Because of the will."

That had to be a lie. He wanted to know for his own reasons. "After your divorce," she whispered. "You wrote to him, and he changed the will. He told me about it. He said he didn't want the others to hate me. His family." *He implied you loved me, that I would end up here after all. Now, don't ask questions, Tage.*

Tage asked no more. "None of your business" was a definitive answer. It was Sarah's answer.

The door to the now-fallen cabin stood closed, and he had to remind himself that rubble lay beyond. Though the bed had been buried, the mattress stood against shelves on one wall of the studio, already dry. It must have taken superhuman strength for her to rescue it, although she'd left the box spring.

The linen lay in a heap in the corner.

He saw them in bed together. What was a consenting adult anyhow? Arthur had died when she was twenty-three.

Tage had made love with her after the funeral.

And known.

The darkness stole through him. Sketchy recollections long past. The year Sarah was in Lapland was hard to remember. But later, when she was back in the United

States and none of them had seen her for several years...
Arthur had spoken of her—how she was in art school and
doing well. There was nothing improper in Arthur's re-
marking that her skin was beautiful, that her hair was long,
that she'd grown tall. Yes, still shy. *Not with me, of course,*
Arthur had said, sounding pleased and confident.

Sarah was in college, grown up.

Hearing Arthur talking that way, you had to conclude
that he was very proud of her, that he loved her like a
daughter. He always had, you told yourself. It wasn't any
different from how he'd talked about Sarah when she
was—fourteen.

That really wasn't a hard-on you heard in his voice.
Surely, other people—your parents—would notice if it
was. They knew him well. He'd carried you on his shoulders and brought you presents when you were small. He
was a respected anthropologist. A friend of your father's.
A friend of yours.

So you forgot the sound of his voice talking about his
stepdaughter until you finally saw her again and made love
with her yourself, and then you spent twelve more years
saying nothing, until one night she wouldn't marry you.
After you'd asked her about Arthur, after she'd said yes,
there had been sexual intercourse, you keyed on the rest
of what she'd said, the best of what she'd said. The worst
of it, too. *As a consenting adult.*

Those words absolved you. And damned her.

Tage wanted to kill someone. Not Sarah. And Arthur
was already dead, of chlorine gas. What more could you
ask for?

He screwed the lid on his Thermos, stuffed it in his
pack. Sarah had come for help with Moses.

"You need to start reading." He spoke to her wheel,
never looking at her. "I'll put some books and articles in
your room. And remember what I said." Standing, he

faced her. "Don't give Moses any command unless you know you can make him obey."

Sarah nodded. She found no danger in watching his face, because he wasn't looking at her but past her. She twisted around in the chair to see what had caught his eye.

It was just the pile of sheets.

CHAPTER FIVE

LARS IS MY SON.

Why had he told her? Somehow, she'd always believed Tage had no secrets—or that she knew them. Married and divorced when he was young... Lars *looked* like him but that had seemed unremarkable in his brother's son.

A pail of kaolin tipped over and rolled on the floor. Moses was playing tug-of-war with a towel stuck under bags of clay. Her car was probably buried in snow, probably wouldn't start. She should have asked Tage for help with it. She'd have to ski back to the house with Moses. They should go now before the weather worsened.

Lars is my son.

He hadn't told her that on a whim. But why had he told her?

In front of her eyes was an unfaded image of Arthur standing by the window, gazing out at the lake, then at her.

You mustn't let it hurt you, Sarah, what we've done.

Moses lifted a leg on her wheel.

She wound her scarf around her neck and tucked it into her sweater so Moses wouldn't find the ends. He'd almost strangled her once. She avoided wearing her hair in a braid for similar reasons.

As she zipped her parka, snow flew sideways past the window. Would the schools call a snow day, send the children home?

Lars is my son.

Tage had never told her any secrets before. Was he asking for help?

Yes. He *had* asked, in so many words. But she wouldn't be any help. Was he desperate or something?

No. He just loves you.

Great. All she needed was to hear Arthur's voice making Obi-wan Kenobi pronouncements in her head. *Feel the Force, Sarah.*

What she felt, still, was anger. About the salt kiln. It was too much like theater. A mask firing in the kiln. A tragic accident of the sort no coward would choose.

It was too much like Arthur.

When he saw the leash, Moses ran through the studio, hiding under tables. It took her fifteen minutes to get him outside and put on her skis. The road looked like the rest of the world, white and ice. The wolf dog did not pull her but stayed close, as though expecting her to know the way. She skied, and ice stuck to the bottom of her skis, slowing her. Arthur had smiled at her questions about Tage. *Have you met Tage's wife?*

No. I'm sure she's not as pretty as you, Sarah.

But she is Saami. And that would matter to Tage.

It really wasn't true. It had mattered to Tage's brother.

Maybe it had mattered to Tage when he married Marit. Or perhaps Arthur had meant to make her feel better. He'd never tried to keep her from loving Tage.

She felt Arthur skiing beside her, heard him say, *I always wanted to see you with Tage. You mustn't be foolish about the past. If you want Tage now, take him. He's yours. You've been afraid too long.*

It was the kind of thing Arthur had said in life.

Like that night on the lake. *Trust your feelings, Sarah.*

Ice hit her face, encrusted her skin. The wolf dog, the warmest thing in the day, the most visible, padded beside her.

And she remembered something else Arthur had told her. *There's nothing wrong with fear, unless you yield to it. All dishonor is born in cowardice.*

But Sarah was a stutterer. Coward was her middle name.

And dishonor was her close friend.

THE RADIO SAID SCHOOL was let out because of snow. Tage had already sent his assistants home and was returning a cocker spaniel he'd been training in the dome to its kennel when the phone rang. The office was beside the front door, and he picked up the phone on the way out.

"Good Dog Kennels, Tage speaking." As he spoke, he switched radio stations for the dogs, finding Christmas music.

"Oh, thank God you're there. You've got to help me. I can't take it any more. I'm going to put him down. God, if this can't be fixed, we just have to get rid of him." The woman sniffed. "Oh, I can't believe what he *did!*"

"Ma'am, please tell me your name. I can't counsel you on the phone, but I'll be happy to set up an emergency appointment."

"He *chewed* my Peña."

A painting. One dog in his practice had climbed onto the owner's bar to get at a picture he wanted. Another had climbed on a dresser to reach pillows on a high storage shelf. "Would you like to make an appointment? We'll see what we can do about the destructive chewing."

A figure opened one of the glass doors, entered the dome. Sarah.

"Yes!" said the woman on the phone, and he had to remember what they'd been talking about. "Today."

He pointed out the weather.

"All right. Tomorrow? Oh, God, do I bring him? We can't even trim the Christmas tree. He makes off with everything and won't give it back. He has a hoard. We've given up on glass balls—he'll kill himself. Though maybe that's not such a bad idea.''

Struggling to concentrate, he finished the conversation, got the information he needed. When he hung up, Sarah pushed herself from the wall and came toward him.

''I have to get Lars and Lobsang,'' he told her. ''Do you need something?''

Her mouth moved slightly. Not a block. Shyness.

The space between them closed a little, though he wasn't conscious of moving, just of seeing her hair up close, seeing the different shades in a single lock. Wanting her lips. ''Would you like to come with me?''

''Yes.'' Her fingers grasped the bottom edge of her pumpkin-colored parka, and she spoke at somewhere past him.

Tage kept his hands to himself. ''Let's go. We'll see how your wolf dog does in the car.''

THE HEATER IN THE 4Runner hummed quietly as Tage drove through the misty snow on the mile-long stretch to the highway. Although eventually Moses should learn to sit on the back seat without disturbing the occupants of the car, for this trip Tage had installed the steel car barrier he sometimes used for taking dogs to shows, confining Moses to the back of the Toyota. They hadn't heard a sound from him.

''He's being good,'' Sarah said.

''Two minutes. Quite a track record.''

She punched his arm.

''Last night, I noticed him licking his paws. He'll give himself sores. It's boredom—he needs a bigger place. Today I asked Lisa, one of my assistants, to sort through some information I'd downloaded from the Internet. I put the articles in your room. We've decided he needs a large compound with a peripheral fence to keep children from coming close. He also needs a companion, or two, maybe some of my dogs.''

At the highway, he flipped on his turn indicator. The road was empty. Mary's Bonnet Lake stretched along the other side, fingering into the woods. On the lakeshore, Tage's nearest neighbor, a hunter, had erected a life-size nativity in a lean-to. The accompanying lights were a foggy glow in the darkness.

He turned onto the snowy road. A school bus crawled toward them from the other direction.

''I've seen your place in Sneffels, Sarah. You don't have room for what I'm talking about. But we can build something here, for now, while I'm training him.''

Sarah unzipped her parka. With the heater on, she was too warm. ''How m-m-much will it cost?''

''It's a business expense. Don't worry about it.''

Thousands, thought Sarah. *It will cost thousands of dollars. And what will that mean?* Perhaps that Tage was willing to take care of her, as Arthur had. Silence filled the car, became the wet sounds of the windshield wipers, of tires in the snow.

His voice broke the quiet. ''You can stay as long as you want.''

Sarah pressed her hand to her forehead, shut her eyes and rested her arm against the door. She knew she didn't have to answer.

SARAH WAITED IN THE CAR with the engine running while Tage went into the elementary school to get Lobsang. When they emerged, the tiny child scuffed her boots on the snowy sidewalk, her face clouded and unhappy. Tage carried a paper bag that probably held her school things. Through the snow-dotted passenger window, Sarah tried to read his face, but his head was lowered. He was talking to Lobsang.

When he opened the back door to help her in, the child saw Sarah and grew suddenly alert—almost happy.

"Hi," said Sarah. It was a word she could almost always say.

As he fastened her seat belt, Tage told Lobsang, "Sarah came with me to get you." Obviously, he was speaking so that Lobsang would hear English and become accustomed to it.

Lobsang folded her hands over the buckle and stared at Sarah, who still peered around the headrest, trying to smile.

Sliding behind the steering wheel, Tage put the car in gear. He should have thought of a backpack for Lobsang earlier. Maybe she even had one in her belongings that he'd brought from Jokkmokk. He hadn't really unpacked, hadn't set up her room.

As though it would all go away if he didn't deal with it.

As though he could still return both children to Sweden.

On the way to the junior high school, they passed houses decked with lights and tinsel. Quietly, Sarah studied the decorations. She and Tage had celebrated Christmas together in the past, in Sneffels, always quietly, with kisses and hot drinks by the fire. Trimming the tree together, exchanging small gifts. One of his carvings for her. A special mug or serving bowl for him. An afternoon skiing in the mountains, seeing Christmas in each other's eyes.

There would be no more of those Christmases, thanks to Lars and Lobsang. Christmas was a family time, and now these kids were Tage's family. She couldn't just hang around like a poor relation. Children, especially these children, needed commitment. Permanence. What Sarah's grandmother had given her when no one else would.

The 4Runner stopped at the curb outside the junior high, and Lars, in Saami clothes, saw them and said goodbye to two girls. One had a ring through her nose and four more in one ear. Lars grinned as he hurried toward the car.

Then he saw Sarah.

It *was* seeing her that changed his expression.

Tage twisted in his seat to unlock the back door for Lars.

Sarah observed their eye contact, how the boy's gaze darted away, how Tage's lingered. Tage's expression belonged to a man who wanted to know his son.

Lars shut his door, hunted for his seat belt.

"How was school?"

The silent shrug was a brush-off.

It had to hurt, but Tage just turned front, checked traffic and pulled into the storm as the wipers continued to whisk the snow aside. With a questioning glance, Sarah reached for the radio. Reba McIntyre was singing "Away in a Manger," and Sarah sang with her.

In the back seat, Lars measured the white mountains of snow piled on the roadsides. A snowplow swept by, spraying white at his window. Sarah's voice blended with Reba McIntyre's, husky and easy to hear. The words weren't any he knew, though he recognized the melody.

Christmas carols.

Lars choked down sadness. Lobsang was staring at the back of Sarah's head and swinging her legs against the seat. When his sister suddenly looked at him, Lars asked her in English, to practice more, "Did you like school?"

She frowned, then reached for the paper bag on the floor of the car, rummaged through it and pulled something out.

It was a real mess, made of pipe cleaners colored green and little white pompoms and pieces of green felt shaped like leaves. Lobsang held it between two fingers and regarded it as though it smelled bad.

As the car slowed at a light, Lars said, "What is it?"

Lobsang shrugged, looking close to tears.

Sarah turned in her seat, and so did Tage. Even Moses

had found the courage to peer through the mesh at the children, particularly Lobsang.

On the radio, a choir sang, *"Oh, tidings of comfort and joy, comfort and joy..."*

"I know what it is."

Tage started, and both children stared at Sarah.

Oh, God, thought Sarah. *Now I have to say it.* She planned the word in her mind. It began with one of the most difficult sounds in the English language.

A horn blasted behind them, and Tage noticed the green light and pulled into the intersection.

"It's what you kiss under," she said.

"We don't do that in Sweden." Tage headed down the road that would take them home.

"Oh."

His heart felt sore, as though he'd overused it. Sarah wouldn't say "mistletoe" in front of Lars and Lobsang. They were children, yet she didn't want them to see her stutter.

When a woman had such a weakness, she was vulnerable. When she craved a parent's love, she was even more vulnerable. A young woman as imprisoned by her stutter as Sarah was couldn't really be a consenting adult. Not with the only parent who had ever seemed to love her.

"Mistletoe," he told the children for her. "It's mistletoe. In this country, people hang it in doorways or somewhere in the house, and if someone passes under it you can kiss her."

Something made Sarah reach into the back seat and take the mistletoe from Lobsang's fingers. "It's nice." She smiled at Lobsang and said words she knew she could utter. "I like it." She held it where Tage could see it.

He nodded, approving. "It's good, Lobsang."

Sarah returned it to the child. Mollified, Lobsang put it back in the paper bag.

As his uncle's girlfriend faced the front again, Lars glared at the bag. Great. A kissing tradition. Well, now that they'd seen Lobsang's art project they could all forget about it—he hoped.

Behind him, the wolf dog whined.

Lars said, "Hey, Tage, can we really go to a dogsled race soon?" Surely Sarah wouldn't want to go. It would give him a chance to be alone with his uncle.

Tage shifted gears, slowing for ice on the road. "I saw a flyer this morning for the local races. They start this Saturday. Every Saturday morning all winter. We can go, but you'll have to practice between now and the weekend."

"Okay." Winning a dogsled race would make him feel much better, Lars figured. Something had to make him feel better, sometime.

IT WAS STILL SNOWING when they got home, but Lars went at once to find Snutte and took him into the dome to do some training exercises Tage had suggested.

While Sarah led Moses back to his kennel, fighting with him as he pulled toward the house, Tage carried Lobsang's paper bag inside. After filling Moses's water dish, Sarah followed and found Tage and Lobsang in the living room. Lobsang held a picture book, obviously checked out from the school library, and she was pointing at a photograph on the wall beside the alcove. The photo showed Tage's family and a tame reindeer wearing a bell about his neck and pulling a sled.

One of Arthur's photos.

Curious, Sarah stepped down into the room.

When Lobsang pointed at the picture on the front of her book, *The Night before Christmas*, Tage smiled at Santa's coursers and sleigh. "Reindeer." He sat on the edge of a spindle-back Mission chair, coming down to Lobsang's eye level. "Reindeer don't fly, and no one lives at the North Pole."

Lobsang seemed thoughtful, and Tage reached up to the built-in shelf unit behind him for the globe, which sat beside the silver halfway trophy from the Iditarod. "Globe. Say it. Globe."

Her mouth formed the word. "Globe."

Tage grinned, and she grinned back. He turned the globe to show her various countries. "This is China, where you came from. Here is Tibet."

He's watching her eyes, Sarah reflected. *He wants to know if the name means anything to her.* It didn't seem to.

He moved the globe again. "The United States. Here. Minnesota." He indicated the house, the surrounding area. "And this line up here is the Arctic Circle.

"Now, although the Arctic Circle is a straight line on the globe, it's imaginary. And it's not fixed but it moves. Let me explain." Meeting Sarah's eyes briefly, he hurried past her to the vestibule to get a well-chewed ball from the boot bench. He switched on a lamp, which became the sun for the purposes of a science lesson. He demonstrated the orbit of the earth around the sun and hastily defined the elliptic inclination and explained its relationship to the arctic circle. "Forget about that for now," he told Lobsang with seriousness. "Let me tell you about the Midnight Sun and the winter twilight. You will be amazed."

She listened with her eyes wide. Comprehending nothing, Sarah decided. But Tage must know that, too; he was teaching Lobsang the language by using it—and showing a certain respect for her, establishing a touching honesty, by sharing knowledge. It seemed to set a precedent that the things he would say to her would be important and true.

Her own eyes sought out the trophy again.

Parents—guardians—*should* do that. Sarah eyed the

Iditarod trophy, and her thoughts wandered. He'd never mentioned Nome or the awards banquet she'd skipped. But not writing her for three years had told her how he felt. Maybe.

Sarah, what are you doing here?

"So the Arctic Circle is also the southernmost point at which the sun does not set on the summer solstice and does not rise on the winter solstice. The further north you go—" he indicated on the globe "—the longer are the continuous periods of day and night. On the North Pole, it is day for six months and night for six months. There is no land there, only shifting ice packs. No one could live there, but that's where people say Santa Claus lives. The fellow in your book."

Lobsang took a seat in another of the room's Craftsman chairs and thoughtfully turned pages.

Tage leaned forward, forearms across his knees. "Now, Santa Claus is a myth, a story. In Sweden, children are told that on Christmas Eve the gnomes who live under the floorboards come out and bring them gifts. These gnomes are called *tomten.* They aren't real, either. My father—and after him, my stepfather—he was *jultomten,* Santa Claus. Here in the United States, I will be Santa Claus. Maybe Sarah will, too."

Sarah felt faint. *Excuse me?*

"On Christmas, parents give their children gifts and pretend the gifts are from these imaginary figures. They say Santa Claus flies through the sky with a sled full of gifts for all the good children in the world." A concept that couldn't be expressed to a Tibetan child without sweeping gestures indicating a flying sleigh. "He squeezes down chimneys." Tage crossed the room to the cold hearth. Lobsang followed curiously, and as he indicated the location of the chimney, she ducked her head under the copper hood to peer upward.

It seemed to inspire her with another idea.

Dashing across the living room with the energy of the very young, Lobsang stopped at her paper bag and dipped her hands in. Rustling through papers, she frowned, then smiled.

Uneasily, Sarah rose from the chair. Time to go.

Before she could leave, Lobsang handed her the mistletoe expectantly. Sarah watched her own fingers take the ''sprig.''

Holding it by the red yarn ribbon, obviously the device by which it should be hung, Sarah appealed to Tage.

Silently he took it from her, ducked into the alcove and pulled a thumbtack from his bulletin board while checking the TV monitor. Most of the dogs were dozing.

In this house, few nails or thumbtacks had been pushed into the walls. All Arthur's arctic art was carefully, tastefully placed. Arthur wouldn't have randomly plunged a thumbtack into the wall of a Craftsman home.

Till now, neither would Tage.

He stuck a tack through the red yarn on Lobsang's mistletoe and crossed the hall. Plunging the tack into the flawless cherrywood above the entry to the library was like planting a flag on a summit.

My house. My life.

Lingering behind the Morris spindle chair in the living room, Sarah gaped at the child-made art hanging from the unblemished cherry. When she realized Tage was watching her, she shrank back, hugging herself in her blue-and-white patterned sweater.

''Come here,'' he said.

Sarah made her way to him.

Tage smiled at Lobsang, pretending it didn't matter that he'd caught the loose sleeve of Sarah's sweater, to keep her from escaping. ''This is what we do under the mistletoe.''

A draft of cold from the front door swept over him as

he touched her lips with his. At the feel of her mouth, he remembered Arthur and didn't want to kiss any more.

In the vestibule, a blue-clad Lars removed his boots, unsmiling.

Lobsang, on the other hand, was grinning. She clapped her hands, and Tage lifted her up, held her under the mistletoe and kissed her cheek.

When he looked for Sarah, she was gone, disappeared into the library. Already, she'd settled on the window seat. Knees against her chest, she was watching the snow outside.

Bare feet thumped on wood as Lars went upstairs without a word.

LARS DECIDED HE'D GOTTEN what he deserved. He should never have imagined that he and his uncle and Lobsang would be like a family. Lars had experienced being part of a family, and it wouldn't happen again, and he didn't want it to.

Lobsang, however—she obviously fit into the picture. You could just see it, her and Tage and Sarah under the mistletoe. You could even see that Tage's girlfriend liked Lobsang, probably because she was tiny. Who wouldn't like Lobsang? She was just like a doll.

But a twelve-year-old was different. In the entryway to the dome, there were pictures of dogs from the local animal shelter, dogs for adoption. The woman Critter, whom Lars had met his first day in Minnesota, had hung up the photos. Lars felt like one of those dogs.

Outside the window, snow collected in the branches of the maple. *I hate that tree.*

Numb, Lars remembered how after school he and his father used to drive out to where the reindeer were corralled, and his father had taught him how to read earmarks, how to pick out which reindeer belonged to their family.

Lars had never been sure he wanted to be a reindeer herder when he grew up, but his father had said that was okay.

The day at school flickered in and out of his mind. Becka, the girl with the ring through her nose, was cool, but even she seemed far away now. She wasn't anything that could save him from being stuck in this house where nobody cared about him.

Someone knocked at the door.

His uncle. It had to be. Lars answered in Swedish before he remembered that he should always practice English around here.

Stepping inside, Tage shut the door, stepped over a box and sat on the bed. "What's up?"

There was a way his uncle looked at him that wasn't like the way anyone else in his life had ever looked at him. Lars figured it was because Tage was a dog trainer. He always looked like he expected something. Expected you to be more polite or something.

Lars stared back at him, like, *So, yeah, what?*

"Sarah is my very old, very close friend. She's going to be here for a while, in this house."

His uncle had come to the end of the bed. Lars didn't mean to flatten himself against the back of the chair, to back away in general, but Tage could have that effect on you when he was pissed off, which he was now, you could see.

What was he going to say?

"You treat women nicely. All women. All girls. Your sister. Critter and Lisa, my assistants. Your teachers. Sarah."

"What did I do?"

"We say hello. We say goodbye. We say please. We say thank you. We talk to each other. Sarah is very shy. She stammers badly." Tage used the word closest to the Swedish *stamning*, to make it clear.

Why was his uncle's voice changing that way? So what if she stammered? Big deal. She hardly talked anyhow.

Tage wasn't done. "I can't make the things you feel go away. No one can. You have to hold on to the love in your heart. We will try to be a family, the best we can. It won't be what you had before. But we must all try to be good, to be strong."

Lars felt his lips and chin moving, even though he wanted them to hold still. They trembled like he was going to cry or something, which he wasn't. His mouth wanted to say things, and it said them, said the one useful English phrase he'd learned at school that day. Becka had told him it stood for an old English expression, For Ungodly Carnal Knowledge, and the word applied perfectly to his uncle and the stuck-up bitch downstairs, and it was satisfying to say it to Tage, and also to say, "You're not my father. And she's not my mother. We're not going to be a big happy family."

Lars heard the dogs barking outside, heard a branch brushing the side of the house the way it always did. He heard those sounds for a long time, then thought he heard voices downstairs.

He started to wish Tage would say something.

"Do you feel like a man now?"

A man.

Lars had felt like a man skiing after the reindeer herd, looking after Lobsang when it was so cold. Drinking coffee in the morning with the other men.

A sick feeling rolled around in his stomach. No, he didn't feel like a man. He felt like a jerk. A stupid punk.

He couldn't look at his uncle. It was too scary how much Tage looked like an older version of him. His eyes were just like the eyes Lars saw in the mirror every day. It bugged him a lot, bugged him because Tage had been married to... It was really pretty hard to imagine. Much easier to imagine Tage and Sarah, who was obviously Tage's type, really beautiful.

Lars gazed out the windows, and he could almost hear Tage's breath but nothing else except the sounds outside and downstairs. Then the bed creaked. "You may as well unpack."

Staring at the boxes, Lars absorbed that, thought what it meant. When he looked up, his uncle was gone.

Just like that. Like that was all.

CHAPTER SIX

SARAH HAD COME UP to her room planning to shut her door, to be alone, to decide if she really wanted to stay. But the little girl had seen her go and followed her up the stairs. With Lobsang watching her from the top of the steps, Sarah had difficulty closing her door.

The child stepped toward the corner bedroom and beckoned.

The other doors were shut, and Sarah heard Tage's voice from behind one of them, but not what he was saying. Feeling oddly helpless, she followed Lobsang.

The girl's bed was unmade, with a floppy white red-nosed reindeer stuck among the covers. The clothes folded neatly on a corner chair didn't quite obscure the messy stack of children's books beneath them. Several boxes, some unopened, blocked the closet door.

Lobsang picked up a cylindrical packing tube and handed it to Sarah.

After a moment, Sarah removed the cap on the end and peered inside. Posters.

Lobsang made a grand gesture, indicating that the walls of the room were unadorned.

"Oh," said Sarah. She couldn't stick tacks in that wallpaper. Not without asking Tage, anyhow. This was a Craftsman house.

A door somewhere on the upper floor opened, and Sarah glanced into the hallway.

Tage saw her.

Opening her mouth, she tried to find words, easy vowel sounds. At last, as he reached her, she simply handed him the poster tube.

Tage was still hearing Lars's voice.

You're not my father. She's not my mother.

Absently, he wandered into Lobsang's bedroom and tried to figure out what the two who didn't speak wanted. Then he saw what he held.

"Sarah, there are thumbtacks in the alcove. If there aren't enough on the bulletin board, there's a box in my desk drawer."

She left the room and he was alone with Lobsang and his thoughts.

You're not my father. She's not my mother.

No, she wasn't.

Peter had urged him to marry Marit. *Hang onto that one. She's a good Saami woman.*

The good Saami woman had screwed Peter in Tage's bed.

Saami were famous for not fighting, even in the old days. They just disappeared. It was what Tage had done. But in your heart you knew when you'd abandoned your offspring. You knew when you'd taken the easy way out.

He started. A small black-haired child gazed up at him anxiously, seeming uncertain that he would hang her posters.

"Sarah will be back soon. She's bringing the thumbtacks."

SHE SEARCHED HIS DESK drawer and looked for the box of tacks. There were staples. There was a choke chain. There were papers and someone's school photo.

Her school photo.

Good grief, was that her?

To Tage. From Sarah.

Fourteen years old, with braces. She gazed at her own young face. First, it struck her that he'd kept it. Then, that it was in this drawer with photos of...dogs. And thumbtacks. There they were.

Sliding shut the drawer, she remembered the look on his face the night before. It didn't matter if he'd counted her freshman photo as treasure or junk. He might have invited her to stay as long as she liked, but she'd seen his emotions in his eyes when she'd told him she'd slept with Arthur.

Contempt, horror and anger didn't vanish overnight.

Sometimes, they didn't leave at all.

And she only had to carry the box of thumbtacks past Lobsang's mistletoe and remember what had happened twenty minutes earlier to know that Tage hadn't forgotten Arthur even for the length of a kiss.

IT AMAZED SARAH to see him puncturing the walls of the corner bedroom. Winnie-the-Pooh soon hung beside the casement windows. Cinderella and her pumpkin coach hung over the bed.

Holding her stuffed reindeer, Lobsang shadowed him wherever he moved, like a small supervisor. Where she pointed, he hung posters.

Sarah could almost feel Arthur's shudder.

He wouldn't have liked dogs in the house either, particularly Nordic breeds who shed with each step, like Comet, who was distributing guard hairs on the carpet at Sarah's feet. Petting the dog, who licked her hand in response, she watched the back of Tage's Levis as he took another poster from Lobsang.

He's trying to be a good dad, she thought.

"I could—" Sarah was so surprised to hear her own voice that she stopped in midsentence. She used the pause to choose words. "Arrange dinner."

Tage turned, staring. After a second, he said, "Okay. Good. I have an obedience class at six. Let's eat after."

THE WEATHER IMPROVED enough that all his students came. It was the last session before Christmas, with tests, and one woman brought him cookies and another brought him a reindeer ornament for his tree, which he never put up till Lucia Day, the thirteenth.

After the session in the dome, he checked on Anna, then entered the house through the back door and the laundry room to find Lobsang setting the table while Sarah sliced vegetables for egg rolls.

Lobsang placed the last piece of silverware and came to him. He picked her up, then turned to check the TV monitor.

Where was Lars?

Do you feel like a man now? You may as well unpack. After a few hours' reflection, Tage wondered if he'd been too harsh.

"Lobsang, let's find your brother. Do you need my help, Sarah?"

She shook her head.

He couldn't find Lars in the house; Snutte was missing, too, and Tage bundled up Lobsang and went out to the sled dogs' run to look for the herding dog, then into the dome. No Lars.

Just Snutte's tracks and ski tracks, leading down a trail that went past the training field and wound into the woods. The path led up a ridge on the near side of the lake.

Tage carried Lobsang back to the house, told Sarah where Lars had gone and suggested she go ahead with dinner. He and Lars would eat it cold. "If you want, you can bring Moses inside and put him on a long down, sitting on his lead." He'd left written instructions for the long down and Michael Fox's book on wolf behavior beside her bed. "But don't let him off the lead."

Outside, he put on his skis and a headlamp to follow the boy's tracks away from the lights of the kennels.

Lars knew better than to set off and tell no one where he was going. The tracks wandered off the trail, into birch forest. *What are you doing, Lars?* Would Peter have understood?

Tage closed his lips. Regret was a place; you lost your way and arrived there and could only leave after you'd paid an unspecified due. Some people never escaped. But no matter how strong your regret, you did *not* tell a twelve-year-old who had just lost both parents that the man he called Father hadn't conceived him. If that was the toll, Tage refused to pay.

He and Lars could be friends, uncle and nephew, teacher and student. They could never be father and son.

Where was Lars going? The tracks hadn't turned back yet. If Lars kept on in this direction, he would reach the highway. The highway...

Running away?

Tage skied faster, learning what it was to be frightened for his child. Learning something Peter and Marit must have learned long ago.

SARAH FRIED ENOUGH egg rolls for her and Lobsang; she would fix the rest when Tage returned with Lars. She and Lobsang sat down to eat, and a peace descended on the table. It was nice to be with someone who didn't expect conversation. And Lobsang seemed to like egg rolls, too.

After dinner, Sarah retrieved several of Lobsang's books, and impulsively the stuffed reindeer, and carried them to the inglenook by the living-room hearth. Eagerly taking her reindeer, Lobsang sat down on a bench to page through the book.

Sarah brought Moses inside, along with a chew toy Tage must have given him, a canvas thing resembling Humpty-Dumpty. Following Tage's instructions, she measured out a length of the lead, giving Moses only enough freedom to lie down, then sat on the rest of the leash.

He tugged it out from under her.

"N—" *No.* Tage had given her a nylon slip collar and taught her how to put it on Moses. She gave it a sharp tug, as Tage had said to, but the word "no" hung in her mouth. As she tried to say it, Moses yelped and sat down and became surprisingly docile, resting his head on Humpty-Dumpty.

Slowly, Sarah relaxed and opened the book in her lap, Tage's book on wolves. She tried to ignore Moses. Difficult. He was staring intently at Lobsang and her stuffed toy, and after a few seconds he began chewing on his lead. Sarah gave the leash a sharp jerk upward, and he yelped again. She was supposed to ignore Moses during this exercise, so she opened her book again.

He stood and maneuvered in front of the chair. Putting his paws on her lap, he snatched the book in his teeth.

Tage had said not to give a command she wasn't sure would be obeyed.

Pushing Moses away, the book still in the grip of his muzzle, she stood. "Okay, outside."

His tail began to wag, and he jerked the lead from her hand and sprinted from the room, darting across the hall and into the library. In the dark, something crashed. Glass broke.

As Lobsang looked up with a start, Sarah tore after Moses. She couldn't take the book away, but at least she could grab his lead and get him out of the house. Shit, that was a Mission floor lamp he'd broken.

The white tail disappeared through the dining room door into the pantry.

Moses!

She dashed past the Twenty-second Psalm in time to find him with his feet on the kitchen counter, polishing off the egg rolls.

THE MIST-SHROUDED FIGURE waited by the road with his skis and his dog, and he must have just gotten there because no one had stopped yet, and in Manitou people would stop. Neighbors were friendly, and often hitchhikers were motorists in distress. A boy out in this weather with skis and a dog would be picked up at once.

Through the slanting snow, Tage skied toward Lars and Snutte, any anger long since vanished. Lars was safe.

When Tage neared, the boy eyed him indifferently and checked the black road for headlights. An icy wind cut through Tage's wool pants as Snutte greeted him, tail wagging.

"Let's go home, Lars."

Lars put on his skis and led the way into the woods. The pointed tails on his hat bobbed behind him, and Tage found a pace beside him in the sudden silence of snowfall. Their skis whispered in the December night.

"Where were you going?"

The dark figure beside him shrugged as he skied.

The cold was arctic. Snowflakes swirled around blackened skeletons of trees. Tage felt as though the two of them were hanging over a precipice. "When my father died—" he said, then broke off the sentence. "He froze. He got lost on a migration and froze and died. I didn't know why he did it. I didn't know why he hadn't been more careful. I needed him. I felt almost like he'd gotten lost on purpose."

"That's stupid," Lars said as Snutte marked a nearby tree. He knew what Tage was doing. Trying to make it seem like he'd felt the same way when he was a kid. Well,

Tage was wrong. Tage could never have felt this bad. And Tage hadn't been sent to live with an uncle and his girl-friend.

Lars darted a glance at him.

Even though it was night, with no moon, you could see Tage's white-blond hair under his hat. It was long and wavy, almost reaching his shoulders. Lars could make out his features, too. And his eyes. Otherwise, he was all black, like the night.

The kind of jerk who said, *You may as well unpack.*

Snow touched Lars's cheeks and his nose, and Snutte crossed in front of him and Tage. At least his uncle had stopped saying stupid things.

He hadn't really been going anywhere. At first, he'd thought he would just ski into the forest and not come back. Then he'd lost his way and ended up here. It had occurred to him he could hitchhike somewhere.

Branches broke ahead of them, and Lars jumped. *What was that?*

"Stop." Tage grasped Lars's arm. He recognized the shaking of the ground. "Be still."

As Tage gauged his distance to Snutte, measured what it would take to grab the dog, the monstrous horned shape emerged from the trees like a god of the woods and the black dog charged it.

"Snutte!" screamed Lars, into his uncle's glove, which was suddenly covering his mouth. He could hardly see, just hear Snutte's growling and feel himself thrown off the trail, skis and all.

"Don't move."

The ground shook as the moose thundered past.

Holding Lars, Tage watched the animal disappear on the trail. If it came back to fight, they were in trouble. Snutte was getting to his feet again, limping, looking after the moose.

Tage spoke to the dog in Saami, calling him.

Snutte came at once, and Tage caught his collar and removed a glove to check him over. The dog had escaped with a cut on one leg.

While Lars sat up and shook snow off himself, Snutte licked his face. "Snutte. You're all right! You're stupid, you know that?"

Soon, he and Tage were skiing again. Lars thought of the moose and remembered other moose, moose he and his father had seen together in Lapland. A moose his father had shot.

He'd never been charged by a moose before. His uncle was fast. Strange to be held so tightly. Lars couldn't remember his father ever holding him so hard. He hadn't expected Tage to...well, care so much if a moose trampled him. Lars felt guilty and wasn't sure why. Except perhaps because it made him feel good that Tage cared about him like a parent.

TAGE HAD SEEN SARAH this distressed only once before—when they'd gone out to dinner in Colorado and some gallery owner she knew had tried to have a conversation with her.

Flushed, she told Tage, "He ate the egg rolls." While Snutte limped by wearing the bandage Tage and Lars had applied in the grooming area, Sarah showed Tage what was left of the Mission lamp and presented his mauled copy of *Behavior of Wolves, Dogs and Related Canids.*

Lobsang watched anxiously from the doorway of the library, as though worried that Sarah was in trouble.

Tage cracked a smile. "Moses is outside?"

"Yes."

"Penned?"

She nodded.

"Tomorrow morning, I'll work with you and Moses, all

right?'' He handed the book back to her. ''For now, keep reading.''

Sarah fixed sandwiches for him and Lars. As he helped, Tage told her about the moose and also about the reindeer taken from the roadside zoo. Wildlife officials were bringing the corral the next day; the reindeer should arrive Wednesday. They were in some kind of quarantine.

Exhausted, Sarah sat at the table with Tage and Lars and with Lobsang, who wanted Cheerios. When Tage offered Sarah some of Arthur's wine, she accepted. The wine performed alchemy in her veins. It reminded her that she had wanted Arthur and that there had been no blood relationship between them. Mutual agreement. A ritual coming of age, as Arthur had suggested. A second glass softened the edges. This place had been her Avalon always—never Thebes.

After dinner, Tage said it was Lobsang's bedtime, and Sarah made herself scarce. She'd spent enough time with Lobsang tonight, especially since Lobsang had seen her trying not to cry over egg rolls and a broken lamp. After the cleanup, when Sarah had curled up in a chair to contemplate escape, Lobsang had brought her reindeer and put it in Sarah's lap.

No more Lobsang tonight.

Sarah went out to see Moses and lie down with him on the warm floor of his run, feeling the heat from the water piped beneath the concrete. He kissed her face and accepted being petted, and Sarah tried to forget how hard it had been to get him out of the house. He'd picked up the book again and tried to play, waving his tail high in the air, eyes on hers. Growling.

It had made her feel the way stuttering did. Helpless and clumsy.

Now... Well, Moses was peaceful, even if he was entertaining himself by mouthing her upper arm through her parka.

She petted him and withdrew, standing. Immediately, he became playful, jumping up on her. Bracing herself against the wall, she edged all the way to the door of the run. She rubbed his coarse fur and let him kiss her face before she slipped out.

When she returned to the house, Tage was coming down the stairs.

"They're both in bed," he told her.

She followed him to the kitchen, where he poured them each some more wine and turned to her. Their eyes met; they raised their goblets, drank, and gazed at each other again.

Neither of them looked long. The kitchen faucet became more interesting to him than she was. When they moved to the library, it was the same. He paused by the window seat, studying the panes as though he could see something besides night.

"I could leave," she said. She'd been there more than twenty-four hours—enough rest from the drive.

He turned with the goblet at his lips and drank.

Sarah tucked her feet under her on the Frank Lloyd Wright couch.

Tage lowered his glass. "Why did you come with me to pick up Lars and Lobsang at school?"

It wasn't a good time to talk. She was a little drunk. Sometimes that made her fluent, but she lost the single advantage stuttering had ever given her. Silence. Care in speech.

She tried sidestepping his question. "It doesn't seem relevant. We can't even kiss." *Clumsy, Sarah. Just shut up.*

Tage laughed. "You're talking about that?" His eyes indicated the mistletoe. "We can kiss," he promised. "I'm still occasionally disturbed by images of you and my friend Arthur screwing in the cabin. I'm sure it will pass.''

Faint nausea went through her. *So now we talk about this.* Drunk, she wanted to mention the salt kiln, to ask Tage what he thought. Drunk, she was stupid.

There was a sound on the stairs, and Snutte came in the library. He must have let himself out of the bedroom. Tage hadn't brought Comet inside for the night yet, so Snutte came right to the two of them, and Sarah eyed the bandage on his leg. The wound was minor, Tage had said when he explained about the moose.

Tage sat on the couch beside her. The way he looked at her, she wondered if he was seeing her naked. A hard male desire steamed off him. Sometimes, she felt her reaction to him was equally visible, as though she gave off a flower fragrance, an aphrodisiac, her pores emitting the scent of sex.

Arthur had told her something very similar once. That summer night when darkness was so slow in coming.

Shifting against the far armrest and taking more than his share of the couch, Tage said, "How old were you? Seventeen?"

He must have known better. The urge to mention the salt kiln evaporated, dried up by his question—or the way he'd asked.

"You'd like that." She drained her goblet and set it on the maple shelf surrounding the couch. "Twenty-three. It happened eight months before he died. In June."

Tage considered. Sarah's birthday was May Day. Arthur would have been...sixty-eight. "That's a forty-five-year age difference."

"I can add."

"Did you like it?"

The hall clock ticked, and there was a sound on the stairs that Tage thought absently must be a dog, especially when Snutte got up and trotted out of the room. Tage wanted Sarah's answer to his question. He wanted to know if she'd liked sex with Arthur Tennyson.

"Of course."

She'd looked in his eyes to say it, then looked away. He knew she saw the mistletoe. And that she was on the verge of crying.

Of course.

He'd seen Sarah when she was liking sex. It was something far removed from that cool kiss under the mistletoe, the kiss he'd forced on her. The kiss that wasn't.

Was "of course," a lie? Sarcasm? Or candor.

Sarah could no longer speak. Words sloshed inside her. *I think he killed himself.* She stood, grabbing her goblet, knowing she might as well leave. But the wine had made her talkative, and there was still something she wanted to know.

"Wh-wh-wh—"

Stammering.

Tage knew it would be more comfortable for her if he didn't watch her stutter. He watched anyhow—couldn't really help it. She put a foot on the floor, and the muscles of her throat strained as her face twisted grotesquely, flooded with embarrassed color, as she tried to speak.

"Wh-wh-wh-whyyyy did you tell me about Lars?"

Silence cloaked the room, except for the sound of Snutte's nails on the stairs, his tags jingling. Somewhere, a sound like a breath. Tage thought it was his own. "I wish I hadn't. I'll never tell him."

The top buttons of her long undershirt were undone. No bra. Tage saw the outline of her nipples through the cotton and grew hard, painfully hard. He saw her with Arthur. Control sifted out of his pores and slithered away. Feeling it leave, he stood and strode out of the library. In the hall he started violently.

Lars sat on the stairs with Snutte.

It took Tage seconds to speak. "What are you doing?"

Lars dragged himself to his feet without answering.

What did he hear? What did we say?

Had either he or Sarah called Lars his son?

No. Whenever those words were spoken, Tage remembered. So far he himself was the only person who had ever uttered them—except perhaps Peter and Marit to each other. They'd never discussed the matter with him, not since he'd told Marit that he would let them raise the baby as their own.

So Lars must be curious—but he didn't know anything.

Tage waited for questions.

None came. Only a furtive glance.

You shouldn't eavesdrop. Tage didn't say it. His own indiscretion weighed more heavily than Lars's curiosity. Oh, shit, what had they said about Sarah and Arthur? That conversation had been much longer and more frank.

Tage opened his mouth and shut it. Asking Lars what he'd heard would only draw more attention to the conversation—and maybe reveal something Lars hadn't even noticed. As the boy eyed him with cold detachment, Tage hid his discomposure, as he would from an aggressive dog.

Staring into his son's eyes—something he *wouldn't* do with an aggressive dog—Tage asked, "Can I get you something?"

Lars ducked his head, murmuring, "No." Without another word, he slowly trudged up the stairs.

Breath shallow, Tage watched him go. Snutte followed his young master, and when both had disappeared into the shadows of the upper hall, Tage turned back to the library and almost bumped into Sarah. She stood between the cherry panels on each side of the doorway, room dividers opened at the bottom and the top. In the top window of each sat Arthur's raku, and Tage studied one of the vases so that he wouldn't have to see Sarah's eyes. He couldn't remember where he'd been going, what he'd been doing, before seeing Lars.

He knew only that Sarah stood beneath the mistletoe and so did he. That he was aware of it and she was not.

From the corner of his eye, he took in her expression. She wasn't curious about what Lars had heard. She was preoccupied and desolate.

He whispered, "I'm sorry. I'm very jealous. And angry at Arthur."

She whispered, too. Her words tore the floor out from under him and the roof off his head.

"I think he killed himself."

TWENTY MINUTES LATER, Lars still couldn't sleep. Not after the way his uncle had gone white and jumped three feet in the air.

Lars would have felt better if Tage had gotten mad at him for listening. Instead, he'd looked at Lars oddly. What had Sarah meant? What was it his uncle would never tell him?

He shuddered.

Ideas occurred to him that he knew were outrageous. That his uncle had murdered his parents. That he, Lars, had been adopted by Peter and Marit, just like Lobsang.

Oh, God, could that be it? He didn't look much like either of his parents. They both had dark hair, and he was blond. But his grandmother was blond, too. No. If he'd been adopted, he would know, and his parents would have told him. They weren't silly about things like that.

He tossed restlessly in his bed, bothered by other things. He was getting acne, on his shoulders and even on his face. His legs were cramped, and he remembered how his mother used to rub them. She and his father had said the leg cramps were growing pains, and his father had smiled and said, *You're getting so tall, Lars. You're going to be big and handsome, bigger than me.*

The thought made him cry, and in the midst of his tears he recalled his uncle holding him earlier, when the moose went by.

His uncle cared what happened to him, at least.

That made him cry, too, because he wanted his father, not his uncle. He wanted someone who'd known him forever and who... Biting his lips against the sheet, he remembered how his father used to cuddle him in the big armchair by the fire. But his uncle wouldn't hold him that way. Lars didn't want him to. He'd crossed over now, to a place where no one cuddled you, and he was alone, had to stand alone the way his father had taught him.

But I always thought you'd be around.

As tears flooded his eyes again, two paws weighed down the side of his bed, and then Snutte jumped up on the mattress.

Tage had said no dogs on the bed.

So what?

Lars dragged Snutte over to the empty side of the bed. "Down," he said and rubbed the spot between Snutte's head and his back, the spot Tage had shown him, and Snutte lay down beside Lars. Putting his head near the dog's, Lars let himself cry and wished the darkness would go away.

CHAPTER SEVEN

Tuesday

LARS SQUINTED AT THE clock, disoriented. He was in his uncle's house. His parents were dead. And it was only five in the morning.

Tage was there beside his bed, in sweatpants, saying, "It's not snowing. Let's go run the dogs."

Sleepy, Lars sat up part way. Stars still shone outside. *The dogs...* Tage had promised to take him to a dogsled race that weekend. Now Tage wanted to help him train.

He wavered, then abruptly remembered Snutte.

Where was he?

On the floor, sniffing Tage.

It was all right, then. His uncle hadn't seen the dog on the bed.

Lars recalled what he'd overheard on the stairs. Years earlier, he'd overheard his parents talking about Chernobyl, about the reindeer being poisoned, and it had scared him. When he'd finally gotten the nerve to say something about it, his father had told him, *Don't ever be afraid to ask me anything, Lars.*

Did the same thing apply to his uncle, his uncle who had let him go on migration and had held him so tightly when the moose went by? No, it didn't apply. Tage had said to Sarah, *I'll never tell him.*

"Lars?"

Tage had invited him to run dogs. Lars didn't want to

run dogs with someone who was keeping a big secret from him—but sharing it with Sarah. He said, as politely as possible, "No, thanks."

His uncle seemed to jump back a little. A second later, he said, "Not interested in mushing any more?"

Not interested in mushing... The few times Lars had gone out, it was only with a few dogs, never more than three. Even that had felt very fast. Tage had told him that with more than seven dogs, you couldn't stop them unless they wanted to stop. *How many dogs,* Lars had asked, *for the Iditarod?*

"Up to twenty."

Tage had won the silver cup. *There is one valley,* he'd said, *where the wind is always blowing. It blows away all the snow, and you have to run behind the sled for seventy miles, and the rocks tear apart the sled anyhow. By the end of the race, you sleep only a few hours a day. You begin to see things that aren't there....*

Lars was fascinated by this picture. He wanted to run the Iditarod someday, and he knew that he would.

But he had principles. And Tage, his uncle, was holding a secret from him, some bad secret. "No."

His uncle looked at him forever. The room seemed blue and black in the morning, except Tage, who was those shades of blond and brown, who was so handsome.

Tage stood. "If you change your mind, come down. I'll leave in about twenty minutes."

"SARAH?"

The knock roused her from a familiar dream. She was in school. The teacher had called on her to read, and she struggled over the first word on the page. Tried and tried to say it...

It was still dark. Outside the row of windows, the snow

lay like dried icing on the branches of the evergreens.
Things rushed back. Arguing with Tage about Arthur.

*I knew Arthur, Sarah. I knew him differently than you
did. Having slept with you, he would not have killed himself over it. I never knew him to feel remorse, for anything.*

She eased out of bed and grabbed some jeans and
opened the door.

Tage's parka was unzipped. His eyes searched hers
briefly. "I'm taking the dogs out. Lars says he doesn't
want to come, but if he changes his mind, will you look
after Lobsang when she wakes up? I'll be back in time to
get her ready for school."

Look after Lobsang.

It sounded so casual. It didn't have to mean anything,
didn't have to mean that he was somehow inviting her to
share in caring for his children on other occasions. On all
occasions. "If you don't want to do it, say so. I'll wake
her, and she can come with us."

So it really didn't matter.

But he was helping her with Moses, putting her up in
his house. She should repay him somehow.

"It's all right. Go," she said.

What if he thought it was incest? she'd asked Tage.

Tage's jaw had dropped. *What do you think it was,
Sarah? But don't worry about Arthur's conscience working overtime. I'm telling you, the man never exerted himself that way.*

Now his arctic-ice eyes lingered, making sure she was
okay. She wasn't, but the two of them had said everything
last night.

He walked away, starting down the stairs.

No sooner was he out of sight than Lars's door opened,
and the black dog came out, then Lars himself, dressed in
clothing of reindeer fur. Crossing the hall to the bathroom,
he must have seen Sarah from the corner of his eye. Over

the empty space of the stairwell, the railings between them, he lifted his hand in a grudging wave.

BY NOON, TAGE WANTED a drink. After taking the children to the bus, an event that had made Lobsang cry, he'd helped Sarah with Moses, worked on her with establishing positive eye contact and elementary leash work.

All of it had left him feeling uneasy. Moses was an adolescent, and his business was challenging Sarah for leadership. It was a business that would consume his life. Tage wanted to believe Sarah was up to it and knew she wasn't. He gave her the articles he'd downloaded from the Internet, told her to read more in the wolf book and wished for a miracle.

At eleven-thirty, the woman who had called the day before, frantic about a destroyed painting, arrived with Baron, the German shepherd who had chewed it up. While she and her husband filled out a questionnaire in the office, Tage walked over to the stone building to see the dog. He let himself in with Baron, and at the sight of the slip collar and leash Tage carried, the dog lunged at him.

Critter heard the commotion and was in the run in a second. It took both of them to subdue the German shepherd. Tage's arm was torn up, the first bite he'd suffered from a client's dog in three years. His blood puddled on the concrete as he secured the run. "Destructive chewing," he murmured.

"Want me to drive you to the clinic?"

He shook his head. The bite was bad enough that it should be seen, but he wanted to get the owner interview over with. "I'll take care of it."

The wound required a bottle of betadyne to clean and eight butterfly bandages to close. When Baron's owner saw Tage's bandages, she broke down, crying till her glasses fogged. "Oh, I didn't think he'd do it with *you!*"

It was Tage's last appointment of the day. Afterward, he headed for the house to get on the computer and be alone.

Sarah would be out in the studio.

His stepfather had e-mailed him days ago, and he hadn't answered. He poured himself some coffee, and when he checked his mail there were three more messages from Nils-Isak, all polite inquiries as to how things were going. Clearly, his mother and stepfather were wondering how he was managing with the two children.

Trying to ignore what he'd learned about his father's good friend Arthur, Tage wrote back that Sarah had come for help with a wolf dog, that he was teaching Lars to drive a dogsled and that he had hung up Lobsang's posters. Then he shut down the computer and slouched in the chair, swilling coffee and looking at all he could see.

All Arthur Tennyson had given him.

Beneath the sleeve of his flannel shirt, his arm stung and throbbed from the dog bite. Trying to focus on business, he grabbed the phone book. Soon, he'd arranged for a fencing contractor to come out to give a bid on the wolf compound later that day.

Moses...

Thinking about the wolf dog, he squinted at the TV monitor, then opened a drawer in the filing cabinet and removed a shoe box. Pieces of antler and his carving tools lay inside. *Duodji*, Saami handcrafts, were not made by patterns alone. There was technique and an inspiration that came from the materials. Nils-Isak had taught Tage to carve, and now it was second nature. He picked up one piece he'd begun and one of his tools, but the bite had his hand shaking.

A man couldn't ignore where he was.

Numb, he gazed out at the kennels. Lisa was leading a mixed breed out to the training field.

He had come to the U.S. with money from slaughtering his herd. Arthur's bequest had given him a place into which to sink that money, and he'd done it.

Suicide?

Tage hadn't received any of the life insurance money, and he didn't believe Arthur had killed himself. But Sarah did. She'd believed it for *twelve years*. In all those years, she'd said nothing.

The way you said nothing about Lars.

Things like Nome made sense.

Maybe it was Peter's and Marit's death, or maybe it was Sarah's bringing the wolf dog. But suddenly his ordered life had become chaos. Nothing was as it had appeared. This place where he lived was trying to be Arthur's instead of his. It was trying to hold Arthur's spirit, as though Arthur walked among them, keeping him and Sarah apart.

The way Peter's memory would always keep him from Lars.

SARAH SPENT MUCH of the day in the studio with Moses, trying to read about wolves and wolf dogs. The articles Tage had left disturbed her. Children and wolf dogs were a deadly combination; she couldn't help thinking of Lobsang. And owning a wolf dog was different from other types of pet ownership. The liability was great, the animals vulnerable. Their needs were powerful and different from a dog's.

Most of them were put down before they turned three.

On the way back to the house, she passed a workman in the woods talking to Tage. Together, they were marking an area with stakes and string. For Moses's pen? Moses avoided the men, pulling her after him into the trees.

That night, when the children were in bed, Tage asked Sarah to bring Moses inside for a long down. "We'll see how he gets along with Comet and Snutte."

They had their answer soon. Moses and Comet stood with stiff bodies and raised tails, while Snutte sniffed the air, ready to spring into any fight that erupted. As Tage caught Comet's collar, the sled dog went into a frenzy of snarling, and Moses broke from Sarah's hand. Only Snutte, charging in, let Tage shove Comet onto the porch. As he shut the door, he said, *"Moses, no. Snutte, no."*

Seeing his eyes, the wolf dog suddenly sat down, as though undecided what to do next, and tucked his tail beneath him. While Comet whined and jumped on the door, raising Cain, Snutte held himself still, then made a show of forgetting there had been a disagreement. *Yeah, you'll wait till I turn around and start it again,* Tage thought. With his arm stinging and sore from where he'd been bitten earlier, Tage hauled Snutte outside and dragged him and a protesting Comet to the sled dogs' compound.

When he came back inside, Sarah was struggling to keep Moses in his down. She wasn't strong enough to hold the leash in place. Moses finally began to respond to her corrections with soft growls, and Tage muzzled him so she could correct his behavior and they could complete the exercise.

Afterward, Tage said, "I want to try this. Some dogs respond very well to being allowed to sleep in a crate in your room. We'll have to take some care to keep Comet and Snutte out of his way, but let's give it a try."

Moses tried to explore the whole upstairs before they baited his crate in her room with meat. Tage secured the door of the crate with a padlock, gave Sarah the key and said good-night. He was going to bring Comet and Snutte back in.

He left her without ever mentioning Arthur. He didn't need to. As Moses whined in his crate, all Sarah could hear in her mind was Tage saying, *What do you think it was, Sarah?* What do *you* think it was? All she could see was his eyes and in them the horror of a man who had just become father to a little girl not of his blood. A man who had a stepfather of his own.

His eyes said that Arthur had violated a sacred trust.

And so, thought Sarah, *did I violate that trust.*

Arthur had called her sensuous and alluring. *You've seduced me, Sarah.*

She shivered.

Tage was wrong! Tage was wrong about Arthur. Tage hadn't dissuaded her last night, hadn't dissuaded her from believing that Arthur had planned the accident with the salt kiln.

He had convinced her.

She knew Arthur better than he did.

Arthur Tennyson could feel remorse. And he had been seduced.

THE NEXT MORNING, Wednesday, Tage and Lars left early again to run the sled dogs. No sooner had they gone than the doorknob of Sarah's room turned and Lobsang came in. Her small bare feet made a soft sound on the floor, and without invitation she climbed up onto Sarah's bed. Moses whined in his crate.

As Sarah sat up, Lobsang played with her reindeer, combing its straggly white fur with her fingers.

Why are you hanging around me? Sarah wondered. Yesterday, she hadn't even gone with Tage to meet the children at the bus stop. When they'd come home, he and Lars and Lobsang had gone out to watch the people from the humane society assemble the reindeer corral.

Sarah had stayed away.

She felt sick. Each hour that passed made her sicker.

Each hour, some memory shoved itself in her face, and Tage's voice asked, *What do* you *think it was?* She shut her eyes, cringing as she had in the night, half awake, half dreaming.

When she opened her eyes, Lobsang was still there.

What could she do about this child who had become her shadow? Lobsang shouldn't depend on her. Somehow, she had to make the little girl see that.

There were ways to do it.

Leaving for Cairo two days before your daughter turned four. Missing the Christmas pageant when she was Mary—one of the few times in her life she would be on stage, because the part required no speaking. Standing her up in Bath, although the vacation had been planned months before.

The times Sarah's mother had been around were almost as ghastly as when she'd been gone. She'd taken Sarah to Denver to get her hair cut and sometimes permed or colored, whether Sarah wanted it or not. They'd shopped for dresses Sarah didn't want and had posed for studio photographs together. Mother-daughter pictures with the mother who was never there except *for* the pictures.

Sometimes, Sarah sympathized with her mother. Sometimes, she suspected that Poloma had so little to do with her because Poloma doubted her own powers of speech.

A parent should be able to talk.

Sarah needed to be able to talk, to speak to Lobsang about Moses, to explain that she mustn't run when he was loose, that she mustn't fall down near him, that if she did those things he might regard her as prey.

No, Sarah. The answer has nothing to do with language. Moses and that child should not be together.

Moses whined more insistently, and Sarah climbed from bed. She collected the leash and slip collar from the top of the crate, preparing to put them on him as soon as he emerged.

Lobsang got out of bed, too, and stood by the door, watching the wolf.

Don't look into his eyes, Sarah thought. But even if she could say the words, Lobsang wouldn't understand.

She caught Moses's collar as he came out of the crate. When the slip collar and lead were on him, he stepped toward the dresser against the far wall and lifted his leg.

"No!" Sarah jerked on the lead, surprised she'd spoken so fluently.

Yelping, Moses gazed up at her, then darted away, stretching to the end of the lead, trying to get out the door.

Tage had given her a list of rules that would help her establish dominance over Moses. Things like making sure he let her go through doors first.

No such luck. The wolf dog dragged her around the stairwell and down the hall to the bathroom. Finding himself cornered, he seemed to panic, then resort to play, tugging the bath mat from the bathroom, out into the hall and down the stairs.

I'm not going to try to take it away from him.

Instead, she followed him, with Lobsang behind her. While she laced her boots in the vestibule, Moses ate the bath mat. Only when she stood and put on her scarf and parka did Moses seem to realize that she meant to take him outside. Giving up what remained of the bath mat, he tried to flee into the living room, and a tug-of-war ensued.

Sarah jerked the lead sharply. "M-M—" Moses, come. She stabbed her foot into the ground, her breath insufficient to utter the words, the muscles of her chest and throat locked, her lips contorted. "M-M-M—" Oblivious to the child behind her, to anything but the words, she tried to speak.

Moses raised his tail and growled at her.

She had to get him outside, out to his kennel.

The back door?

As she turned past the stairs, into the little passage between the front hall and the pantry, Moses raced past her, skidding on the floor, pulling her along, eager to visit the rest of the house.

Sarah lost no momentum in the kitchen, just continued into the utility room, where a basket of dirty laundry sat beside the dryer. It absorbed the wolf dog's attention, and he snatched one of Tage's wool socks.

Damn it, Moses.

From the kitchen doorway, Lobsang solemnly observed his naughtiness.

Sarah opened the back door, and Moses's head went up. He sniffed the fresh cold air. Dropping the sock, he lunged through the opening, dragging Sarah onto the back step. Beneath the back awning, the wood was coated with ice. Her boots slipped out from under her, and the leash flew from her hand as she fell, slamming her rear end hard against the porch.

Tears stung her eyes. Gingerly she hauled herself up and grabbed the snowy railing with a bare hand to get down to the area behind the house. A cleared path with three-foot drifts on either side led back to the isolation kennels, where Moses was leaping at a high window.

What did he want?

Carefully treading the snowy path, trying to ignore her body's tenderness, she watched him sniff around the stone structure, finally making his way to the door, where he tried the handle and turned it.

Sarah hurried, her muscles moving like sandbags in the cold, her eyes on the leash dragging behind him in the snow. He nudged open the door, but as she caught his leash, he whisked it away. When she grasped the doorknob, the cold metal burned her hand, and Moses darted in, the lead slipping behind him like a snake. Shocked, eyes watering again, Sarah shouldered through the door.

The building had one occupant, in the run at the far end, and Moses stood tall and dominant, staring through the chain link. The dog inside, a sled dog Sarah didn't recognize, lifted her head, sniffing the air, and whined.

Suddenly, Sarah knew.

Sex. It was what had brought Moses in here. Sliding across the ceramic tile floor, Sarah snatched up Moses's leash and pulled hard. "No!"

He turned, snarling, fangs bared, and sprang at her. Like a wall hit by a wrecking ball she went down, backward, and her head slammed the tile floor. Then ninety pounds of wolf dog were on top of her. A wolf's breath and white teeth and retracted lips swept past her eyes, and she was bitten but did not scream. Standing on her, Moses growled, and after some seconds of blankness, Sarah realized she'd emptied her bladder and bowels. Her eyes teared in the emptiness, her back oddly warm on the floor, but she didn't move.

The time went on and on. Feeling the different warmth of the animal above her, the warmth of life, and scenting his breath, she was afraid to move and didn't dare look at him. *You win, Moses. You're the alpha.*

Ages passed that way, before he slowly moved off her, edging back toward the kennel run where the sled dog waited. The bitch held her ground, watching him indecisively.

Motionless, Sarah listened to the tags on his collar and to his breath.

He jumped up on the chain link separating him from the other dog, then stood on his hind legs and nosed up the latch on the gate. It was just like the latch to Sarah's portable kennel at home. He was going to get in.

Sarah couldn't move.

The sled dog whined.

Hearing the gate spring open and bang the kennel wall,

Sarah cautiously sat up. Moses spun around, with tail raised.

Recalling what she'd read in Tage's book on wolf behavior, Sarah looked away. After a long time, she heard him moving, and when she slowly shifted her own head, his tail was disappearing into the run.

Behind her, the door of the stone building opened and two small bare feet, strange against the snow and ice, crossed the threshold.

No! Lobsang, go back.

Sarah shook her head, and the girl came in anyway.

She couldn't get up fast enough. Moses was going to come out. The door was miles away, and she used her body to shield Lobsang, who was so small. As the handle turned under her fingers, she expected to feel the wolf dog slam against her. She knew the force of his weight, knew how hard it would throw her against the door. If she could just push Lobsang outside... And then she had, and the kennel door was shut behind them.

The six-year-old stood barefoot in the snow, gazing up at Sarah, and Sarah saw that her own clothes weren't torn, though she could feel that they were soiled, that her fear had done that. She didn't think she was bleeding, just bruised. Dazed, she nudged Lobsang ahead of her, and the child, with her feet that didn't care about the snow, walked ahead.

The white world swirled, and her stomach revolted.

Halfway to the house, Sarah knelt in the snow and vomited.

WHAT COULD SHE DO?

Lobsang stuck to her like glue, even following her into the bathroom, where Sarah rolled up her dirty clothes and got in the shower, shaking. She had to calm down, had to figure out what to do. It was only about six; Tage and Lars wouldn't be back for another hour, and no assistants would arrive till an hour after that.

Where were Tage's keys to the kennels? She couldn't stop Moses from mating with the dog in isolation, but at least she could lock the door so he wouldn't run away.

She hurried in the shower, her legs vibrating like rubber. He *had* bitten her through her scarf. Blood on her neck. No sooner did she see it on her hand and feel what seemed like a small puncture wound than she forgot about it.

Shutting off the water, she wrapped up in a towel, and the child who'd been sitting on the toilet seat waiting trailed after her to her room.

It took only minutes to dress again and put her dirty clothes in the washing machine downstairs. Then Sarah hunted for the keys, checking hooks in the kitchen and pantry, Tage's desk in the alcove, coat pockets in the closet.

She tried to tell Lobsang. *"K-k-k-keys."*

The brown eyes comprehended nothing.

Maybe in the dome. What if Moses got out while she was looking for the keys? No, if he was really mating with that female it would take a while, wouldn't it? Sarah really wasn't sure.

Whose dog was that? Was it one of Tage's sled dogs? Or a client's?

Oh, shit. Oh, shit. Wasn't there something she could do? Turn a hose on them?

Again, she felt Moses standing on her, heard his growl, the growl of a wild animal. Her legs threatened to fold.

She could not separate the mating pair. But she had to find a way to see that Moses didn't get out.

A chair. Put a chair under the door. It opened outward....

Hurrying, she grabbed a scarred spindle-back chair from the alcove and carried it through the house. *Arthur would have a fit.* Taking a chair outside.

Nausea rolled through her again.

Everything that had seemed manageable, tolerable just an hour before now threatened to overwhelm her. In the utility room, she told Lobsang, "S-s-s—" Oh, she couldn't talk. She couldn't talk, even to say, *Stay here.*

Desperate, Sarah pointed toward the kitchen. *Go back.*

Lobsang went.

Sarah stepped outside and was faint and dizzy when she saw the isolation kennel again. Moses wouldn't come out. Why would he?

But she trembled uncontrollably all the way to the building, even as she fit the chair under the door, trapping the animals inside.

NO SOONER HAD Sarah returned to the kitchen than Lobsang handed her the school library copy of *The Night before Christmas.*

"Oh…" Sarah's throat and chest squeezed tight. *I can't read out loud.* How could she say that to a child who had heard her teacher read to her, who had heard Tage read to her, who had heard her twelve-year-old brother read to her?

She shook her head helplessly, stupidly. It was worse than a bad dream. She wished she could read out loud— not for herself but for Lobsang.

Weakly, she shook her head.

And Lobsang's eyes dropped as though *she* had done something wrong.

Oh, get me out of here.

That was the thing to do. She couldn't keep Moses now. Not after he'd attacked her, not after he'd become the alpha. How could she possibly regain control? Bite him back?

In seconds, she was decided. A minute later, upstairs,

she had her bags on the bed and the drawers open, throwing clothes from one into the other.

Oh, if only she could stop shaking. There was Lobsang again, staring at her.

Her car was back at the cabin. They were going to have to dig it out, and Tage would resent it, would be quietly condescending about her leaving. And the Arthur thing was already happening—imagining Arthur's eyes looking sad, as though she'd let him down.

You let me down, Arthur! I was twenty-three. You were old and wise. If I seduced you, why couldn't you resist?

She hadn't meant to seduce anyone. His lie called itself a lie, but she had been very desperate that he love her.

No wonder Tage thought it was...what he thought. His family was so normal, hers so absent. Even Arthur had gone away, again and again.

She herself made a life of leaving, and it was right, right for those who always slip away in the night or under cover of winter.

This way, she wouldn't interfere with Tage's relationship with his son. As for the little girl sitting on the threadbare recliner in the corner of the room, one of the few pieces in the house that wasn't of the Arts and Crafts period, as for Lobsang...

Tage would be good to her. He would do his best.

You think his best is better than the best you two could do together?

She felt as though Arthur was posing the question, as though he stood by the windows in the light, which was how she always seemed to picture him. It was too easy to imagine him reasoning with her, as he'd reasoned with her after her first quarter of art school, when she'd wanted to drop out because she couldn't stand having to speak to people.

Neither of her parents had attended her graduation, but

Arthur had been there with the gift of a slim gold necklace with a heart on it. *For courage,* he had said. *I'm so proud of you, Sarah.*

Afterward, Sarah had thought of that heart often. Thought of the heart and begun to consider Arthur Tennyson differently.

Her stomach revolted again.

She tossed tights and turtlenecks into her suitcase, hardly folding them.

Too soon, she was done, and she carried the bags downstairs, and when they sat beside the door, she glanced at the child who had followed her and saw Lobsang's face fall. Then, swiftly, the girl spun around and raced up the stairs.

Should I go after her?

Tage could deal with it. Lobsang was his responsibility.

Sarah still hadn't moved when the child came down the stairs again, wearing her parka over her pajamas and rushing, carrying a tot-sized suitcase and the floppy white reindeer with the red nose.

Lobsang thought she was coming along!

Oh, no, Sarah, just Mother is going. You stay here with Grandmother, darling. Mother will be back. Don't worry...

A pink suitcase with Barbie on it... Bunny, her rabbit...

"I have to get out of here," Sarah whispered into the hallway as Lobsang reached the bottom step.

Averting her eyes, the little girl walked past her with the small suitcase and reindeer, set them beside Sarah's, and opened the lid of the bench to find her own shoes.

The sound of stomping on the porch blended with Tage's low voice, soft laughter, and some happy tone from Lars. The latch clicked and they came in, an older and younger version of each other.

Tage was glancing down and he remained fixed in that

position, fixed on the suitcases. His gaze shifted to Lob-sang, who seemed suddenly fearful, then to Sarah.

She expected him to demand an explanation. Instead, as the door closed behind Lars, Tage's blue eyes widened. He moved in two quick strides, and his hand was on her face and her neck. His voice was quick, too. "What happened?"

Moses and the dog in isolation rushed back to her mind. "M-M—"

His fingers were still on her jaw, his face so close to hers. Her knees buckled, and she caught herself, stayed upright. Grabbing his sleeve, she pulled him with her, through the passage beside the stairs.

How could she explain about Lobsang? Maybe he'd think she was trying to steal Lobsang.

No, how stupid, Sarah! You'll explain. You can explain anything to Tage.

What she couldn't do was let go, with either hand, of his forearm. He was so big. By the time they'd reached the utility room, she'd sorted out some words. "In isolation."

Tage tore past her, leaving the back door swinging behind him.

MOSES AND ANNA were lying together, smiling, sated, and Moses wore a new confidence, looked at Tage with keener eyes.

You attacked Sarah to screw my best bitch.

His legs felt unsteady.

In this kind of fight, a fight for sex, Mother Nature usually left only one survivor. The victor.

The door of the building clicked, and Tage shook his head at Lars. *Don't come in.* Never losing a sense of the wolf and the dog, of what they were doing, he moved carefully toward the door himself.

Outside, he locked it with a key.

"What happened?" asked Lars.

"Moses must have bitten her." He envisioned an alpha wolf after the kill. Teeth bared, gums bloody.

God, Sarah.

Lars followed him back to the kitchen, where Sarah was pouring milk over Cheerios for Lobsang. As she put the milk away, Tage grabbed first-aid supplies from under the sink and soaped a washcloth.

A moment later, he made her sit down so he could wash the wounds. His left hand held her right, against her knee, as he cleaned the puncture marks. Already the breaks in her skin were surrounded by bruises.

By the laws of nature, Moses should have torn her throat out, done to her neck what Baron had done to Tage's arm. *Sarah. God, Sarah...*

The children watched them, and Tage felt their presence and all the things that couldn't be said. So he told her, "I need your help," and he touched her face until she looked at him. "I can't leave those dogs, not together that way. I need you to drive Lars and Lobsang to the bus stop and then come back here. Are you all right to drive?"

Her chin nodded.

And he did lower the washcloth so that he could hold her, even under the children's eyes.

CHAPTER EIGHT

"COME ON, LOBSANG. We have to get on the bus."

Lobsang shook her head and clung to the edge of the back seat, eyes on Sarah.

"*Lobsang*. We're going to be late." Lars opened her door. "Look the bus is waiting. He's waving to us."

Sarah switched off the engine and unfastened her seat belt. She hadn't had a chance to explain to Tage about the suitcases, but Lobsang had remembered. She'd refused to dress for school until Sarah went upstairs with her.

When Lars tried to lift her from her seat, Lobsang shook her head and crawled away from him, across the back of the 4Runner.

"Sarah, make her come," Lars said. "She'll make the whole bus late. He's going to leave without us."

The cold bit Sarah's face, a friendly fair-weather cold. With a gloved hand, she opened the back door.

Lobsang's eyes filled.

She's afraid I'll leave.

Sarah remembered her own Barbie suitcase. Her mind saw Tage's silver halfway trophy from the Iditarod. People should not desert each other.

If she promised Lobsang she wouldn't go, would the tears stop?

I can't promise.

She felt Tage's arms around her, the way he'd held her just a half hour ago.

I can't promise.

Drawing the door open further, Sarah lifted Lobsang down from the seat, then handed the child her backpack. Lobsang cried, and her tears froze on her cheeks.

The school bus driver honked.

Sarah clutched Lobsang's hand, led her toward the bus.

Lars trudged across the fine-packed snow beside them. He rolled his eyes and tossed his head, like, *Why do I have to be seen with these people?*

Grumbling, "Come on, Lobsang," he took her hand in his and led her up the steps of the bus.

The doors shut with an unmistakable, unforgettable sound. Sarah waved at the faces in the window, at Lobsang's desolate face, half grieving, half scowling back.

TAGE POURED SARAH some coffee, which was what she'd said she wanted, and listened to her story about Moses and about how frightened someone could be. Now the wolf dog was back in his own run, Anna safe in hers.

Copper brown betadyne stained Sarah's throat and face but didn't hide the puncture wounds and the bruises surrounding them. "When Critter and Lisa get here, I'll take you to the clinic." He would have his arm looked at, too. The dog bite had turned red and troubling.

"Wh-wh—" Blinking, lips quivering, she studied the tabletop and finally whispered, "Why?"

"Rabies shots."

Sarah started. *Rabies shots!* Moses had received all his shots, but she'd learned in the articles Tage had given her that the shots didn't necessarily work. She'd learned other things, too.

"No! He doesn't have rabies. You'll have to re-re-report it, and they'll take him away. They m-m-m-m-m-*mm*might kill him!"

Tage's heart strained in his chest. One of his mentors in

dog-training had once said, *You don't know a person until his dog bites him—or one of his kids.*

When Sarah cried that someone might kill Moses, Tage thought, *You are very fine. And you are going to have rabies treatment.*

Sarah saw his expression. Sometimes a man's eyes could tell you when you weren't going to win.

She jumped up. "I'm taking him. I'm going. I'm not your problem."

"You're my biggest problem." He caught her wrist, and she was in his lap, held tight there, his arms pressing hers to her sides.

Sarah remembered everything she'd read, how hard it was to get a wolf dog back once the authorities took him. She shook her head, fighting Tage, helpless. Who would listen to her? If it became a legal battle, she would lose, just like that. They would kill Moses.

She could feel Tage watching her face, and she tossed her head away, tried to stand. *I don't want you to hold me this way. I want to be in control.* Unspoken words built inside her, and the fact that she couldn't say them was why she wanted him to let her go. He was too strong. And he could make himself understood, and she could not. Not about Arthur. Not about Moses.

Oh, Tage, don't hold your head against mine like that.

"Rabies," he said, "is fatal. And you, who have fed your pet roadkill, are going to have postexposure prophylaxis rabies shots. We will do our best to satisfy the law without letting anyone take Moses, but it is likely he will be quarantined for ten days."

"He'll b-b-b—" She tried again. "B-b-b— He'll act shy. They'll think he has r-r-r-rabies."

"I have an idea. This is what will happen. The hospital will call the sheriff. And when the sheriff arrives, we'll make sure he finds that Moses is perfectly quarantined here. Maybe he'll be allowed to stay. All right?"

She didn't realize she'd been crying till she needed to wipe her face. He did it for her, with his lips. Just brushing her cheek. She saw his eyelashes up close, and he drew her closer.

In silence, she felt the strength of his chest, his heartbeat.

And the magnitude of her own crime.

"P-p-p-p-please let me go."

He did, but his hand held her arm, steadying her till she was on her feet, then guiding her back to her own chair. Even then, his ankles imprisoned one of hers, as though to keep her from running. "Tell me about the suitcases."

Sarah downed some coffee, silent. It took a while to get it right—what she wanted to say. "I can't t-t-t-train him. I'll p-p-pay you to keep him. If you would."

Shit. *Don't do this, Sarah. Don't run.* "You don't want the state to take him, but you want me to?"

"Yes. You'll take good care of him. L-L-L—" There was more, drowned out by the silence of a block. "L-L-Lob*sang* just p-p-p-*paaccked*. On her own."

It wasn't about Moses at all.

And he needed to think of Lobsang. Lobsang liked Sarah. If Sarah was going to leave, it was his duty to get her on her way soon, before Lobsang could become any more attached to her. The kind of relationship he'd had with Sarah in the past was no longer acceptable. When you were responsible for children, you couldn't let a woman walk in and out of your life whenever she pleased.

Tell her that, Tage.

He knew what would happen if he did. She would pack her car and drive away. Tage worded an ultimatum and couldn't say it. If anyone had asked him to justify his silence, he couldn't have done that, either. He could only have pointed out that this morning, on the way to the utility room, trying to say what Moses had done, she'd held onto him in a way she never had before.

People didn't go through life needing no one.

And Sarah had no one. Except him.

HE TALKED FOR HER at the clinic, and Sarah let him. He told the emergency room doctor about the bite and stayed with her while the doctor cleaned the wounds and injected them with vaccine. She would have to receive a series of shots over the next five weeks. The hospital would notify the authorities of the bite. Then the doctor looked at the German shepherd bite. It had to be opened again, scrubbed, flushed. He was given antibiotics and told he'd behaved like an idiot.

Tage didn't care.

He walked close to Sarah as they left the clinic.

"Now we go take care of Moses," he said, as he held the passenger door of the 4Runner for her.

It was a quiet ride home, passing Christmas decorations and then familiar lakes and woods.

Sarah watched his hand each time it reached for the stick shift. He hadn't said she should go. He hadn't asked her to stay.

But she knew when they reached the house, the first thing she'd see was her bags in the vestibule, demanding attention.

It seemed wrong to leave when Moses's future was uncertain.

It seemed wrong to stay any longer—because of Lobsang.

On the highway, Tage stopped at his mailbox to get his mail, then turned down his road. Sarah watched a snowshoe hare spring across the white, in front of the car, and disappear into the birch forest. When they reached the end of Tage's road, the kennels appeared, their Christmas lights brightening the day. He'd decorated two fir trees as well.

It was a winter wonderland. Just like the song said.

He pressed the automatic garage door opener. Silently, he drove past the training rig, drove inside. The door groaned shut, and they were in the dark. He killed the ignition, looked at her, and didn't say whatever was on the tip of his tongue.

Sarah caught his wrist, then felt stupid, like she was throwing herself at him.

His arm moved, his hand took hers, and they sat there in the car in the darkened garage. The shape of his pickup with the dog boxes on it was a shadow beside the 4Runner. Shelves on the walls were filled with cardboard boxes and unused dog crates.

"I'm s-s-s-sorry," she said, "about Nome." Finding usable substitutions, she added, "I've outstayed my welcome here." As usual, it wasn't precisely what she meant. What she meant was, *I know you don't feel the same about me any more, now that you know about Arthur.*

He imagined her in Arthur's hands. The things Arthur must have done. His own life would be death without her.

Embraces over the gearshift worked better than holding hands. He said the only thing he knew was true. "I love you."

Sarah held on hard, her hands molding against his back. She hadn't heard him say that for a long time, and when he'd said it, it had never meant anything. "You" had never been her. He hadn't known her.

This time was different.

Awful and sweet.

He was talking, against her hair. "You're like Moses. The first time I looked in his eyes, I knew no one could train him. We can only learn to live with him the way he is. Your way is to come and go. Unless I fall in love with someone else and marry her, this is your home, and you can come and go from here as you like. And I'll build a pen for Moses and keep him for you."

Sarah's heart pounded. *Unless I fall in love with someone else and marry her...* She forced herself to relax. Everything was okay. Tage was saying they could be friends, like always. But maybe better. She would be some kind of aunt to his...children. She could come and go as she pleased, as was comfortable for her.

His hands moved her head, and she saw the shadows and planes of his face. His fingers were in her hair, then gently smoothing one of the bandages on her neck. His lips said, "But I want one favor just now. A promise."

She nodded. Whatever it was, she would do it. She would do anything for him. And she knew what he was going to ask just before he said it.

So did Tage. Maybe it was the fact that she said, "Okay," at the moment he tried to speak that made him miss a word or two. He'd only wanted her to stay. The words that came out were, "I want you for Christmas."

AT FOUR THAT AFTERNOON, Sarah drove Tage's 4Runner down his road to the bus stop. When he'd asked her to pick up the children because he had a client coming, what could she say? Anyhow, she really didn't mind. Anna had been moved to the whelping shed so that Moses could be quarantined in the isolation kennel. Tage had hung quarantine signs on all the windows and doors, warning people away. The building was locked, the key labeled with a large red ticket that read QUARANTINE.

The trouble he'd taken touched Sarah. She was happy. And safe. Why she felt safe now, safer than she'd ever felt in her life, she couldn't imagine. Maybe it was just because someone had said to her, *This is your home. You can come*

and go, and I'll always be glad to see you when you return.
Maybe it was because *he* would not leave. Maybe it was
because Tage had said he loved her.

She arrived early at the bus stop, but it was only ten
degrees out, so she left the engine running and waited in
the car, watching the snow fall on Mary's Bonnet Lake,
watching the lights around the life-size nativity Tage's
neighbor had erected. An ice-fishing shack sat on the middle of the lake, and a figure with a pipe stepped out of it.
He lifted an arm, waving toward the car. She waved back,
wondering if he could see her. He must think she was
Tage.

Minnesota. She loved Minnesota. She loved *her home.*

Arthur came and went from her mind, leaving tension
behind, and she set the thoughts away from her, not wanting to hurt the day.

The bus appeared around a curve and exhaled to a slow
stop. By the time the brakes sighed and the doors swung
open, Sarah stood outside the Toyota. She didn't want to
see Lars's surprise at who had come to pick him up. She
didn't want to know his negative feelings. This way, he
could notice her first, could react before she ever saw him.

The two figures were coming down the aisle, shadows
behind the windows. Only the top of Lobsang's head
showed, and Sarah heard other children's voices in the bus.
"Lob-ster, Lob-ster..."

What was that about?

A horn sounded in the road. A vehicle had come from
the other direction and stopped, because of the school bus,
but its turn signal was flashing. An official seal on the
driver's door identified it as a government truck, and it
pulled a trailer containing livestock.

Reindeer.

I'm blocking the road.

The children had stepped down to the snow, and Lars

was scowling back at the school bus. He gave someone in the bus the finger.

"Lars!" gasped Sarah.

The bus driver called out the door, "Do that again, and you won't ride this bus."

Cringing, Sarah tried to corral both children toward the 4Runner. Lobsang's mouth was a down-turned bow, and her little chin shook. Oh, good grief, she was crying.

"Wh—" *What is it?* Sarah crouched beside her in the snow, trying to ask.

Lars glared at the bus as it drove off. "They make fun of her name." He said it as though Sarah should have known. *"Idiots."*

It was natural to hug the little body, and Lobsang's arms gripped her neck so tightly that Sarah had no choice but to lift her up. She wanted to thank Lars for standing up for his sister, but did you thank a kid for giving someone the finger?

Anyhow, he'd noticed the reindeer. Striding past Tage's car, he waved to the rangers from the Division of Wildlife, and the men in the cab of the truck waved back, then smiled at each other, probably over the boy's colorful clothing.

"Move the truck, Sarah! The reindeer can't get through. If I had Snutte right now," he said, swinging open the passenger door, "he could herd them down the road without any help."

Hurriedly, Sarah buckled Lobsang into the back seat. The little girl had stopped crying, but her expectant expression troubled Sarah. She looked as though—well, as though she thought Sarah could do something to fix her situation.

Pretending not to notice, Sarah got behind the wheel.

"Hurry," said Lars, tapping his fingers on the armrest.

Backing the 4Runner out of the way, Sarah let the government vehicle and trailer turn down the road.

Lars twisted impatiently in his seat. "Lobsang, you tell those losers that if they tease you again, I'm going to beat the pee out of them."

As Lobsang's grave eyes held him to the promise, Sarah started to spin the wheel, to follow the trailer. But yet another vehicle was turning into the drive, a white Cherokee with a bar of lights on top.

It was the sheriff.

Coming for Moses.

THE BUSINESS WITH the sheriff's deputy seemed to take Tage only minutes. Before Sarah knew it, the officer was climbing in his car and driving away.

Tage joined her, where she waited with Lobsang at the edge of the house. She'd been afraid to stay too far from where Moses was, afraid he'd be led away. "I trained his German shepherd. Everything's fine. Let's go see the reindeer."

They walked down the snowy road behind the kennels and out to a clearing in the woods not far from the lake, where the corral stood. Beneath the snow grew the thick moss called reindeer lichen, and already the reindeer were pawing through the white covering to eat it. Lars and Snutte walked freely in the enclosure, Snutte looking purposeful, Lars authoritative.

When she'd visited Lapland with Arthur, Sarah had seen reindeer. She remembered how their antlers were warm and covered with velvet, how before rutting, the velvety exterior peeled away and hung like cobwebs from the blood-filled antlers.

These reindeer were unlike those she'd seen in Sweden. They were skin and bones, and when they were penned one of the rangers gave Tage a bag filled with medicines. Diseased as well as skinny, Sarah saw.

Hanging close to his uncle, Lars also listened to the rangers. Only when they left did he venture back across the snow to the small herd.

Tage accompanied the men to their truck and joined Sarah and Lobsang. "What do you think, Lobsang?"

The child didn't answer, didn't need to. Clearly, she was enchanted by the reindeer, whatever their state of health.

Tage picked her up. "Let's go see the reindeer, Lobsang."

Solemnly, the brown eyes gazed ahead at the animals, and soon Lobsang's brother joined her and Tage. It was Lars who guided her small hand over an antler.

Watching the three of them from outside the corral, Sarah wondered what had happened to the joy she'd felt such a short time earlier. Hugging her arms around herself, she slipped away, into the trees.

A HALF HOUR LATER, she was hand building a vase to fire in the raku kiln when barking distracted her. "Haw!" someone yelled. Beyond the studio windows and the glassed-in porch, a dogsled raced out onto the lake in the late-afternoon sun. Three dogs pulled it, and Lars drove the sled.

Unable to resist, Sarah washed her hands, drew on her sweater and stepped out on the windowed porch to see better. The brilliant blue of Lars's tunic contrasted with the snow, and he rode the sled runners with the balance and grace of a natural athlete.

A shadow cut out some of the light from the side of the porch, and she jumped. Tage grinned at her through the glass. On skis, he pulled a sled carrying Lobsang. As he came around the front and stopped at her door, Sarah opened it.

"Hi."

Lobsang was on her feet, plunging through the snow to the porch.

"I thought she might like to see what you do on your wheel."

The other two explored the studio while Sarah began wedging some clay, preparing it for the wheel. Pausing in front of the glaze pails, Lobsang studied their labels.

Tage squatted beside her. "Kaolin," he read. "Feldspar. These are for Sarah's glazes. They make the colors on her pottery."

The specter of Arthur hung in the air.

Lobsang touched the letters on the labels.

She must be learning her letters in school, thought Sarah. Tage and Lars both worked with her at night, teaching her first-grade words. *Look. Father. Mother. Sister. Brother.* No one in Lobsang's life would confuse the words "stepfather" and "friend." Sarah waited for Tage to read the labels on the pails again for Lobsang, but he had glanced toward the window. "Oh, no."

Opening the door, he went back out on the porch to watch Lars. The sled had crashed against the far lakeshore, and the dogs were tangled in their lines, waiting patiently in awkward poses for someone to free them. "Sarah, keep an eye on Lobsang, will you?"

LARS WAS MAD AT the dogs. No, he was mad at everything.

He'd almost felt like things weren't too bad at school; then those jerks had made fun of Lobsang on the bus and Tage had sent Sarah to pick them up, and now the dogs kept getting tangled. It was Jedi's fault. He was a silver Siberian husky and pretty young, Tage had said, but Tage thought he could be fast and that he was pretty smart.

Lars thought Jedi was the stupidest dog he'd ever seen.

He really wanted to hit him, but he knew his uncle would never let him near his dogs again if he did.

So what?

Maybe if he went back to Sweden his grandfather would tell him what the big secret was.

When he almost had the lines straightened, Jedi crossed under the gangline again to wag tails with Boots. Good grief, they were going to tip the sled, the stupid dogs. *While I freeze trying to get them untangled.* At least the lead dog, Molinka, wasn't making things worse. She was smart.

Spotting Tage skiing across the lake, Lars gave up on the tangle. His uncle would sort it out.

But when he reached Lars, Tage said, "Oh, no. *You're* going to do it." Taking off his skis, he glanced at the dogs and the sled. "Unhitch Jedi. That will solve your problem."

"But look at Boots!" As he spoke, the cold seemed to make Lars's voice do something odd, made it go away. Or so it seemed to him.

His uncle didn't appear to notice. "Boots will get himself back into line once Jedi is out of there."

Lars followed the advice, and as soon as Jedi was off the gang line, Boots got himself back into place. "You're stupid, Jedi," Lars said and waited for Tage to get mad at him. Nothing happened. His uncle seemed oblivious, maybe not even thinking about him.

What is it he's never going to tell me?

It was on the tip of his tongue to ask, but then he saw his uncle gaze back across the lake, and suddenly he felt afraid of him. And suddenly he missed his parents enough to make him cry. The dogs were jumping around, and Jedi was squirming while Lars tried to hold him, and suddenly Lars just let him go.

Tage started and grabbed the dog by its harness. He

seemed to notice Lars, as though he'd forgotten he was there.

"You take them home," Lars said. "I've had enough." *I want my mom. I want my dad.*

Dragging Jedi, his uncle came slowly toward him, looking in his eyes, and Lars was bothered by how much Tage's eyes were like his own. He jerked his head away. He really had to get out of here. He just had to be alone.

Tage took Lars's gloved hand and guided it through Jedi's harness. "You always feel better," he said, "if you finish what you start."

Straightening, he turned away and started putting on his skis.

And Lars hauled Jedi around to his side of the gang line, to hook the tug line to his harness.

Eyes tearing in the cold, he said to his uncle, "What's the big secret anyway? What is it you won't tell me that you'll tell Sarah?"

His uncle stared like he'd never seen Lars before. "What are you talking about?"

Lars stepped on the runners of the sled. He was going to bash Jedi with the snow hook if he tangled the lines again. "I heard you in the library. There's something you wouldn't tell me."

Tage turned white again, the way he had outside the library.

His breath steamed in front of his face, and Lars's eyes steamed, too. They steamed in fear, because his uncle said, "I will tell you. For now, take the dogs home."

WHEN TAGE RETURNED to the studio, most of the daylight had faded, and he half expected Sarah would have taken Lobsang back to the house. But no, Sarah sat in the overstuffed chair with a notebook and Scotch tape, while Lobsang stood over her shoulder.

"Chair," pronounced Sarah slowly, handing the girl a piece of paper with the word CHAIR written on it. She had affixed transparent tape to the piece of paper. Pointing at a metal folding chair, she said again, "Chair."

Lobsang hurried across the floor, ceramic dust clinging to the fur on her boots, and taped the label to the chair.

Tage closed the door softly. *I heard you in the library.* Now he had to tell Lars. He'd promised.

They saw him, and Sarah instantly flushed, her skin darkening against the white bandages on her throat. Lobsang pointed proudly to the sign on the chair.

"Chair," he said. "Good for you."

Sarah's color intensified. It took Tage a moment to focus, to figure out why. She was teaching Lobsang and felt shy about it. Instinctively, he knew Sarah wouldn't be able to say the next word she attempted—because of his presence.

He left again, going out in the snow to watch the lake and the woods turn dark blue and black. He didn't want to think about Lars.

He thought of Sarah's stutter instead.

Years ago, he'd heard a radio program about Annie Glenn, the wife of astronaut John Glenn. She'd had a disabling stutter; he'd seen it portrayed in the movie *The Right Stuff.* But she'd found some kind of speech therapy that worked. Couldn't Sarah?

She had to have tried things....

Oh, come on, Tage. Her mother doesn't remember to call her on Christmas Day. When she was a kid, Sarah used to go two or three years at a time without seeing her.

As for her grandmother... Well, grandmothers sometimes had old-fashioned ideas. Sarah's father had never been on the scene. Which left one other person, a well-educated resourceful person, who should have seen that Sarah received the speech therapy she needed.

Who hadn't done it. Who'd done other things instead.
The lake grew darker. And darker.

As a consenting adult.

He wondered if she was lying, leaving out the worst.
He knew she was scared. And he knew in his heart that
telling him had changed her. She'd said the truth out loud
for the first time and seen his face—seen the face of a man
thinking, *Sarah, that's incest!*—and now she knew what
she'd probably never admitted before.

He worried about her.

And about Lars.

How Lars would take what he had promised to tell him.

CHAPTER NINE

Still Wednesday

LARS HAD NOT HUNG UP a single poster, nor unpacked a box. He kept his clothes on top of the boxes.

This all struck Tage when he entered his son's room that night.

Should I have helped him unpack as I helped Lobsang?

He had thought a twelve-year-old boy would want to do the job himself. The truth came forth. Lars hadn't reconciled himself to staying. On some level, he hadn't accepted his parents' death.

It wouldn't make this moment easier.

Lars sat by the window in his pajamas, petting Snutte. Fifteen minutes ago, Tage had said, *You should get to sleep. I'll be right up.*

Lars knew why, you could see. He hadn't forgotten what he'd asked Tage on the lake. He'd been silent through dinner, had done some homework and come downstairs to train Snutte in the dome. Whenever he passed Tage, it had been with an anxious glance.

And here they were.

Tage shut the door and sat on the end of the bed.

Would this become a ritual for the two of them? Sitting in these spots for father-son talks?

"This is going to be hard to hear."

Like a soldier in his first battle, Lars stared back at him, clearly terrified but refusing to bow to it.

You're a wonderful boy.

It was Peter's doing.

"Your mother was married to me when she became pregnant with you." Speaking, Tage felt the intense clarity and simplicity of the words. He felt their horror for Lars. It was a confession of desertion. "She was pregnant when we divorced. She loved Peter, and I thought that together they'd be better parents for you, that it would be easier than your having a father and a stepfather. But you are my biological son." When Lars's face didn't move, when he just continued to stare, Tage added, "That's what I told Sarah I would never tell you. I never expected you to ask."

Lars could not speak. He couldn't think. Tage his father? He said the first thing that came to mind. "You're not my father! My father is my father."

Tage held back, made sure Lars was finished. He wanted to cut in with every word. Finally, he said, "I know that. That's why I never planned to tell you. It's irrelevant. Peter is your uncle. I am your father." He covered his face with his hand. "That's not what I meant to say. Peter is your father. I am your uncle." God. Of all the times to blunder.

The boy looked sick. Snutte lay at his feet, head on his paws, yet seemed aware of them both.

Things came to a man at such a moment. Especially when he loved a woman whose father hadn't cared about her. A woman who had known one male model in her life...

I abandoned you, Lars. I'm sorry.

He tried to tell himself again that he'd meant everything for the best.

It wasn't true.

He'd been twenty-four years old, and the last thing he'd wanted was entanglements with Marit and Peter over a child when it could be avoided. The last thing he'd wanted was anything that would force him to deal with Marit and Peter again.

That was why he'd given up Lars.

Lars stared at Snutte's black fur against the hardwood floor. Was Tage waiting for him to say something? There was nothing to say. Tage's secret didn't seem like a lie, but Lars couldn't think of a single thing to say. Now, all of a sudden, everything was different. It was like Tage had stolen something from him. Tage had slept with his mother. Lars didn't like that. He didn't want him around, didn't want to be around him.

The room seemed brown and gold; all the lights in this house were like this, turned things orange, except for Tage, whose eyes were blue even in the wooden house. Blue like Lars's eyes.

Tage said, "I've never thought I could take the place of your father. Peter was your father in every way that mattered, and I know he'll always be the father of your heart. But you asked me, and I can't lie to you."

What does he expect me to say? Lars wondered. *That he's made me feel a lot better?* A new notion occurred to him, and it was worse than all the others.

Even before he was born, Tage had decided he didn't want him. And now Tage was stuck with him.

"I want to go back to Sweden and live with my grandparents," Lars said.

Tage stared at him in that way, that way that made you look down.

Lars didn't look down.

Tage said, "No."

Without letting himself even blink, Lars said, "You don't want me. I don't want to live with you. I think you're a bad person." Having said that, he found he couldn't face his uncle—his...his uncle—any more. He bent over to pet Snutte.

Watching Lars's head, the hair that had grown long enough to drag over his eyes, Tage swallowed the words he wanted to say. *Your father slept with my wife.* No. Lars was twelve years old, and Peter had been a good father to him. Some things you did not say.

He thought of Anna running in deep snow. He pictured other dogs, his Iditarod dogs, pulling so hard against the wind, dragging a disintegrating sled across the Farewell Burn. Dogs who did not give up.

Though your lover had slept with her stepfather and your son thought you were a bad person and you suddenly had responsibility for a wolf and eight sickly reindeer and a Tibetan child who couldn't speak English, you did not give up either. You tried to be as fine as a dog.

"Lars..." The word was hesitant. He waited, waited for Lars to look up.

Lars kept petting Snutte.

I need you to unpack. You need to unpack. Please unpack. Unpack these goddamn boxes!

Swallowing, Tage said, "I'll wake you at five tomorrow. You can set up your room."

Lars exercised his new vocabulary again, and Tage felt as he did when a bossy dog growled at him. His instincts took over. Indignation took over. He saw his own hand reach to the back of Lars's neck, yank him upright until Tage could see his eyes. They were his own.

"What did you say?"

Lars repeated himself.

"Say it again."

Lars punched him in the face—or tried to.

It was easy to knock his arm away. "You're slow."

The next one hit Tage's neck, and he grabbed both wrists and felt lengthening bones, a child becoming a man. Lars was biting his lip, crying and trying not to.

"I am your father." Tage pushed the long slim arms

back at Lars and let him go. "I gave you life. Don't ever talk that way to me again."

HE LEFT LARS'S ROOM and stood in the hall, shaking. Every door was shut. Sarah had drunk two glasses of wine and turned in even before Lars, and as Tage watched, the light disappeared from under the door he'd just closed. The bed creaked, and dog tags jingled. Tage smiled a little.

Good Snutte, he thought. *Take care of him.*

After a time, Tage wandered past the stairwell and railings to the window seat in the upper hall.

He sat, leaning back against cherry paneling beside the casements, and studied the moonless night, the winter constellations hanging like icicles in the branches of the maples. His breath fogged the frozen window. In a while, he might go get some of the cold coffee still in the pot downstairs. He might get the box of antlers or another box that held small pieces of hardwood cut from dead tree branches and bring them up here to carve. But for now, he would just sit and listen to the closed doors.

To make sure everyone was all right.

IT WAS SO QUIET, he could hear the downstairs hall clock tick and every breath Comet took. He'd brought the dog in an hour before, to join his vigil. The sled dog had sat alert for some time, asking what was wrong, then had finally stretched out on his paws without sleeping.

Tage carved from a block of maple.

He didn't like what was emerging from the wood, but it wouldn't stop coming. The wood had its own life, its own wish, and Tage had been taught from a young age to fulfill the wish of the wood, the wish of the antler. He'd been taught that being able to do so was the power of the craftsman.

They were slender, primitive—no, primal—figures.

Joined in a tortured dance. One was large, the other small. It was love and reluctance and weakness and seduction and evil. Small arms around the other's neck. A bowing together and arching apart.

He was afraid Sarah would see it.

He knew he would give it to her.

At 4:00 a.m., he violated her room and her sleep, wondering if he was treading where another had, if Arthur had ever crept into her room at night to see her face, her body. Because of that, he didn't look at her, even to see if she awoke. He set the thing the wood had wanted to be on her night table and went away without glimpsing her skin or her hair or knowing if she was safe in her bed.

Thursday

IT WAS THE FIRST THING Sarah saw when she woke. Her eyes focused on the raw maple.

For a long time, she didn't touch it.

She got out of bed and dressed before she picked it up. She loved it and hated it, and she zipped it in the pocket of the woolly pile sweater she wore, to keep with her all day.

When she glanced toward the window, the snowy owl sat in the tree. Sarah repositioned the recliner, relaxed in the chair and put up her feet.

She cried a little because this was her home.

Because Tage had said so.

TAGE WISHED HE'D HAD more sleep. The day had begun in a battle with Lars over unpacking boxes. Tage had won, but now Lobsang refused to get dressed for school. He had set out her clothes for her, as usual, then gone out to exercise Anna and feed and check on Moses in quarantine, to bring the wolf dog more chew toys. When he returned,

Sarah's door was still closed and Lobsang sat on the edge of her bed in her pajamas.

"What is it?" He looked over her clothes to make sure he'd selected the correct articles and that everything was clean. He thought it was even an outfit Lobsang liked. Pink corduroys and a white shirt with matching pink trim at the cuffs and neck and a white sweater with pink and turquoise accents. Something Marit must have picked out...

What kind of clothes would Sarah have chosen for an adopted daughter?

Sarah would have made sure Lobsang chose.

Maybe Marit had, too. Anyhow, these clothes didn't explain why Lobsang wasn't dressed or why she looked like life was a funeral. Days earlier, he would have chalked it up to the turbulence of her existence, but she'd been happy this past week.

Behind him, a door latch clicked.

It was Sarah, framed against the windows behind her, against the maples.

"*Godmorgon,*" he said softly.

She came toward him, her hair still uncombed. Her fingers caught his nearest forearm. "Thank you."

"Lobsang won't get dressed for school."

Sarah glanced at him. His tone admitted confusion. His blue eyes avoided her gaze. She saw he hadn't shaved. His shoulders, his body, swept past her impatiently, Saami blue brushing the sleeve of her sweater.

Sitting against crumpled sheets, Lobsang met Sarah's eyes and pursed her mouth in a small frown. It was a ladylike expression of hers that meant something wasn't to her satisfaction. Uneasy, feeling stupidly flattered by being singled out for this silent communication of Lobsang's, Sarah edged into the room.

"*Lob-ster,*" said Lobsang. "*Lob-ster, Lob-ster...*" Her eyes filled with tears.

Comprehending, Sarah looked up, to try to explain to Tage.

Lars appeared. He brushed past her the way Tage had, to step inside. "What's wrong? Why aren't you dressed, Lobsang?"

"*Lob-ster, Lob-ster!*" Her few tears became a choking sob, and she drew her legs up onto the bed, burying her face in her knees.

"I told you— I will beat them up if they do that again. Idiots," he told Sarah, repeating his observation of the day before.

"What?" Tage asked. "What is this about?"

Lars glared at him. "People make fun of her name."

Sarah remained on the threshold. Through the window, beyond the other three, she saw snow drop from one of the maples. *S-S-S-Sarah! S-S-S-Sarah, come play with us. Why don't you want to play, S-S-S-Sarah?*

She blinked.

Lobsang craned her head up at Tage, silently begging, *Please help.*

"I told her," Lars said, "that I would beat them up."

Tage looked so tired. Sarah crept past them and found a spot by the window. She unzipped the pockets of her sweater and stuck her hands inside and felt the wood.

"No Lobsang." Lobsang's voice startled them all. "No Lobsang. No Lob-ster. Ugly."

"Your name?" Tage crouched beside the bed, a hand on the mattress beside the little girl. The cuff of his Saami tunic with its five inches of red braid embroidered with minute flowers fascinated Sarah only slightly less than his hand itself. His lightly tanned skin and strong fingers...

Carving hands.

"Ugly," Lobsang repeated.

"If she doesn't like her name," said Lars, "she should name herself something else."

"Oh, there's a good suggestion."

At Tage's biting response, Lars drew back, nostrils flaring.

"It *is* a good suggestion." Sarah clapped her hand over her mouth. Had *she* said that?

Tage's head spun, and he stared. "No. It is *not* a good suggestion. When you don't like things, you can't just change them."

He seemed to wait, as though expecting her to answer.

She arranged a sentence. "I can't change how I talk." Or the things I've done, Tage. *I can't change it, Tage!* "A name can be changed."

Lars was staring, seeing her as the freak she was.

Her face grew furnace hot, and she measured the dust on the baseboards beneath the window.

"It doesn't make a person strong," Tage said, "to avoid things that are difficult. A name is important."

"Ugly," said Lobsang. *"Lob-ster. Lob-ster!"*

Her brother threw himself onto the double bed beside her. "It's all right. We'll make things right."

Lobsang gazed at the twelve-year-old as though he could get her the moon if she wanted it.

"It's easy to be strong," Lars told Tage, "when everything is easy for you."

Out of the mouths of babes, thought Sarah. But Lars was wrong if he thought everything was easy for Tage.

Lars couldn't know. Couldn't imagine.

Climbing off her bed, Lobsang went to a pile of books on the seat of a wooden chair in the corner. She extracted a paperback from Sweden. Sarah recognized the illustration on the cover. She'd had the same book as a child— in English. *Little Bear's Friend.*

Lobsang returned to the bed and presented the book to Lars. "Emily," she said. "Lucy. Pretty."

The little girl named Emily. Her doll named Lucy. Sarah

remembered them both. Her grandmother had read her that book.

"Would you like to be called Emily?" Lars asked.

"Lars." Tage gritted his teeth. "Her name is Lobsang."

"Ugly!" Lobsang yelled at him. "Ugly name!" And she burst into tears all over again.

"I bet you do everything the hard way," said Lars, "just for the fun of it."

Tage didn't respond, and a moment later the adolescent rolled onto his stomach and began picking at a small hole in Lobsang's sheet.

Sarah suddenly recalled herself. These kids were Tage's responsibility, not hers. He'd said she could come and go from his house as she liked, but he hadn't invited her to help raise these children. Not since things had changed. Naming was important, as Tage had said. This situation was none of her business. Stepping around Tage, she headed for the door.

He grabbed her wrist from where he still half knelt beside the bed. "Oh, don't run off, Sarah." His teeth reminded her of Moses's, when the wolf dog smiled.

"She's probably getting away from you," Lars muttered.

Sarah said, "It isn't anything to do with me."

Tage slowly released her.

Her chest hurt like fire, the aftermath of speaking. Or maybe it hurt from not speaking. She thrust her hands in her sweater pockets. One of them wrapped around his wood carving.

Oh, Tage. Oh, Tage.

The words burst from her pinched chest. "I am not agreeing with you. About Emily."

"Why do you talk that way?" On the bed, Lars sat up, an inquisitor.

Panic embraced Sarah, filled her.

What did he mean? Had she stuttered? Or had he noticed that she tried to use words that started with vowels?

Glancing at his son, Tage tried to make out if Lars had been sincere in his curiosity or if he'd just planned to embarrass Sarah. *Sincere,* he concluded. Which was moot. Sarah's face was scarlet, and Tage knew she probably couldn't even think clearly, let alone talk.

He wanted to throttle Lars. Lars, who had said, *It's easy to be strong when everything is easy for you.*

Lobsang's face still glistened with tears, and her nose was running.

Sarah's color had not faded.

He turned to Lobsang and asked, "Do you want to be called Emily? Or something else?"

He never knew what Lobsang understood, but she seemed to grasp this question, because she nodded emphatically.

She'd mentioned the name Lucy, too. But the woman beside the door, the woman Lobsang liked so much, the woman who had gone to the excruciating effort of speaking on this issue, had an easier time saying words that began with vowels.

"Emily?"

She nodded again, hard.

Tage stood and lifted her off the bed to hug her, and the action filled him with hatred and disgust for Arthur Tennyson. He knew he hid it and knew also that Sarah must know what was in his mind. He told the child, "Emily you are."

ON THE WAY to the bus stop, Tage explained why Sarah talked so strangely—that she didn't like to say words that started with certain consonants. Lars only half listened, because he was thinking about the night before and what his uncle-father had said. *I gave you life.*

So what was the big deal? Half the time he wished he'd never been born anyhow. Well, he'd put away his stuff this morning, but he hadn't hung anything on the walls. The room was a prison cell, and he wanted Tage to know he thought so. Somebody had chosen a stupid place to plant that maple tree. The climbing limbs were even too far from his window. He really hated that tree.

His mind wandered. He found himself thinking about breasts. Becka's breasts and also Cindy Crawford. If he *did* hang up any of his posters, he would hang up Cindy Crawford.

Sarah also had nice...

The thought became immediately uninteresting. She was Tage's girlfriend. Whatever that made her, she wasn't someone Lars wanted to think about the way he thought of Cindy Crawford.

What was going to happen to the wolf now that it had bitten Sarah? "Does Sarah's wolf have rabies?" he asked hopefully. His voice startled him. In the middle of the question, it did a strange squawking thing. It sounded like he had a cold or something, except that his throat didn't hurt.

Tage took his eyes from the snowy drive—maybe to see what had made the weird sounds. "Probably not. The quarantine is a legal thing. We're going to build him a compound. Maybe let Anna stay with him."

"Are they going to have puppies?" If so, the puppies could be his sled team. Lars could have a team of wolf dogs.

"No," said Tage.

"You know already that it didn't work?"

"If it did work, it doesn't matter. We can't have a litter of wolf dogs."

Was he serious? If Anna had gotten pregnant... Tage was going to kill the puppies. Somehow.

Lars had never heard anything so horrible in his life. "We could have them! Give them to me! They'll be my dog team."

Tage shook his head. "No wolf dogs."

"Molinka's part wolf. You can tell."

"It's a question of example. You notice I'm building a special pen for Moses? It's not because we need it, Lars. That sled dog compound is escape-proof, and I could give Moses part of it and take him out every day, make sure he gets the exercise he needs. But anyone who sees Moses knows immediately that he is a wolf. And I am spending thousands of dollars to make sure my clients see that wolves don't make good pets, that it is a big deal to have that kind of animal in your life. That he just might grab someone you love by the throat. But if we breed wolf dogs, one of my clients will assume they make good family pets."

"For a dog team! Molinka!"

"No. This isn't about us. It's about other people. We're careful with Lob—Emily and I teach her how to behave around dogs. We don't leave her alone with them, don't leave her alone at all, don't even let her in with the sled dogs. When wolves, even some dogs, see the natural running children do, it triggers their prey instinct. Lars, I've seen a musher slip and his dogs tear into him. If Emily fell down where Moses or—"

Lars flipped around to peer at his sister in the back seat. "He thinks the wolf could eat you, Emily." His voice cut out again, on "eat." What was going on?

As he rubbed his neck, his uncle—*uncle,* that's how he'd have to keep thinking of him—slowed the car at the bus stop. When Lars glanced over, Tage said, "It doesn't last forever."

Lars swallowed. Oh.

Oh.

He'd heard all about this in school—in Sweden. Of course, Tage... If Tage knew what was going on about this, about his voice, he probably knew other things that were happening, too.

Feeling exposed and strange, Lars watched the school bus pull up to the stop. He was glad to get out into the cold. He felt like breaking things. He wanted to cut down that tree in front of his window. He wanted to call the humane society and stop Tage from killing the wolf dog puppies. He wanted to forget all about what Tage had told him the night before.

And most of all, he wanted his mom and dad.

It was really so hard just to go on.

LATE THAT AFTERNOON, Sarah was in the studio when she heard a "Whoa!" from outside. Not Lars. Tage, driving five dogs.

As he anchored the sled, using a snow hook, she hid the object she'd been examining, Arthur's mask. She stuffed it under a towel on the wedging table and tried to look like she'd been doing something else.

Nothing she'd tried making today had worked out. She fingered the wood carving in her pocket, the carving she'd spent most of the day examining, along with the mask. For a while, she'd stood outside by the kilns. That morning, she'd discovered something interesting.

She always went out of her way to avoid Tage's assistants, but when she skied out to the studio that morning, she'd passed the reindeer corral, and the assistant with the long gray hair, Critter, was petting the reindeer. Sarah had never seen Critter up close before.

Now that she had...

Well, the woman Tage called Critter was Arthur's friend Clare. Critter was the woman who had found Arthur.

Did Critter know who *Sarah* was?

Arthur had introduced them once, and Sarah had seen Critter at the funeral, and that was it.

It was seeing Critter, seeing Clare, that had made her go out to look at the salt kiln. It was why she couldn't ignore the mask.

She went outside, into the snow and bright sunlight, and the long white surface of the lake shone at her face as the sinking sun cast long shadows from the building.

Tage had been waiting for her to come out. The dogs were restless in their harnesses, eager.

"Wh-wh—" She ground her foot into the snow. "Wh-wh-wwwhere are L-L— Emily and Lars?"

"I asked Lars to watch his sister." He studied the lake as though there was something to see on its surface. "I had to tell him the truth, and he has taken to being rude, so he can't drive the dogs today. I came to ask you to make Christmas presents for me to send my family in Sweden. Bowls, plates and cups. And to bribe you with a dog-sled ride."

"Okay. Let me get my coat."

She hurried back into the studio. As she bundled up, her eyes strayed to the towel that covered the salt-glazed mask. She left quickly.

IT HAD BEEN A BAD idea, Lars saw now. He'd spent math class figuring out how to fell the maple tree. He hadn't known it would take forever. If he walked away now, would anyone notice? Probably. The tree was right in front of the porch, and he'd already chopped a big wedge out of just the wrong side. The wedge was angled toward the parking area. Anyone coming up the steps couldn't miss it.

Okay, well, he would keep going, and it would be worth it. He would be able to see out his window.

"Lobsang—Emily, I mean—you get on the porch."

Lars pointed. He still had some more to cut out of the parking-area side before he started on the other side, to make it fall over, but why take chances? He had to be careful so the maple didn't fall on the kennels or on Lobsang. Emily. Boy, it was hard when a person changed names.

"Stay on the porch," he repeated. "This tree is going to make a huge crash." He tried to make this clear to her with his hands.

From behind the stone planters that ringed the porch, Emily nodded solemnly.

Okay, she was safe.

Well, his arms hurt, but at least the blade of Tage's ax was sharp. Lars returned to the maple trunk and swung the ax again, feeling very strong and really very good.

As HE DROVE THE SLED, Tage kept his eyes on the path ahead and on the dogs, but that didn't stop him from seeing the woman in the basket. She held his carving with her gloves.

Oh, Sarah.

The next time he looked at her, she had put it away.

He stopped the dogs at the far shore, catching the snow hook around a slender maple to anchor the sled. He helped Sarah up, so she could stretch her legs.

The sun had brought out freckles on her smooth olive-toned cheeks. Her mother was one-eighth Choctaw. Occasionally, Tage thought he saw this in Sarah's face. Her flushed lips were still. For some things, some times in life, there were no words.

No words to say about her and Arthur.

He hugged her through all her clothes, in the privacy of the wilderness where there were no children close by, only dogs panting in their harnesses, wanting to run. He pushed some of her hair out of her face, and she trembled.

They looked at each other's mouths and did not kiss.

When she broke away a little, he said, "Want to drive?"

"I... I can't give...v-v-v-voice commands."

"I'll run alongside and give them. You can stand on the runners. It's harder than it looks, and five dogs is—well, no one starts with that many. But you're a good athlete. You'll be able to do it on the lake. I'll show you how the brake works. It won't stop the dogs, but it might slow you down some."

"Okay." Her eyelids were lowered; he could only see her lashes. But it took her less than a second to grab the handlebow and step on the footpads, made from pieces of bicycle tire that he'd secured to the tops of the runners. *Ah, you've wanted to try this, haven't you?* He'd uncovered a secret about her. "Say the commands with me, when I give them. For practice." He knew she could do it. Speak in chorus. Sing. Whisper. "Here's what they are—"

"I know them," she said and grabbed the snow hook.

He caught her arm before she could release it from the tree. "Not so fast." Her eyes were glowing. Oh, she wanted this. "Whatever you do, even if it tips, don't let go of the sled...."

CHAPTER TEN

THEY STAYED OUT ON the lake for more than an hour. Twice the sled went over, and both times, Sarah hung on, letting herself be dragged until he could stop the team. The sound of her laughter rang out over the snow, over the lake. It was a sound he'd almost never heard before. He was sure she didn't know how much she was smiling, that her eyes were spitting stars. The wagging tails of the happy dogs were reflected on her face.

The sun had disappeared behind the trees when he took her back to the studio, let her close it up, then gave her a ride back to the house in the basket of the sled.

She helped him put away the harnesses and feed the sled dogs. Her cheeks were flushed, and when she crouched to pet Jedi and be kissed on the face, Tage squatted beside her. Her eyes darted at his, then down.

He gave her his arm to hold as they both stood. Behind the chain link fence, the woods painted color on the snow. Grays for tree bark, orange-red for berries on the mountain ash. Everywhere they'd been today, everything they'd done, Arthur Tennyson had made possible.

Tage hated Arthur Tennyson.

He wasn't jealous anymore because time brought everything into a clearer focus. Time allowed him to remember small things about Arthur. Had his own parents ever whispered suspicions? Or had no one seen Arthur's intentions?

Tage had seen. At sixteen, he hadn't known what he

was seeing. Or maybe everyone had known and was gagged by the possibility of shame among them.

Sick, he hid his emotions. *I should have protected you Sarah. I didn't know.* "You're a good athlete," he said again. "You're a natural musher."

Her glance accused him of lies. He hadn't lied. She *was* a natural. But her stutter would never allow her to drive a dog team alone.

He said, "Let's go make dinner."

They came around the back of the stone kennel building, and Sarah's eyes hollowed. Tage saw, too. The porch seemed naked. A raw, awkward stump jutted from snow scattered with sawdust and splinters. Beside it lay the fallen giant, its trunk ending in a ragged break like a limb torn from a socket.

All else was silent and still, implement and lumberjack both out of sight. The stump spoke to Tage; it was a personal affront. It said, *I don't care what you think.*

No. It said, *I do care.*

A second before, all the trees in the forest had worn the stamp of Arthur Tennyson. But the tree lying in the parking area, the tree that had been subject to such an amateur hack job, had absolutely nothing to do with Arthur. It was Tage's tree. And someone had cut it down.

"I...don't m-m-mind it."

"I do," he said.

LARS HUNTED THROUGH the Lego box for a flat six-by-two piece. He'd started out showing Emily how to build with Legos, but now he was making a fantastic spaceship. Someday, people would build passenger planes faster than the space shuttle. This plane... This plane was very fast. It sped over Emily's Lego house, which was actually an enemy ammunition storage facility. But this was a peace plane, on surveillance.

His sister looked up at him. She was an alien...no, a meteor of great size. He needed to warn the space station, so they could use the disintegrator to blow it up. He stood to fly the ship out of his room and make the jump to hyperspace in the upper hallway. "Whoosh..."

There were footsteps on the stairs.

There was his uncle's head.

No. Tage wasn't his uncle. He had to remind himself.

Lars lowered the spacecraft, carried it back into his room and put it in the Lego box. He should have taken Emily to see the reindeer. Then they could have stayed out until dinnertime.

Or he could have left Emily inside and tried to see the wolf. If he could make friends with the wolf, maybe Tage would see that they really could keep the puppies.

"Lars," said Tage from the doorway. "Please come outside."

THE GIRLFRIEND WASN'T around, at least.

Lars paused at the bench in the vestibule to put on his boots, not taking time to pack the sedge grass nicely, just pulling them on, even though Tage acted like he had all the time in the world.

They went out onto the porch, and the sight of the long kennel building greeted them, and beyond that rose the dome. Everything looked brighter and more cheerful, Lars thought. He hoped his uncle—

Tensing inside, he prepared to defend his actions.

"Did you cut down that tree?"

"It blocked my window. I thought I'd build something with the wood."

"You could build a house with the wood."

Lars stole a glance at the tree. It was large. When it had fallen and the earth had shook some, he'd begun to get a bad feeling.

"That is my tree."

Something about the way Tage said it made Lars look at him. His uncle—*yes, he's my uncle; he's not my father*—gestured over the expanse of the forest that surrounded the Craftsman and the kennels. When he did that, and when he spoke, he reminded Lars of a picture of the handsome Norse god Frey from one of his schoolbooks in Sweden.

He acted like he thought he was a god, too. "These are all my trees," he said. "Whispering Wind Lake is my lake. Those are my kennels. And those sled dogs are my dogs. This house is mine. The room you sleep in is mine. Virtually everything here is mine."

Yes, so what's the point?

Lars couldn't quite make himself say it.

"Someday, if you work hard to be very good, all of this may be yours. And you may cut down all the trees you want."

Lars had to address that. "I don't want to cut down any more. Just this one."

"Well, you're not done with this one. It's blocking my parking lot. *My* parking lot. Do you know how to run a chain saw?"

"No." It seemed like something worth learning, though. Maybe he could cut up the tree with the chain saw.

"You're going to learn. I have two chain saws. I will use one, and you will use the other, but they are both mine. The food you eat tonight will be mine. The bed in which you sleep is mine. The sheets on that bed are mine. From the goodness of my heart and a sense of responsibility for your well-being, I share these things with you. If you wish to acquire anything of your own that you don't already possess, such as your own team of dogs, you should cooperate with me."

Lars found he couldn't look away from Tage's eyes. He began to like the fact that his eyes resembled Tage's.

Frey, the god of sunshine, smiled down at him like something that could overcome the darkest winter. "Because everything here is mine."

THEY COULDN'T MAKE much headway on the tree before dark. Tage figured it would take them the whole next afternoon to move it. Then he'd call the mill to come pick it up. They could mill it and kiln dry it, and he would help Lars make something from the wood.

And now Lars could see out his window.

And Tage could see what was his. These things of his life did not belong to a dead man. They were his. He had altered the landscape. Now his son had changed it more. This place was his, Tage's. If he had to piss on every tree in the forest to make it so.

In the dining room, taking some of Sarah's plates from the china cabinet to carry into the kitchen, Tage thought, *These are mine.*

Arthur couldn't have eaten off these plates for more than a couple of years. They weren't the work of a freshman in art school. Sarah must have been at least twenty when she made them. *I have owned these plates since 1986. More than ten years. They are mine.*

This table is mine.

This hanging lantern chandelier is mine.

This pantry is mine.

Lars, my son, is mine.

A heady and wonderful thought.

He paused at the threshold to the kitchen.

Comet was certainly his.

Emily was his responsibility.

And Sarah...

She turned at the counter. "Emily, hand me that towel."

She pointed, and Emily ran to snatch up the towel and bring it to her.

Tage set the plates on the table, came up behind Sarah and hugged her.

"Wh-wh—" Her fingers gripped his forearms but she didn't try to pull him off her. Whatever she'd meant to say, she left unsaid.

They stood like that, and her breath warmed his hands, but even holding her close he knew she wasn't his. Sarah had never understood, except perhaps from her grandmother, what it was to be treasured. He didn't think she'd ever treasured anyone else either.

He'd been right to say she was like Moses, because Moses was a wolf without a pack, as Sarah was a woman without a family, without loved ones. Moses deserved more—the companionship of his kind. And so did Sarah.

If he wanted her to be part of his pack, he must win her. The usual methods wouldn't work. Tage couldn't tear the throat from a ghost.

All this territory was his. But Arthur was not gone. He had left his sign, indelibly, on Sarah.

LARS FELT GUILTY. Not because he'd never returned Tage's keys after Tage gave them to him to retrieve a handsaw from the wood shop behind the garage. Not because he'd used the keys to get into the quarantine kennel. Not because the wolf had eaten the scraps Lars had given him through the chain-link gate on his run.

He felt guilty because he'd liked running the chain saw with Tage.

He felt guilty because he'd been having fun.

And maybe, because if he had to have a father all of a sudden, it could be much worse. Standing on the porch, listening to Tage go on about everything that was his... And *then,* and *then* Tage had said, *Someday, if you work hard to be very good, all of this may be yours.* And Lars could tell it wasn't a bribe to make him like Tage. Obviously, Tage didn't care if Lars liked him or not.

It's just because I'm his son.

As Lars put some more meat through the fence, carefully keeping his fingers on his side, his parents became very clear in his head. He remembered them strongly, and he sat down on the tile floor and tried to stop thinking about them.

When would it get better?

It had to stop sometime.

"Lars!"

He froze, his pulse suddenly racing. That was Tage. Looking for him. It must be dinnertime.

The wolf seemed to be listening, too.

Lars wavered to his feet, hoping the top of his head didn't show through the windows. *Don't come in here!*

Creeping toward the door, he listened for footsteps, but there were none. Where had his uncle called from? He waited and waited, until he thought he heard Tage calling from somewhere farther away, and then he slipped out of the kennel in the dark and carefully locked the door behind him, leaving the place as he had found it.

"THERE YOU ARE," said Tage.

He had just come in the house, too, Lars could tell, and the way his eyes looked, like they could reach inside Lars and find out what he'd been doing, was troubling. He and Tage had collided in the dining room. In the kitchen, Sarah was singing "Santa Claus Is Comin' to Town," and Emily was singing with her, which was pretty funny. You could tell Emily really believed *jultomten* could see her when she was sleeping and that he knew if she'd been behaving herself.

Yes, it was funny, like the curious way Tage was looking at him.

Tage said, "Where are my keys?"

"Oh. Right here." Lars gave them to him.

"Thank you." Tage scrutinized his son. He'd been up to something. No, surely not so soon, after... He thought of the tree. They would make something wonderful out of it, together.

He smiled at Lars, thinking, *Mine. You are mine.*

In the kitchen a minute later, just to hear himself say it, he told Sarah, "When you make those dishes for my parents, I think it should be some like these. Like mine."

She'd been preparing to move the salad bowl to the table, but she stopped, transfixed by the two goblets in his hands.

His stomach lurched.

She was white, and he knew her expression had nothing to do with his dishes having once been Arthur's. He was an idiot. "On second thought, I'd prefer to give them your plain stoneware. My mother loves blue."

But Sarah shook her head, already arguing with him, already saying it was okay. "No. No, it will be good to fire the salt kiln." As though to herself, she repeated, "It will be good."

His hand circled her nearest wrist. With Sarah you didn't always need words, which was good, because he suddenly sensed Lars watching them from the doorway.

Sarah's dark eyes lifted and held Tage's. She squeezed his hands, and he told himself it meant she wouldn't fire the salt kiln alone.

Friday

IN THE MORNING, Sarah stacked her reduction kiln, which she would use for bisque firing. A kiln had stood in the same place before. She had only to attach four 100,000 Btu burners, arrange her shelves, and she was in business. Since Tage had refused to let her pay for the tank of propane, at least she could make a great set of dishes for his folks.

Salt-glazed ware.

She'd heard Tage perfectly. The mountain ash dishes—the plates, the bowls, the tumblers, the goblets—were his. She liked that idea. Arthur had hardly used them. He'd been in Iceland, then in Sweden and Norway, for many months after she'd given them to him.

Perhaps for Christmas, she should make Tage something else to go with them.

She began wedging clay for the pieces for his parents. He had said four place settings would be fine. She would make plates, bowls, tumblers, goblets and a couple of serving bowls. Tage had also asked for candleholders for his sister and her husband.

It was an hour later that she sat down at the wheel, with a Christmas CD on.

As she centered the clay, the sight of her own hands hurt her eyes, and she felt sick in her own skin. She saw another pair of hands over hers. Felt them. Squeezing the clay. Lifting it. His thumbs on hers, guiding them.

She shuddered, stopping the wheel.

I never used to feel this way.

She'd thrown hundreds of pots, and it had always been fine. Just as she'd made love with Tage so many times, and that was fine.... A lie. She'd never made love with Tage. She'd never been that *present.*

Never since the very first time, with Arthur. On that night when darkness was so long in coming.

Saliva filled her mouth. She didn't want to name or classify what she'd done with her stepfather. The only man in her life with whom she'd had any close connection. Poloma had been married many times, but Sarah had met only one of her husbands, besides Joel Calder.

What do *you* think it was, Sarah?

She kept wanting to scream. What she had made okay, what Arthur's eloquence had shaped into a strange and almost mystical part of her past, had come closer, had come into a shaky focus where she remembered feelings she had forgotten.

I can't think about this. I can't think about this.

She couldn't, if her life depended on it, shape a single pot.

I have to. I have to do this for Tage.

Dogs barked in the woods nearby.

"Gee!"

Sarah jumped up, tapped the *stop* button on the CD player with the toe of her hiking boot and ran to the sink. Quickly, she soaped her arms and snatched up the closest towel.

The glassy surfaced bearded mask with its varicolored texture screamed up at her. She grasped the edge of the wedging table.

It was all right, Arthur. Anyhow, it was my fault. It was my idea.

There was a change in the light. The room was brighter, and Tage came in. He saw the mask.

He said, "It always bothered me that you wanted that."

"I w-w-w— W-w-w—" She took another breath. "W-w-w-w-*wwwwant* to drive the dogs."

He spun, as though expecting to find Arthur in the studio, perhaps through the door into the next room, coming in from the kilns.

Tage's gaze fastened on her wheel, on the clay centered there.

It stuck in his mind, that clay on the wheel. She'd been out here all morning. Now she was going toward the door, acting like Comet did when he hadn't had enough exercise, acting like she needed to run. Before he'd known about her and Arthur, he'd said they should lean on each other. She was leaning now, but he knew it wasn't by choice.

She needed him.

He went to hold her up.

THIS TIME, HE LET HER drive the dogs on the road in the woods, but he insisted on quitting sooner than they needed to. They cared for the dogs and put away equipment together. He stopped to feed Anna—he would run with her later—then walked Sarah back to the studio. On the way, he said, "If you need to talk, there are counselors."

She put a hand to her head, as though her head ached.

The broken cabin came into sight.

They trod the path around the building to the lake side and went, through the porch, back into the warm ceramics studio.

"Sarah?"

She was staring at the mask.

He tilted his head toward the overstuffed chair. "Would you like to sit a while?"

She shivered. Nodding, she moved toward the chair, and he sat first and reached for her. She could make herself into a ball against him while he unzipped her parka and reached inside to hold her closer.

But she couldn't say a word. The words wouldn't come out, not because of her stutter. Just because she couldn't say how it had been that night with Arthur. She couldn't explain a detail like a first kiss. She definitely couldn't tell Tage, *It was like we were in love.*

Recollections swirled in her mind. She let them come and go away. They were of all the things one could think were love.

A man she'd always known looking into her eyes and saying, *Ah, Sarah. Are you sure you want this?*

Love was standing on the sled runners or hanging onto the handle bow and running behind the sled, and a man ran with you, and when you said the same thing at the same time it was possible to talk. Dogs listened to you.

Tage didn't touch her hair, and she was glad. He didn't kiss her. She would have had to get away.

But against her head, he said, very low, "You do certain things so you won't stutter. You use words that aren't the words you want to say. Sometimes, you don't talk at all. I wish you wouldn't do that. It's important that I know all the things you want to say."

She shook her head. *No. No, Tage.*

"You don't think I've seen you stutter?"

"Not *much*," she whispered, then crunched her eyes shut. Nothing like this had ever happened before. Not for years. There had been one speech therapist in high school... But Sarah had escaped unscathed, without having to talk.

Tage's arms were easing her around to face him, and Sarah kept her head down, her eyes closed.

"Look at me."

His voice got her attention as efficiently as it did his dogs'.

"I have seen you stutter many times. I have seen what happens to your face. I have seen you grind your foot into the floor. You blink. Your lips and nose quiver. I know when you rearrange sentences so that you won't stutter. If you think you've hidden any of this, you're mistaken."

When he saw her reaction, the horrible reddening of her face, he knew she *had* thought she'd hidden it.

She tried to get up, and he let her. She was a woman, not a child. She wandered across the studio and into the second room, where the window over the sink let her see the lake.

Sarah shivered. *I can't stand this. I can't stand it. Why was I born this way?* A person who could talk well could do anything. A person who stuttered was forever at the mercy of others.

Or else, forever alone.

Behind her was a shelf of raku pieces. She even recognized a bowl she'd made years earlier, when Arthur was teaching her about raku. She grabbed it and hurled it to the floor, wishing it would break against concrete instead of softer linoleum.

It broke without the satisfying shatter she wanted to hear.

There was some kind of raku statue, too.

Arthur had made it. *Arthur!* Wanting to scream his name, she flung the piece as hard as she could against the place where someone had never put baseboards on, against the space between the pale green walls and the linoleum.

Everything shimmered. Every color ran.

A moan came out of her.

A tea bowl. She didn't care that he'd made it and wouldn't make anything again. She broke it over the edge of the sink.

There was a twenty-inch salt-glazed plate, a decorative piece with some Norse god type of shape in the center. The glazes had run to gold in places. Glazes that could not be replicated. With a scream, she hurled it against the wall, chipping out a chunk of plaster, and then she sank down on her knees and cried.

Everything shimmered. The colors around her were like glazes beginning to look wet in the fire of the raku kiln. *I want to talk. I want to talk like other people.*

She held herself, gasping, and cried as hard as she

wanted. There was ceramic dust in her hair, on her face and clothes.

Incest began with a vowel. It was a substitution. For a parent's love.

Tage... She didn't call to him. She never would. You couldn't need people.

She got up and dragged the sleeve of her parka across her face. The Gore-tex was dirty. She hunted for a towel, but they were all in the other room.

Tage shifted, leaning forward in the chair, his forearms on his knees. When she went by, he lowered his head.

Sarah picked up the mask from the wedging table and hurled it to the floor.

It broke precisely in half, down the center of the nose, and she saw that when it had fired, one side had fired pale, the other dark, an oxblood glaze gone wrong or running. It still screamed. The mask had meant something to her once. It didn't any more. Just the thing she couldn't *know*.

Tage had said Arthur never felt remorse.

Maybe it was her last effort to see Arthur as a hero, to hope he'd killed himself with chlorine gas and gone to such dramatic lengths to make it look like an accident.

She didn't know what a hero was.

She didn't even know if when a hero's stepdaughter kissed his mouth, he would walk away. She didn't know if Arthur had kissed her first. Such touches were lost details.

She remembered Tage. She'd been going to wipe her face.

She washed in the sink, face and hands, and dried herself with the towel that had covered the mask. She said, "He came out here with w-w—" The stutter was going to make her scream again. *I have to tell him. I can't do it this way.* She could whisper like her mother. *No!* Her heart hissed the denial. She could speak in chorus with others.

Everyone should know the chorus of this very old play, but Tage couldn't.

She sang. Tunelessly.

"He came out here with wine in the evenings. It was June. We watched the sun go down on the lake and went swimming. Sometimes, we took the canoe. It was Midsummer's Night. We were in the water, and I kissed him. It was my fault, you see."

In the chair, Tage watched her face. He had seen eleven cycles of the seasons on Whispering Wind Lake. Summer. He saw loons and heard mosquitoes.

"I don't think he'd thought of it himself."

Trust me, he had, thought Tage. A man who'd never thought of it would have sent her for counseling. But her words let him see precisely what Arthur had done.

And Tage let her sing. No word was too difficult anymore—just two words beginning with vowels, two words she never used. One of them was the name Arthur. The other was what they had done.

She shifted to sit on the folding chair, and he didn't offer her the better one. He didn't want her to know he was there. He was just the audience, and her head was in her hands, and she was singing, on one or two stark notes, of the first time Arthur had looked at her and how his hands had touched her. All the ways he had touched her.

Tage wanted to curl in on himself. There was something in this…this thing she sang that shrank his soul. Not made it small but made it cringe, made it crush like tissue crumpling itself, made his soul cry, *Oh, my God! Oh, my God!*

Arthur had entered her.

His own mouth tasted like a hangover, like morning.

Tage saw the clock rather than thought to look at it. The school bus would be pulling up to the road right now.

Sarah had moved to the floor, where she leaned against a leg of the wedging table.

He said, "Come with me to the bus. We're late."

She let him take her hand to help her up.

Then he bent and took up the two pieces of the mask and hunted for a bag or something to put them in. He found a paper bag half filled with some trash—plastic bags that had held clay. He put the mask inside with the other refuse and wrapped it up and tucked it under his arm.

He held the door to the screen porch for her.

Outside, the air was bright, sunny. The lake shone, beautiful and bright.

He caught Sarah's eyes and he told her, his voice feeling warm, "You know, that is my lake."

Her smile was pretty and red eyed.

"And these are my trees."

Sarah saw him there on the shore with the sky reflected on snow and ice behind him. His eyes were like a bigger sky, his hair like sun. His shoulders were broad enough to carry her sins. And his face told no lies.

Arthur was gone.

These are my trees, he had said, as though he was king here now.

And he asked, "Would you like to cut one down?"

Light Returns

CHAPTER ELEVEN

Still Friday

KNEELING IN THE SNOW, Sarah sawed at the trunk of the spruce, just above the bottom ring of branches so that the tree would grow back. As Tage held the trunk, bending it away from the cut, Lars and Emily crouched to see how far the saw had worked through.

"I'll help, Sarah," Lars offered.

"This is Sarah's tree. You've had yours."

And as soon as they got this one home, Lars and Tage would finish sawing the maple. The mill truck was coming to pick it up the next day, Saturday, the same day workers were coming to construct the wolf compound. The day of Lars's first dogsled race. Sarah hadn't been in Minnesota a week; it felt like a year.

Among the spruce needles, she wondered if Tage would forgive her for letting Lars cut the rest of the tree. She gave him a questioning glance.

He peered at her through the branches. "Tired?"

"A little."

He stepped back, gestured to his son. Sarah scrambled out from under the twelve-foot tree and handed Lars the saw.

"You're sure?" Lars asked.

She nodded. "Thank you."

As he tackled the last inch of sawing, Emily wandered away from the others, to see the reindeer. Lars and Tage had harnessed two of them, using harnesses made from equipment Tage used for dog training. Encouraged by Snutte, the two called Blitzen and Dancer had pulled an empty stone sled to this spot, a half mile from the corral.

Fingering Tage's wood carving in her coat pocket, Sarah kept her eye on Emily, making sure she didn't stray too close to the animals. They had horns and hooves. But something stopped her from picking up the little girl. It seemed presumptuous. Emily was Tage's child.

And Sarah felt unfit to care for her.

If she hadn't been born that way, as a stutterer, her parents had contrived to make her that way. Arthur had sealed her fate, sealed it with a kiss and more.

No. I sealed it.

"That's it." Tage slid the tree off its stump. It stood ten feet tall, and the bottommost boughs stretched eight feet across. His eyes found Sarah's. "Do you like your tree?"

She nodded. Sawing through the branches, she had sympathized with Lars's instinct to cut down the maple. But the evergreen symbolized eternity, a continuance of life. A return of light.

She shivered. The nights were still getting longer.

Emily gazed at Tage with an interested frown. The word she spoke was Swedish. *"Jultomten."*

"Not till Christmas," said Lars. "He'll be Santa Claus for Christmas. But now we have a tree."

"Reindeer." Her boots almost disappearing in the snow, Emily pointed at the reindeer, then at Tage. *"Jultomten."* She laid her finger beside her nose and nodded and waved, like Moore's jolly old elf, then faced Lars with a defiant expression. "Santa Claus!"

"Yes," agreed Tage. "I will be Santa Claus on Christmas Eve."

Pressing her lips firmly together, Emily regarded her brother with an expression that meant, *See? I told you so.*

Lars adjusted his Saami hat just a bit. "She doesn't really get it."

"It's all right." Tage smiled at him, proud of the kind of brother Lars was. "Let's get the ropes and take this home."

THEY LEFT THE CHRISTMAS tree in a bucket of water against a wall in the training dome. Tage and Lars worked till after dark sawing branches from the maple and preparing the limbs and trunk for pickup by the mill truck. Sarah made pizza for dinner, and after dinner, while Tage read to Emily and helped her practice saying words, Sarah closed herself in her room. The owl was in its tree, and as she sat down to watch, she glimpsed a shape passing on the ground below, beneath the branches. A light from the house—from the dining room, perhaps—cast a rectangular glow and the figure passed through it.

Lars.

Where was he going?

The path behind the house led to only one place. The isolation kennel, where Moses was quarantined.

Surely Lars couldn't get in without a key.

Sarah switched off her bedroom light, trying to see into the darkness. Tage used ultraviolet lights in all his kennel buildings to reduce the spread of any infections.

When the door of the isolation building opened, Sarah saw the light.

Hugging herself, she wavered. Her relationship with Lars had taken a turn for the better, she thought. If she told on him...

She touched her neck. She'd removed the bandages, but the bruises and puncture marks remained. And she had many shots to go.

She left her room and crossed the hall to Emily's. The

door was open, and inside Tage and Emily sat in the chair by the window. He was reading a book to her. *The Mitten.*

Sarah spent several moments trying to work out substitutions.

When Tage's eyes reached her, the afternoon came back. "L-L-Lars is in the isolation kennels."

He stared but didn't question her, just scooted Emily off his lap and walked out of the room.

Frowning, Emily began to close her book, then changed her mind and held it up to Sarah.

Sarah shook her head. "I can't."

Emily's expression of displeasure intensified. She shoved the book at Sarah again.

"No." When was the last time she'd had to read aloud? High school. The only way to play it had been rude refusal, and she'd been sent to the dean's office, and then the speech therapist had gotten involved....

Disappointed, Emily closed her book and picked up her reindeer and sat by the window. *You're not my friend,* she said without words.

Sarah didn't know anything to do but go back to her own room and shut the door. She felt stupid. Tage had to take care of everyone, including her, and how could she help when she couldn't even talk without stuttering?

Lying on her bed, she relived the time in the studio, the summer night by the lake, and began to shiver so badly that she had to get between the covers. There, her memories came to claim her.

TAGE WASN'T AFRAID for Lars, and he wasn't angry. He was just tired. He had looked after dogs for years, but suddenly three people needed him, all of them badly. What he really wanted was for Lars and Emily to go to sleep so he could find out how Sarah was doing. They hadn't been alone since that afternoon, since she'd told him about Arthur.

The kitchen light burned through the utility room; outside, it illuminated Lars's footprints in the snow. Tage paused to examine all the tracks to and from the kennel. Was this the first time Lars had been here? He didn't think so. He should have noticed tracks before, but his own footprints, made at night, then covered by snow before morning, had eliminated the smaller ones.

He opened the kennel door, and when he went in Lars was inside Moses's run with the gate shut. The boy started.

Tage thought, *I should have been afraid.*

"Goodbye, Moses." Lars squeezed out of the gate while Moses tried to follow him, then reattached the padlock Tage had used to secure the gate.

Tage held out his hand, and Lars gave him the keys and wouldn't look up.

He's scared this time.

Tage made himself be patient. He pointed out the quarantine sign on the door, the warning Do Not Enter. He reminded Lars that Moses had bitten Sarah on the throat, that it was amazing he'd done so little damage; he could have killed her. He explained that his being allowed to keep Moses in quarantine was a matter of trust. He was standing on his business reputation, and his business reputation stood on the success of this quarantine. Should Moses escape or injure anyone, anyone at all, his business would suffer.

He told Lars that Moses had opened the door of the isolation kennel before, that he'd opened the gate when it wasn't padlocked. That perhaps he'd already seen that by overcoming Lars he could escape. He just hadn't chosen to do it yet. He hadn't been a prisoner long enough.

Tage let them both out of the isolation kennel and locked the door.

He said, "We're not going to the races tomorrow."

The young mouth fell open in dismay that anyone could be so unfair.

Unsurprised, Tage said, "I told you yesterday that you should cooperate with me. You decided not to. You chose to do something you knew you shouldn't."

"I don't have to do what you say."

It wasn't quite a challenge. It reminded Tage of the kind of dog that constantly tested him, constantly tried to see if he could be the alpha. Lars was too smart to say what he'd said in a rude way. He'd said it in a testing way.

"That's true," Tage pointed out. "But you'll be happier if you do."

IT WAS AFTER EMILY'S bedtime. Tage found her still in her room, playing with her reindeer and a puzzle on her bed. Sarah's door was shut. After he'd said good-night to Emily and left her room, he stood outside Sarah's closed door for a long time, wanting to knock. The light had gone out only since he'd come upstairs to tuck in Emily. She couldn't be asleep.

But she wants to be alone, Tage.

Behind him, a latch clicked. As Tage turned, Lars stepped out of his room. They saw each other across the stairwell, and Tage was glad of the shadows in the upper hall. Maybe Lars couldn't tell that he was standing outside Sarah's room like a dog getting ready to scratch on the door.

Trying to look like he'd just left her room, he turned to go downstairs, wondering which of them was the adolescent.

HE COULDN'T SLEEP and sat in the inglenook with Comet, watching the fire and trying not to drink wine. He'd already checked his e-mail and found more messages from

Nils-Isak. *Say hello to Sarah from us. I hope she's doing well. Good luck with the wolf. Your mother is sending a Christmas package....*

He tried to imagine his stepfather's reaction if he knew about Sarah and Arthur. Arthur had understood the Saami community, had pitched in to help neighbors. Sarah had learned to make hearth bread with Tage's mother. She'd gone with Tage to take a *lavvo,* a tent, to some men on migration.

It was how she'd fallen through the ice.

Shadows collected around him.

Was Sarah avoiding him now?

She's all right. She's holding up fine.

The stairs creaked. Comet's ears perked up, and the dog dashed from the living room. Tage rose silently, hoping it was her.

It was.

She wore a long undershirt and sweatpants. When she reached the foot of the stairs, he told Comet to go lie down and drew her against him. Her breasts pressed softly against his ribs. Her hands held his sides.

When he moved to see her face, she didn't look away from him. They stood just feet from where he'd kissed her the last time, the kiss that failed. When he lowered his head this time, she lifted hers.

Sarah's hands groped from his arms to his shoulders as she felt his mouth. She'd never been aware of how his lips felt before. She'd never let herself feel what a kiss really was.

Some kisses were quiet violence. Some spread slow sickness. A sleeping sickness from which it hurt to wake.

Tage's eyes knew everything. They gave her permission to feel awful while she kissed him. To kiss him and remember another man. To relive other kisses. The willing dance of a dark spell.

Her throat crawled.

She held him harder, felt his tongue.

"Come in here," he said.

The two benches on each side of the hearth that made up the inglenook afforded a kind of privacy. A place to kiss. To control anger when he remembered things about her, remembered things only a lover would know. The thing he recalled most was that she was easily seduced.

Nothing was more exciting.

With one leg on the bench behind her, he supported her back as he kissed her. The fire brought red to her cheeks. Her eyes seemed large and darker than ever.

He hated Arthur Tennyson.

He wanted to say, *And you, Sarah, are also mine*.

He would never say such a thing to her. She was her own. He was a visitor to her body. He found the inside of her mouth again. Some sounds could not be heard, and her cries were like that. Like whistles only a dog could hear. Tage felt the change in her breath and knew she was moaning, crying out.

She shifted on the bench, a warm and exciting shift against his thigh and his groin.

"Sarah."

She heard what her name meant. She felt him dragging her closer. His hand touched between her legs.

Not this. Not now. It felt so good and so dreadful.

"Can we go upstairs?" she asked.

"Yes."

On the steps, she held his arm as if they were climbing a mountain. As if she were very old or very sick.

THE OWL STILL BLINKED outside her window, its eyes supernaturally bright. Sarah was used to its being there. In the mornings, she sometimes spent nearly an hour at a time studying its black-tipped white feathers.

Tage locked the door and took her to her bed. They lay on the spread to kiss again, and the mattress creaked gently beneath them.

"Sarah. You've told me about you and Arthur. If you need to feel those things, if you need to remember them when we make love, to relive them somehow, it's all right."

She sat up. Shaking, she drew off her shirt and lay down, feeling the air on her breasts, and shut her eyes.

The time passed very slowly, as time passes in pain.

Like an initiate, she knew that sometime the ordeal would be over.

It was sickening to be so aroused. When their bodies were joined, she couldn't bear for him to move. She begged him not to, and he held still, but the feelings rushed in and out of her anyway, like a dreadful pulse. Another man, first sex. Another man inside her.

"Don't move."

He did.

"Don't move."

When he did, she cried, and he didn't kiss her. Then he did, and everything became as bad as it could be.

FROM THE FOOT of the bed, he gazed out at the owl, his shoulders and the muscles in his arms silhouetted against the window. The starlight left a satin film on his skin.

She huddled in the sheets. *I have to get out of here. I can't stand it. I have to go away.*

She'd promised she wouldn't. Till Christmas.

And how do you think he feels, Sarah? How do you think he really feels?

She saw that she could never repay him.

"Tage." As she sat up, he turned and came back to her. He put his hand behind her on the bed and rested on it, giving her an arm to lean against. But even beside her, he watched the owl.

Tage didn't want to talk about what had just happened. He didn't want her to talk about it. They both knew what had occurred, and there was no need to put words to it. He didn't dream for a moment that sex would be magically innocuous the next time. It would take a long time and many times.

And he would think about the salt kiln, the way she must.

When he'd first kissed her tonight, at the foot of the stairs, he'd known how sex would be. He had allowed it to happen, had told himself he was *giving* to her by letting her have her thoughts and feelings against his body. He hadn't counted on knowing so much.

He hadn't counted on becoming Arthur.

He felt like he'd been bitten by a rabid dog and there was no antidote.

"I wish I could repay you," she whispered.

It was the final sickening thing, embarrassing words. He withdrew. "You can't repay love. No one expects it."

Sarah arranged the sheets over herself, hiding. He'd been there, now. Now, he knew her. He talked about love, but he could not love her. Who could?

Outside, it was winter. It seemed as though the sun would never come.

"I thought if we just made love it would be better," she whispered. *I need to leave. I need to leave, Tage.*

She'd promised to stay, and now leaving seemed cowardly. She was feeling her way in the dark, trying to discover where she really wanted to go. She knew only that in her whole life she'd never done anything that mattered to anyone else, except something that might have made one man kill himself, and other things that had made Tage unhappy.

Once, at fifteen, she'd screamed at her grandmother, *I'm n-n-never going to do anything that m-m-m-matters. I might as well be dead.*

Her grandmother had said, *Well. You'll be a lady. That's fine.*

She envied Tage. He trained dogs and people needed their dogs trained.

During the past week, there had been times she'd felt very strong. Most of them had happened behind his dog-sled, giving commands in chorus with Tage.

"Do-do-do-do you think I could get over my s-s-s-s-sssstutter?"

The owl's wings flapped once, and he was off, flying past the windows and out of sight.

Tage broke from the darkness he and Sarah had shared. He stopped licking his wounds.

"Yes."

Nothing in his face let her get away.

"There is no reason," he said, "why you should stutter. There are dozens—hundreds—of stuttering therapies. One of them will work for you."

No hesitation. He'd thought about it before, she could see.

"Why have I never said anything?" All the hatred Tage felt infused one sentence. "Because I felt certain that Arthur Tennyson had. You were his stepdaughter. He was a Ph.D. I trusted that he would have given you every help he could. But he didn't, did he, Sarah?"

Oh, shit, he'd made her cry.

I never knew you, he thought, *till this week.*

"He helped m-m-m-me be-be-become a potter. He took me places. To Lapland. Skiing. It's all I've ever had. I can't hate him. And look what he gave *you*."

"I've been looking all week, wishing he'd given it to someone else. But now it's mine. And his gift doesn't oblige me to respect a man who seduced his stepdaughter.''

"I s-s-s-seduced him! And I wasn't his stepdaughter any more.''

"Who decided that?"

"I did.''

She wanted badly to vindicate Arthur. If she tried any harder, Tage reflected, she might succeed. He wanted to warn her of that, but he didn't warn her. He remembered well enough the things she'd told him Arthur had said. He'd recognized each sentence as something Arthur would say. He understood seduction. "If you were a man, you would see this more clearly. But I can ask you, if you left this house today, would you come back in ten years and have sex with my son?"

She flew out of the bed and began dressing.

She was crying.

He didn't care. Sarah needed to see. "You promised," he said, "that you would stay until Christmas."

"I didn't—" The block lasted perhaps five minutes. By the time she finished the sentence, he'd forgotten how it began. "P-p-p-*prom*ise to stay and be insulted."

"So stay and fight."

"I *can't* fight. Not with—"

Words, thought Tage.

She never said it. The block didn't allow the sound.

He said, "Tell me who you are. Say who you are, Sarah. Say what you believe in."

She buttoned her jeans, let her shirt drop down her body, covering her. "I've n-n-never—" Another long, agonizing silence. "*Pppplay*ed games with you. I have always loved you. I knew I w-w-w-*was*n't the right—individual for you."

They weren't talking to each other. Tage stole off the bed and grabbed her.

She shook free in one impatient movement.

Tired, so tired, of trying to talk and not being understood, Sarah hunted in her pack for notebook and pen. She wrote out directions for cab drivers. She could write this to Tage with no light at all.

Eyes watering, sitting on the edge of the recliner, she scratched out blind clauses. "I am Sarah. I want to talk. What you just said to me can never be forgiven or forgotten."

She ripped out the page, crumpled it up and threw it at him.

Tage rolled on his stomach and turned on the bedside lamp. Her words went all over the page, but he could make them out. Her last sentence frightened him. She'd misunderstood. He'd spoken for comparison's sake.

And the muddy comparisons had to go on. "Arthur can be forgiven, though?"

"It was—" A long time later, she said, "*Mmmmyy* fault."

The windows reflected his body, his nakedness, and the shape of the lamp shade. He avoided the reflection. "Sarah, why are you angry at me for what I said about Lars? Why is it disgusting to you? *Because it should be.* You are a very beautiful and enticing woman, and you were beautiful and enticing at twenty-three, but trust me, Sarah. You were never in your life sufficiently irresistible to make a good man forget that you were his stepdaughter and that you regarded him as a father. There is a clear line on this issue, *and Arthur Tennyson crossed it.*"

Her face was wavering oddly, her eyes flooding. She whispered, "I've never heard of a potter killing himself in a salt firing. Tage, he would have had to *try.*"

What was he supposed to say? He didn't trust himself to say anything she could understand.

Except, "I hope you're not leaving."

Sarah shut her eyes and drew her feet up against her in the chair. She was ashamed of herself for having contemplated leaving. She wasn't going anywhere. She just shook her head.

He switched off the light but stayed where he was.

It was quite a while before she returned to the bed. Even then, she walked around to the far side and didn't remove her clothes. But she groped across the tangled sheets with her hand, and eventually his fingers closed on hers.

Tage was still seeing her scrawled words in his mind.

I am Sarah.

I want to talk.

The white space was the lack in her life. No pack—no family—and no mission.

"You can't leave," he said. "You owe me some dishes. For Christmas."

Invisible, Sarah shut her eyes. How would she touch wet clay again?

Tage embraced her. He was warm; recollection, wretched. "Come downstairs. I'll read you a story, and then you'll sleep."

"Okay."

He pulled on his pants, and they went down. While Sarah stoked the fire, he poured them each some wine.

Then, while she lay on one of the benches in the inglenook, her knees up, vulnerable as a dog on its back, he leaned against the side of the opposite bench, with his feet on the seat, and opened a book he'd picked from a shelf in the library. *My library. My book.* He smiled as he turned the pages.

"'Marley was dead: to begin with,'" he read, satisfied. *Dead. Dead.* "'There is no doubt whatever about that....'"

THEY SLEPT IN SEPARATE rooms that night. He pretended it had to do with the children, with setting an example. It was more complicated, wound up in the fact that he'd become Arthur in her arms. He refused the role. Arthur was dead. *There is no doubt whatever about that....*

In his own bed, Tage recalled the clay she'd centered on her wheel but had never shaped into a pot. Arthur's ghost was more persistent than the ghost of Jacob Marley or Christmas Past or Present or Future. He was Arthur Eternal. For her, he surely lived in the clay. And beside the lake.

How did you kill such a ghost? How did you make the haunted one a part of your pack? Part of your family...

The answer was obvious. Sarah had to slay Arthur's ghost; he was hers. She had to destroy him with the weapon she'd never had. Words to say no. Words to find a love that didn't require sex with a parent. Words to end the constant jeopardy, the helplessness of her life. Words were power, and when Sarah could talk without stuttering, when she was no longer shy, she could rid herself of Arthur's ghost.

He breathed in the dark.

I want to talk. Her decisions, her choices...

Even if she learned to speak without stuttering, it wouldn't happen overnight.

And while she was vulnerable, she shouldn't be alone with her ghost. Not in his house. Not in his woods. Not in the studio, even now that the mask was in his Dumpster, going the way of dog waste.

There was a sudden jingle of tags on the floor, and Tage glanced at Comet's shape, illuminated because the security lights from the kennels blazed in the night. "You?" he said. "She'd never get any work done with you there."

But all dogs needed a mission.

And Comet was quite a distraction.

Tage put his face near the edge of the mattress, and the

dog kissed him. Behind the red mask, Comet's blue eyes seemed insistent. Mischievous. Willing.

Why not? If Comet was too active, there were other dogs. His kennels were full of dogs who could benefit from time spent in the company of a woman with the patience to sit at a potter's wheel. To sit on a dog's leash and ignore him.

If that failed, there was always Anna....

Anna, don't be pregnant.

Preventing a litter of puppies from entering the world wasn't something children could understand. As it wasn't possible to simply abort a litter. It would mean a hysterectomy for Anna. He could never breed her.

So, what if he kept the wolf dog cubs? What if he let Lars raise them, as Lars wanted to do?

The wolf compound rendered most objections inconsequential. But one always remained.

Tage had told Lars "no."

Some words were just for dogs. Some words were for children, too. Some words, a very few words, were absolute.

Everything he'd said to Lars about this litter of wolf dog puppies had been that way. Final. Giving in would raise doubt about who was in charge.

He had to stick by his word.

And hope Lars did not hate him for it.

Saturday

WORKMEN ARRIVED IN THE morning to construct the wolf compound. It spread over almost two acres. The eight-foot-high overhang fence, laid with ground wire to discourage digging, was surrounded by a perimeter fence, to keep children from going close.

Sarah skied past the construction project on her way to the studio. She kept a distance, speaking to no one.

She expected solitude in the cabin, but she'd barely removed her skis when Tage showed up with Comet. He was followed by Lars and the reindeer, pulling Emily on a sled. While Lars took his sister across the lake, Tage asked Sarah if she would help him by keeping Comet in a long down for a half hour.

"It will help him. Maybe he'll be able to stay inside during dinner."

Without stealing food? Sarah doubted it, but she agreed to help.

Tage waited while she arranged the leash and made the first correction to Comet's curiosity about the studio, his trying to visit the kitchen. At her slight jerk on the lead, Comet squealed like he was being murdered, which was just what Tage had expected. Histrionics and lies. For a moment, the dog sat calmly, like the picture of canine decorum, and then he spotted a movement in the corner of the room. His catapult through the air burned the leash out from under Sarah. Aghast, she saw him catch the chipmunk and swallow it whole.

"Sled dogs," said Tage, to Sarah's open mouth.

She remembered a dead chipmunk in a shoe box. Arthur comforting her. His lips brushing her cheek.

Comet, devourer of things that moved, returned to the wheel, flopped down and shut his eyes. *Comet the "Dog, Exterminator."*

Sarah wet her hands with water, and the clay was just clay.

Tage lingered, observing from the overstuffed chair while she shaped a bowl and applied the slips and glazes that would bring out the mountain ash design.

"When are you going to fire?" he asked.

"I don't know..." She tried to say *Friday?* and the

word stopped in her mouth. She could see it there and could see nothing else.

Tage saw more—her eyelids blinking and nostrils quivering, one foot pushing into the floor as though to push the word out. When she did make a sound, the effort stretched her mouth unnaturally.

"F-F-F-Ffffriday?"

The American Speech-Language Hearing Association said stuttering wasn't a medical condition or disease; the United States Food and Drug Administration said it was. Tage had read that it was caused by a defect in the auditory feedback loop; stutterers hear their own voices delayed.

Grabbing the folding metal chair, he got up and came over to the wheel, on the opposite side from where Comet lay.

Sarah centered a new ball of clay on the bat. The wheel hummed.

"Sarah."

"Yes."

"If you want to overcome your stutter, I think you can."

Sarah dipped her hands in a Tupperware container of water and pressed them to the clay, forcing the clay upward, into a cone. It was hard to talk while she worked. Finally, she lifted her hands and stopped the wheel. "I'm—" *Sorry for last night.* The words were so present in her mind that she almost felt if she *thought* them hard enough Tage must realize what they were. She held her breath, couldn't let it out the way she couldn't get the word out. "S-s-s-s-sooooorrry. For last night."

"It's all right. It doesn't matter." The morning sun had chased away the darkness, for the short length of another day.

"Tage... *How?*"

How could she learn to talk without stuttering. "That

depends on you. I can look on the Internet for therapy programs.''

Sarah hated therapy programs. When you relapsed after a therapy program, you felt more stupid than ever. She declined.

''What do you *want,* Sarah?''

She concentrated on the word she wanted to say. ''A—''

From his chest to his abdomen, Tage was tight, rigid. He made himself relax and wait. He resisted the urge to hold her, to try to kiss the word out of her. A minute passed. And another.

Comet opened and shut his eyes.

''Bbbbook.''

A book.

''Do you know which one?''

''Any one.''

He believed. In her. In miracles. ''On Monday, Sarah, you will have a book.''

CHAPTER TWELVE

LARS RESENTED MISSING the dogsled races, but even more it bothered him that Anna might be pregnant and he might not get to keep the wolf dog puppies. He wanted those puppies to be part of his team more than he'd ever wanted anything. Anything *possible*...

Tage had books about wolves and wolf dogs, maybe books he'd gotten because of Sarah's wolf. Lars took the books to his room and read them whenever he could. He was most interested in the books that were actually about wolf hybrids. One of the books worried him a bit. It was true that wolf dogs had attacked, even killed some children. But that was true of dogs, too—didn't even have to be sled dogs. He'd heard Critter and Lisa talking the other day about an English sheepdog that had attacked some boy. Still, he wouldn't want anything to happen to Emily.

How could he convince Tage to let him keep the wolf dog puppies?

Tage...

Whenever Lars had the disturbing thought that Tage and his mother had really had him—instead of his mother and father—he just tried to make the thought go away. What was he supposed to tell people at school? Was he supposed to tell them that his uncle wasn't actually his uncle but was really his father?

Half the time, people called Tage his dad anyhow.

Maybe he should just stop correcting them.

But wouldn't that hurt his own parents? If they knew?

Why had Tage left him when he was a baby, why hadn't Tage wanted to be his father? It wasn't something you could ever ask. Especially because now Tage was only taking care of him because Lars's parents had said he should be guardian if they died.

Don't forget that, Lars.

He still decided he wasn't going to correct people any more when they called Tage his dad.

These things were on his mind every day, but one thing had gotten much better. He could see out his window. Every morning he went and stood by his window and looked out. And sometimes he heard Tage's voice when he'd talked like Frey....

Sometimes he heard Tage saying, *And someday if you work hard to be very good, all of this may be yours.*

So he had to be good, but he also had to get Tage to agree to keep Anna's puppies. He couldn't make friends with Moses right now, because Moses would be quarantined for another week. But he did wonder something.

Did *Sarah* know what Tage planned?

How did she feel about wolf puppies?

Lars found himself smiling at his father's troll drum. Of course! The woman on the drum. He didn't need to get rid of Sarah. He needed her help. She wasn't so bad once you got used to her, anyhow. And he'd figured out something about her. Tage would give Sarah anything she asked for.

Anything at all.

LATE MONDAY AFTERNOON, when Sarah returned to the house to change out of her clay-encrusted jeans, she found a gift-wrapped package on her bed. A glance told her there was something in it besides a book. Before she removed the paper, which was covered with reindeer, she opened the white envelope. The card had a wolf on the front.

Inside, Tage had written, *So you can see the face I love.*

The mirror was bird's-eye maple, with a smooth handle. The book was *Self-Therapy for the Stutterer,* and Sarah knew why he'd given her the mirror.

So that she could watch herself stutter.

She stretched out on her stomach with the book, and she'd only skimmed the table of contents before she closed it. *I can't do these things!* Stop all avoidances, let herself stutter, maintain eye contact.... So, do you want to keep stuttering, Sarah, or do you want to get over it?

She clutched Tage's mirror, remembering the other thing he'd carved for her so recently. That carving lived in the pocket of her parka, never far away. But she had hardly handled it since the night she'd made love with Tage. She'd been making pottery instead—the salt-glazed ware for his family in Sweden and raku pieces for pleasure. For independence.

She read Tage's card again.

She opened the book.

I'm going to do this. I'm going to get over this. I know I can.

It was some time later that she heard someone come in. Emily climbed up on the mattress beside her and toyed with the wrapping paper.

"Santa Claus?" she asked.

It seemed ordained. She had just read that she must practice speaking, and here was someone to speak with. Sarah couldn't remember everything she'd learned, but a few rules she'd read had stuck with her. She must talk slowly and deliberately and let herself stutter. She could try drawing out the starting sounds of words and sentences for as long as a second each.

"Tttaaage … gave … it … to … me. Thhiiings … to … help … m-m-m—" *Relax, Sarah.* She knew she was flushing. Emily gawked. "M-m-meee … s-s-s-stop … s-s-s-s-sssssssstuttering."

Emily's frown became a delighted smile. "Tage," she said and clapped her hands. "Santa Claus!"

"N-n-n-no." Sarah resisted her usual impulse, to quit the conversation, to not bother arguing. "Tage is not—" She'd gone too fast. *Slow way down and let yourself stutter, Sarah.* "S-S-S-S-SSSSSaaanta Claus." She felt stupid and embarrassed.

She also felt free.

I'm going to win. I'm going to get better.

Emily pointed at the wrapping paper. "Reindeer?"

"Yes." Sarah wanted to read the stuttering book some more, but for now she could practice talking. "Let's...go...see...the...r-r-r-reindeer. And Tage."

But before she stood, she picked up the mirror and looked in it. Her own brown eyes stared back. Her nose. Her mouth. *He loves me.* Her eyes felt hot. She remembered Arthur kissing her mouth and made herself stop remembering. She watched her lips in the mirror. "It's a ppppretty m-m-m-*mirrr-or.*"

Oh, God. Oh, God. Do I really look like that? Her nostrils vibrating, her mouth so...awful.

"Sarah."

The cry of distress caught Sarah's attention. Emily was another mirror.

Sarah wiped her eyes. "I'm...okay."

"Tage," Emily said gravely, as though Tage would make everything right, as though Sarah should count on him.

Sarah set the mirror on the bed with the book and her card.

"Let's...gggggo...ddownsssstairs."

LARS HAD BEEN HOPING to corner Sarah in her pottery studio after school, but she wasn't there. Then Tage found him and asked him if he'd like to run the dogs. They could take two sleds, so he could practice passing on the trail, practice passing for races. There would be races on Saturday, which was Lucia Day, though nobody celebrated Lucia Day here, and Tage had promised to take him to Lake Gegoka on Thursday after school so he could try the actual course.

Dinner was his first chance to talk to Sarah, and Lars wasn't sure how to do it with Tage there. He considered it as he gnawed on a piece of pizza and watched Emily pick mushrooms off hers. While he was still thinking, Sarah said to Tage, "I ... haaave ... ffffour ... mmmmore ... ppplates ... to ... mmmmake. After that, I ... can ... ffffire ... them."

When someone talked like that, you really couldn't help staring. Why was she being such a freak? Lars had seen her stutter once or twice, and that was bad enough—embarrassing for everyone. But what was this all about? He couldn't help saying, "Why are you talking that way?"

Then he remembered he wanted her on his side and he also wanted Tage on his side, and now Tage looked like he was going to kill him, and Sarah was getting all red, the way she did. She might look like a model sometimes, but other times she was really a mess.

He didn't know why he'd bothered asking her, since it was obviously going to be one of those times when she just didn't answer.

But she said, "I'm ... tttttrying ... to ... ssssssstop ..."

Boy, *S* was a real challenge for her, you could see. Oh, wow. Now she was going to say "stuttering." This should be good.

"Sssssssssssstuttering. Ttttalking ... this ... wwwway ... is ... sssssupposed ... to ... help."

Help make you more of a freak, thought Lars. Good grief, Tage was catching it, too. The way he looked at her, you'd think she'd won the Nobel Prize. A second later, he went down to the cellar and came back with a bottle of wine. He brought out two ceramic goblets she'd made.

"Lars? Would you like to try some wine?"

Wine?

His father would never have let him try wine. His father said too many people were alcoholics. Tage drank wine, but Lars didn't think he was a drunk. "Yes, please." The word "please" shot off into the stratosphere on a high-pitched squeak.

Good grief. No one around here could talk right except Tage. *This is going to be the longest year of my life.*

Some people, like his friend Becka in school, said that in a year he might feel better about his parents. But he'd asked Tage, and Tage had said, *You'll have to see. Things will never be like they used to, Lars.*

One thing about Tage. He didn't tell lies.

And he didn't offer Emily any wine, either. He gave her grape juice.

Lars forgot about the idea of discussing the wolf dog puppies tonight. He would ask Sarah later, when she wasn't so busy looking into Tage's eyes. After dinner, he was going to hang up Cindy Crawford....

TUESDAY MORNING, SARAH bisque-fired some raku pieces she'd made—a decorative pot, a bottleneck vase, two abstract sculptures and a candleholder—and in the afternoon she glazed and fired them. She was about to check the kiln to see if the ware had sintered when Lars appeared with Emily and one of Tage's old lead dogs, Molinka. Lars wore a skijoring belt, and Molinka had been pulling not only him but also a Flexible Flyer carrying Emily.

"Whoa! Whoa, Molinka!"

When she stopped, Emily jumped off the sled and Lars hustled out of his skis. He tied up Molinka, then he and Emily trooped into the lean-to. Part of the back of the shelter was gone because of the cabin falling, but the kilns were still well out of the snow.

Sarah opened her mouth to tell Emily the kiln was hot. She blocked. Grabbing the little girl, she searched for substitutions and remembered not to use them.

"Emily ... you ... can ... get ... bbbbuurned. Ffffire ..." Making sure the child stayed back, Sarah carefully opened the door—a hinged door attached to the kiln's angle-iron frame—to show her the flames and the glowing bricks and pottery inside. Ordinarily, she wouldn't have opened the door in the midst of firing, using peepholes instead, but she wanted Emily to know the kiln was hot.

"Wow!" exclaimed Lars as Sarah checked the ware inside. Everything had turned a dark gray.

"How can you take those out?" Lars scrutinized the pieces she'd made. "Do you have to wait for everything to get cold?"

Once, Sarah would have shrugged. "No." Shutting the door, she forced herself to talk. "Let ... mmmeee .. turn ... up ... the ... burner." She did, opening it all the way, then straightened. "I ... take ... them ... out ... with tongs." *Talk more, Sarah.* "I ... can't ... ttttalk ... ww while ... I'm ... doing ... this. I'll ... explain ... things .. after."

"Here, Emily. Come here." Lars held his sister by her coat and stood back. Sarah checked in several trash cans halfway buried in the floor of the lean-to. What in the world? One was full of wet leaves, and she rustled through them, then moved away and spent a lot of time making sure her hair was tied back with a ponytail holder so it wouldn't get loose, then putting a hat on, too, over all of it.

The trash can bit was weird. Maybe it wasn't just her stutter that was the problem with Sarah.

He started to get bored but thought he should be polite

and pretend to be interested because he wanted her to be sympathetic about the wolf dog puppies. But after a few minutes, he felt like asking, *How long will this take?*

The bricks were turning orange, and Sarah peered through a gap to see what was going on inside.

Lars said, "Can I look?"

She came to hold Emily, and he went to look in the hole. It was really hot in there. The things inside looked different, like the glaze was turning shiny but also like it was coming off the pots. Lars wondered if it was working right. He really didn't want to see Sarah get embarrassed if they turned out ugly. Maybe he should take Emily and leave, so that she could be humiliated in private.

Sarah didn't seem worried. While he came back to hold Emily, Sarah kept checking the peepholes, then closing off some of them with pieces of that weird yellow brick, then adjusting the flue. Flames shot from between the bricks.

Holding his sister tighter, Lars said, "Is everything, uh, all right?"

Sarah nodded happily. Gosh, he never saw her smile like that.

After about a hundred years, she took some big old gloves off the wall and grabbed some iron tongs from a hook. With a glance at Lars, as though to make sure he was holding Emily, she cautiously opened the door.

Lars didn't breathe.

The pots and her weird shapes were all shiny, incredibly shiny. He watched her use tongs to lift one of the weird shapes from the front. It had turned purple and red. She put the thing she'd made in the can with the wet leaves and begun dumping more leaves on it. A cloud of smoke went up in front of her, and Lars couldn't see her till after she shut the lid.

She's nuts! he thought. *Does Tage know his girlfriend is nuts?*

He wasn't sure if he should be worried or relieved when he saw Tage skiing toward them on the road. What would Tage say.... Sarah was setting that beautiful pot in a bunch of pine needles!

But Tage smiled as he took off his skis. He walked around behind the kilns, outside the lean-to, staying out of Sarah's way as he joined Lars and Emily. *Don't you think she's crazy?* Lars wanted to ask.

Sarah turned off the kiln. "I ... put ... them ... in ... those ..." She started turning red and blinking and stuff. *Here we go,* thought Lars. *So much for getting rid of her stutter.* He wondered if she was going to say anything before Christmas.

"Mmmmaterials ... for ... r-r-r-reeeduction. It ... takes ... oxygen ... from ... the ... mmmetals ... in ... the . . . clay ... and ... the ... glazes ... and ... changes ... the ... colors."

"Oh," said Lars. Now that it turned out she knew what she was doing, he wished Tage hadn't shown up. When was he going to have a chance to ask Sarah about the puppies?

He decided it was time to make friends with her. He'd tell her how cool the pots were, and then maybe sometime when Tage wasn't there he could tell her about Anna maybe being pregnant and see what she said.

THAT NIGHT, while Lars was upstairs helping Emily learn English words, Sarah asked Tage, "Could ... I ... sssseeee ... MMMoses?"

"Of course."

They went out together to the isolation kennel. When Moses saw Sarah, he stood tall, watching her through his amber eyes. In the past, he would have jumped up on the gate, wanting her to let him out. Now, he just watched her.

Sarah swallowed. Nothing would ever be the same between the two of them. It was her fault.

She'd felt this way before. Once before. Sometimes an event happened between two individuals and changed everything forever.

"I'll move him to the new pen when his quarantine is over," said Tage. "Speaking of which, do you have another shot tomorrow?"

She made herself say, "Yes. There ... are ... fffive, I ... think. I ... need ... to ... bbbbuy ... a ... tape ... re-re-re-recorder ... too."

Tage guided her out of the kennel and locked up. "And I need to buy Christmas presents. We'll go together."

When they went upstairs, she slipped into her room and shut the door, and Tage knew she was going to practice speech. He had Emily go brush her teeth and put on her pajamas, and then he tucked her in with her reindeer.

"Sarah good-night," she said.

It was a request she'd never made before. Sarah always vanished at Emily's bedtime. He'd forgiven her for Nome and other disappearances. But he hadn't forgotten. That was the problem with Sarah—with Sarah and him. He had a memory. And twenty-three was not a child. "Sarah can't tuck you in now. She's busy." Before Emily could ask for Sarah again, he changed the subject. Knowing he wouldn't get an answer, he nonetheless said, "Is there anything you would like for Christmas? A present?"

"Sarah?"

"Sarah is busy. No Sarah."

Emily said, "Fa-ther." One of the words in her workbook of English words. "You—fa-ther. Sarah. Mo-ther."

"Are we still talking about Christmas?" Tage asked, alarmed.

"Christmas present," said Emily and smiled. "Thank you, *jultomten*."

AT SOME POINT, he realized Sarah wasn't coming out of her room again that night. Resisting, resisting *wanting* her,

Tage went out to see Anna. Seeing Anna reminded him of Lars, that Lars wanted Anna's puppies.

If she's pregnant.

Tage donned aluminum snowshoes, made smaller for running, and took Anna out on the trail to the lake, running with her in the cold and the dark, running past the studio. He resisted going in to look at things Sarah had made, the raku pieces she'd fired the other day.

He felt feverish, almost chilled, and chalked it up to Sarah.

Arthur must have enjoyed watching her work, too, the way she looked with her hair in a messy ponytail, those long undershirts she always wore unbuttoned at the throat, loose over her breasts. In the summers, shorts showed her long legs.

Don't think about it.

Someday, when she was ready, she would turn to him.

Did Arthur think the same thing, Tage?

A distant howling caught his attention. Wolves.

Anna ran on, indifferent, and he ran with her.

Emily wanted Sarah to be her mother. There were things you couldn't explain to a child. One of them was that you could love someone deeply, as much as you could love, and know she loved you the same way, but that it was a love that would be shattered if you tried to make her yours before she had become her own. You definitely couldn't explain all the ways a woman had been used in her life or that love didn't need a storybook ending to be real. You couldn't explain that you tried hard not to resemble another man—and found yourself becoming more like him every day.

Because Sarah needed you.

And you were waiting, waiting till she was seduced.

THE TEACHER CALLED on her to read, and Sarah opened the book and read in her new, slow way. The book was a children's book, *Good Night Moon*. People began tittering, and Sarah said, "I ... have ... to ... r-r-r-read ... sssssslowly. I'm ... llllearning ... not ... to ... sssssssstutter." She left the classroom and went to the ceramics room. Arthur was there, and he kissed her.

She awoke, shuddering. On the lake, she had kissed him; she had initiated it. They had been standing close in the water. Yes, she had kissed *him*.

The morning afterward, Arthur had told her, *It's what you think it is, Sarah. If you think it's wrong, that is the power it will hold over you.* She'd left a few hours later. It was the day she'd learned to leave.

She got out of bed and looked first for the owl. He wasn't there. In the light of a new moon, she fished in the pockets of her parka and then the sweater she'd been wearing earlier that day. She found the carving, the wood Tage had shaped into an image that made her body ache.

She took it back to bed and lay there, not sleeping.

Tage had told her she could wake him anytime. But it had become important not to awaken him, not to need him.

She turned on her light and found the mirror he'd given her and practiced saying difficult words to it. "MMMMMoses." Her nostrils still flared. If she concentrated, she could stop it. Then she could feel how normal felt.

Dog tags jingled in the hall, and there was a knock at her door.

Her heart rushed. "Ccccccome ... in."

Slipping inside, letting Comet in, too, before he shut the door, Tage saw the carving on her mattress. He shivered. The fire in the hearth had died. She was petting Comet, and he said, "You cried out."

Clear white showed around her large brown irises. She

lowered her eyes, and he didn't trust her and wondered how he could ever know her or trust her. If humans didn't judge, how could they protect themselves and their families? Yet he believed in withholding judgment, believed that very little was his to judge. He could only judge what she had told him.

She insisted it was her fault.

He could only judge what had happened between their bodies so recently. Maybe that was more true than words. Seeing and feeling horror and helplessness within her. He portioned out blame to her birth parents. He tried to convince himself that Sarah could change. That she'd already begun to change.

"TTTTage ... I ... wwwwant ... to ... rrrrread ... to ... you. A ... Christmas ... Caaarol."

They had only finished the First Stave on the night he'd read to her. She'd said they should save the rest for the kids. He had said there would be other Christmases.

"Let me build up your fire." He was coming down with something. After he'd built the fire he said, "I'm going to make some *glögg*. Do you want some?"

"I'll help." She drew on some leggings and followed him out of the room. He stopped in his and emerged drawing a worn Norwegian sweater over his head. It struck her because she'd seen him shiver in her room.

Comet came downstairs with them. While Tage pulled *A Christmas Carol* out of the bookcase, she went down into the cellar.

There were things there she hadn't expected.

Arthur was there, and she had to sit down on the stairs. *Try this one, Sarah.* Every night, he'd brought a different bottle down to the lake, at sunset.

Her pulse raced. It raced in terror, terror of seeing. Summer nights drinking wine by the lake, going out in the canoe. A heart necklace. A heart for courage.

"Sarah?"

She jumped.

Tage was behind her on the stairs. His legs surrounded her, held her, comforting as a firing kiln. From where he sat, he reached for a bottle in a nearby rack and withdrew it.

"You're ... ddddrinking ... his ... bbbest ... ww-wwines."

"My wines. And this isn't one of the best." His arm, stretched across her chest, relaxed her and chased the fear away.

"He ... poured ... mmmmeee ... mmmy ... ffffirst ... ggglass ... of ... wwwine ... in ... Lapland."

Tage saw it—the memory. He'd been there. Everyone had been a little shocked, because his family had viewed alcohol askance. Something to be guarded against. But they'd let him have a glass, too.

Shaking inside, both hot and cold, he tried to remember details. How Arthur had treated Sarah. They'd all thought of him as her father. A different kind of father.

Chilled, Tage held her tighter. He didn't want to learn that she hadn't told him everything. He didn't want to find he could think even worse of Arthur. Tage might never have spoken if he hadn't felt feverish. His mouth moved against her hair. "You should have counseling, Sarah. These kinds of things make people mad."

She knew he meant crazy. Sometimes she was afraid for herself, too. "Mmmmaybe."

"Did he ever touch you when you were younger?"

She shuddered. "No. I ... ddddon't ... think ... it ... occurred ... to ... him. Till ... later." *Hold me, Tage.* "You're ... wwwarm."

"Let's have some *glögg*."

They poured the wine in a pan and heated it on the stove. They added raisins, cloves, cinnamon, ginger and blanched almonds, and while it all simmered, Sarah opened *A Christmas Carol*.

"Wwwhen ... SSSScrooge ... awoke ... it ... wwwas ... soooo ... ddddark ... that ... l-l-l-looooking ... out ... of ... '' She blocked.

Tage's arm was around her, in an absent way. He must be impatient. The block was very bad. She couldn't say this word.

Bed. Bed. She tried to stutter through it as she did with other words. Eventually, the word came out. "Bbbbbed ... he ... could ... sssssscarcely ... ddddistinguish ... the ... t-t-t-transparent ... w-w-w-wwwwindow ... ffffrom ... the ... wwwwalls ... of ... his ... chamber.''

She concentrated so hard she didn't notice when Comet lifted his head and trotted out of the room.

"He ... was ... endeavoring ... to ...''

Tage watched her face, listening to the story. Most people spoke at a rate of one hundred and fifty words a minute. To get over her stutter, Sarah was talking at between forty and sixty. It was okay with him. He'd never enjoyed being read to so much.

The only struggle was to keep from interrupting and saying how much he loved her.

"Ttttwelve! ... It ... wwwas ... pppasst ... two ... wwwhen ... he ... wwwent ...''

Lars could smell spice halfway down the stairs. From the bottom step, he heard the faint sound of speech. Without knowing why, he tried to be quiet. In the hall. In the pantry. When he could see in the kitchen door, he was glad he'd made no sound. He felt like he'd walked in on something he shouldn't see.

They were sitting together with their heads close, and Sarah was reading in her slow way. How could anyone listen to it?

"The ... clock ... wwwas ... wrrrrong ... An ... icicle ... mmmmust ... have ... got ... into ... the ... w-w-w-wwworks."

He couldn't see Tage's face because of the way he was sitting, because of his hair, because he was looking at Sarah or the book.

His stomach strangely warm, Lars eased back into the pantry. For a second he remembered how he'd wanted to drive Sarah away, and now he felt ashamed. He really shouldn't try to chase her away when she was such a freak and Tage liked her. Some other guy probably wouldn't be so nice to her about not being able to talk.

Tage really did like her. Why didn't they get married or something?

Back in the library, Lars petted Snutte and Comet.

I'm really hungry. It was why he'd come downstairs.

Okay, I'll make a bunch of noise and go back in.

He cleared his throat loudly. "Hey, Snutte, you're a good boy!"

The sound of reading in the kitchen stopped, and Lars whistled a Christmas tune as he left the library and went through the dining room to the pantry and the kitchen.

Tage checked a pot on the stove while Sarah held her place in the book.

"Hi." His voice cracked. Embarrassed by the sound and the thought of Tage being in love with Sarah the freak, Lars avoided conversation and went to the bread box. He was going to make a huge sandwich. Huge.

Then an idea occurred to him.

You could see Tage was all caught up in her right now. It was the perfect time.

He asked Tage, "Do you know yet if Anna is pregnant?" As he spoke, Lars watched Sarah's face. It was hard to tell what she thought because she wouldn't look up.

"No. I'll get an ultrasound at twenty-one days." Tage ladled some of the stuff from the pot into mugs and set a mug in front of Sarah.

Lars sniffed the spice. *Glögg.*

As though reading his mind, Tage shook his head. Not twice in one night.

Disappointed, Lars opened the refrigerator and began removing everything that looked like it could be put on a sandwich. Mayonnaise, mustard, pickles, tomato, ham, cheese ... Glancing at Sarah, he asked Tage, "How are you going to kill the puppies?"

That got her attention.

"Wwwwhat ..."

Come on, Sarah. You can say it. What puppies?

"P-p-p-p-ppppppuppies?"

Feeling relieved that her stutter was over, Lars took the milk carton and a bottle of Hershey's syrup from the refrigerator. Chocolate milk.

"Some puppies that may not even exist. Moses and Anna." Tage sat beside her again.

Lars felt hopeful. You could see Tage had one thing on his mind. Yep. Sarah was the ticket. Her eyes turned all huge. Perfect.

"If Anna is pregnant, I'll take her for a hysterectomy," said Tage. "An abortion isn't possible. I'd hoped to breed her. I still do. Cross your fingers."

"Cccccouldn't ... sssshe ... have ... the ..."

Puppies. Lars wanted to stomp his foot. Good grief, Tage was patient to listen to her. "Puppies." The word popped out of his mouth before he could stop it, and he thought Tage was going to get up from the table and murder him.

"Don't interrupt. Ever."

Lars got the picture. Don't *ever* interrupt *Sarah.* Okay, he could live with it. He could even live with her being around forever, *if she would just make it so he could keep the wolf dog puppies!* Thinking of it, he said, "Anyhow, they're really called cubs."

Sarah had given up talking, and Tage was really going to kill him.

No, he was still caught up in Sarah, now that they could have conversations. "What would we do with them?"

"You ... bbbbuilt ... that ... bbbbig ... c-c-c-c-cccccompound."

Lars wanted to tell Tage, *Could you please stop looking at her that way? I'm getting embarrassed. There are other people present—me.*

"I don't want a zoo."

"They could be sled dogs," Lars said.

Tage glared.

Sarah blinked at him. "Wwwhy ... not? Don't ... Eskimos ... use ... wwwwolf ... dogs ... to ... ppppull. . . sssssleds?"

"They don't have to set an example for hundreds of clients with children who might think wolf dogs make good pets."

"Yeah, killing puppies makes a much better example," Lars murmured.

"I already said 'no.'" Tage looked at him that way that always made him look down.

Even Sarah shut up, like she didn't want to challenge him, either. But you could see she wasn't finished thinking about it.

Tomorrow, thought Lars. *I'll bring it up again tomorrow.*

Anxious to keep on her good side, he waved his hand at the book. "Don't let me stop you from reading."

He was very surprised then. She drank some *glögg* and opened the book.

"He ... ttttouched ... the ... sssssspring ... of ... his ...

re-re-re-repeater ... to ... correct ... this ... most ..." She was stuck again. It was like a little kid trying to read, like teaching Emily to read, but worse. "P-p-p-p-ppppreposterous ... clock ..."

Oh, good grief, they were holding hands under the table. Did they think he wouldn't notice?

He was going to have to eat somewhere else. That was all there was to it.

WHEN LARS BEGAN to carry his plate out of the kitchen, Tage said, "Where are you taking that?"

"My room."

Tage pictured food particles decomposing under the bed. He stood, picking up his mug and Sarah's to fill them again. "Eat in here. We'll leave you alone."

"Turning in?" Lars asked with a little too much interest.

"No."

An hour later, Tage wondered just how many sandwiches Lars was going to eat. His body ached, and he wanted to go to bed—with Sarah. She'd stopped reading some time ago, and he'd refilled their mugs and found Lars still eating, as though he considered it his duty to empty the refrigerator.

The fire in the living room felt good, anyway. There was a rug on the tile of the inglenook, and Tage and Sarah lay on it with the mugs of *glögg* and he kissed her. Her leg settled between his, and from his back it was so wonderful to see her face above him.

"You're so pretty." Shutting his eyes, he felt her mouth again, felt her tongue sliding between his lips. His mind was careful, confining itself to Sarah. Kissing Sarah. Feeling her breasts brush his chest. Shifting her body where he wanted it. Holding her and feeling her take over.

He heard Lars whistle to Snutte and go up the stairs.

He opened his eyes. Low, he said, "Let's wait a while and go up."

"Okay." Sarah studied his aquamarine eyes. She said out loud something she'd only whispered in the past. "Your ... eyes ... are ... like ... fjords."

His lips curved, and she saw his wolf smile. She kissed it. She drove the things she didn't want to think about from her mind. The *glögg* had relaxed her. She rolled off him and placed her hand over the bulge her body had covered, the distended front of his sweatpants. "I ... love ... you ... Tage."

His arms suddenly held her very close, very hard, and Sarah knew the power of speech.

She'd never told him she loved him before.

IT WAS POSSIBLE TO MAKE love for the first time even though her body had performed the same act many times before, with the same man.

It was okay. There was enough light coming through the windows of the sleeping porch that she could see him, and it was safe to feel. While Tage, with his Iditarod contender's body, lay beneath her, joined to her, while her face felt his heat, while her breasts were close against his chest and his heart, it was possible to set aside the fact that her first lover had been her stepfather Arthur.

For seconds at a time, sometimes a minute or two, it was possible to forget. His voice helped.

"Are you all right, Sarah?"

"Yes."

A comfortable shifting. Excitement and heat. "Still?"

"Yes." Everything steamed. "I feel so close to you." She could barely hear her own voice. But he heard it, she knew.

Lips on her cheeks. "We're so close. So close."

Kissing, moving more, together. All good. Good and simple. *Hold me tighter, Tage. I want to be closer.*

His head went back, and she heard him say her name. The pillow pressed into her face, and she twisted to kiss his shoulder. His skin was so hot. His throat and neck. Oh, that melting and needing. *Stay in me.*

A sound came out of her throat.

He quieted her, held her down on him. "I love you." His hands…

Oh, closer.

A cry flew out, like a bird darting away.

And then there was a whole flock, carrying them both through a tender place.

HE MUST HAVE A FEVER. She squirmed away, too warm, and Tage said he thought he was coming down with something.

She brought him some orange juice, and he drank it in the dark, then sank back into the sheets with her and slipped toward drowsiness. She covered him up, and he remembered that Emily wanted a mother and he wondered how people learned to be parents when they'd never had parents.

He asked Sarah, "Will you ever tell your mother?"

She was still. "No."

The fever washed all over a vague picture of a woman he'd never met and very clear pictures of her grown daughter. At various times, he had watched Sarah's pursuit of Poloma. Once, Poloma had stood up the two of them. In Denver. Just passing through. She'd be there for a layover.

She'd changed her flight and hadn't called.

Tage had taken Sarah for a hundred-dollar meal and three days alpine skiing in Aspen. He'd bought her things and tried to get her a dog, and all the time she hardly met his eyes.

"Only ... the ... pppeople ... I ... care ... about."
Sarah's voice broke into the night. "I ... will ... only ...
tell ... them."

She used to care about her mother. He knew she still
did but that she'd accepted she would never receive her
mother's love or attention. Poloma had cut the cord of
maternal feeling and damaged a child's love. Maybe that
explained what the grown-up child had done.

That ... and Arthur. Sarah had repeated Arthur's lies.
More emerged each day. *Arthur said* ... Sometimes, she
appeared not to notice the dual meanings, not to wonder
at his intentions. She defended. *He encouraged ... me ...
to ... like ... you. He hadn't ... thought ... of ... me ...
and ... him...* ..

You could only stare silently. Smiling faintly over a man
who had encouraged his adult stepdaughter to love a man
of another culture and language, separated from her by an
ocean, and married to someone else.

Yes, he'd left Tage everything.

The awful blur came again, where he couldn't tell what
was what.

He left me Sarah.

TAGE DIDN'T GO BACK to his own bed, just set Sarah's
alarm for five and arranged more logs in her fireplace and
spread an extra blanket over them, while Comet stretched
out on the floor.

In the morning, Tage had a cold, and Emily had it, too.
After breakfast, she threw up; Sarah touched her cheek and
said she had a fever.

Tage drove Lars to the bus stop. Lars had run the dogs
alone that morning, and on the way to the bus, he said,
"Boots is lame. I don't think he should run this weekend."

Tage made a note to check on Boots when he got home.
Lars's first race would be on Lucia Day, December thir-

teenth. Americans didn't celebrate Lucia Day, but Tage thought it would be nice if their family had a celebration. Unfortunately, their household had no girl the right age to play Lucia and wear a crown of candles and bring the others coffee and *lussekatter* in bed.

Well, they'd bake things, anyway. Light candles, decorate the tree, which still sat in its bucket. Go to the races.

The dog, Tage. Lars needs a good solid team.

"I'll pick another dog." Tage had a dog in mind, Yul, but he'd never run him opposite Jedi. He would take them out that afternoon. This morning Sarah had to go get a shot, for the rabies series; he would need to stay home with Emily.

No. Sarah would ask him to reschedule her shot. She didn't go places like the clinic alone. To do so would mean talking to strangers.

"Could I buy the wolf dog cubs from you?"

Tage braked at the highway. He'd heard enough about the wolf dog cubs. "No. I've spent ten years building a business reputation, and no dog of mine is going to give birth to wolf dog cubs. I don't want to hear about it again."

Lars's stricken eyes gazed back at him. Tage knew that for the first time his son had really heard and believed him.

WHEN HE GOT HOME, Sarah had just taken Emily some ginger ale and soda crackers. He asked, "Want me to call the clinic and change your appointment?"

Her head jerked up. "No. I'll ... go. You ... sssstay ... with ... Emily."

Oh, Sarah. She was brave. She would not leave him. Nome would not happen again.

He dozed on his bed with an afghan over him and the door open, in case Emily should call. When he opened his eyes, it was because Sarah had kissed him.

"You're ... wwwarm ... too."

Waking more, he sat up. "I thought I was getting something, but I feel better." He should check on the dogs in the kennels, see what Critter and Lisa had done, then take Lars's dogs out to see for himself how the team performed.

His skin itched, dry and warm, and a patch on his neck sloughed off under his touch. It reminded him of something—a thought he'd had a while back, now forgotten.

Sarah squinted at him. "Are ... you ... all ... right? There's ... a ... sssstorm ... coming. I ... heard ... on ... the ... rrrrradio."

"I'm fine." He kissed her. "I'll meet Lars at the bus." And run the dogs before the weather turned bad.

SARAH HATED THAT Emily was sick, but everything else was wonderful. She'd actually *talked to a stranger* at the clinic. She hadn't substituted words. She'd let herself stutter. She'd corrected a block. For a minute, she'd even made eye contact and talked at the same time.

And she'd told the nurse that she was talking so slowly because she was trying to get over a stutter!

The nurse had said, *Good for you.*

Sarah had felt so good that she'd wanted to go buy Christmas presents for Emily and Lars—she and Tage had planned to—but she contented herself with stopping at a hardware store for a tape recorder.

Now there was one more thing she wanted to try.

When she brought Emily another glass of ginger ale, she said, "I ... can ... rrrread ... to ... you. Slowly."

Emily reached out with her hands for the books on top of the dresser. She wanted *The Night before Christmas.*

Sarah knew she wasn't supposed to rely on the slow speech to get over her stutter. She should try varying it with more normal sounding speech. *The Night before Christmas* had rhymes in it; it was a poem.

I'll try to read a little faster.

She grabbed the pillows from her room, to put behind her on the bed, and sat down with Emily to try to read.

" 'Twas ... the ... night ..." *Before. Before. Before.*

The blankness and shame rushed over her, worse than ever for arriving unexpectedly. *"B-b-b-before* ... Chrrristma—"

"Tage," said Emily.

Her concentration broken, Sarah glanced over at her. Emily's large dark eyes gazed up at her from her flushed face.

"Tage make better," said Emily. "Christmas present."

Sarah closed the book. Emily lacked Tage's patience. Sarah told herself she hadn't failed, but she couldn't make herself believe it. Thinking of things too awful to share with a child, she told Emily, "Tage ... has ... mmm-mmade ... mmme ... bbbbetter."

SEVEN DOGS. Once Tage had realized that he actually had a couple of hours in which to run dogs, he'd forgotten about checking Lars's team and dismissed the common cold trying to kill him. He had harnessed and hitched seven of his beloved. Comet, Molinka and Oz, Jedi and Yul, Boss and Jo. Tage chose a twenty-five mile route, a loop up low hills, over the Whip Lake trestle, and into the Boundary Waters Canoe Area Wilderness.

There was speed and the necessity of not hitting trees. It awoke him, and he was alive again. Running on the hills. Becoming a dog. Snowshoe hares crossed his trail, and the team ignored the distraction. Tage's foot twisted in a hole, and he kept running, stepped on the right runner, pedaled.

Riding the sled over a lake, he watched Oz stumble and regain his footing just as a dark shape materialized beside them. A beaver.

It was why you kept your lead dogs, even when you gave away the others.

They ran on, straight for the trail up the hill and into the woods.

Icy wind in his face. Alive ...

Sarah was good with the dogs, good on a sled and hardy enough to run behind one and keep up. She was a great natural athlete. Now that she was learning not to stutter, maybe she could race.

She would love to race....

He swayed on the sled, feeling sleepy, wishing he'd brought coffee, abruptly wanting to be in bed.

You've got whatever Emily has, Tage.

He hated to be sick.

A night's sleep would fix him.

The trees on every side reminded him of Arthur, and he had the thought again that he was Arthur to Sarah, that he held the power. Then, he remembered her on top of him the night before. No, she was powerful. He wanted the night to come.

There was a right turn ahead, and Tage called, "GEE!" The dogs took it so fast that Jedi almost hit a tree. The sled skidded through the curve like the end of a whip, and Tage's automatic movements on the runners met a watery feeling in his legs and head.

The trail shifted again, and darkness appeared before him, the black bark of a spruce. He didn't really feel the impact.

CHAPTER THIRTEEN

"WHERE IS TAGE?" Lars asked from the doorway.

Sarah glanced up with a start. She'd left her door open so she could hear Emily, who had gone to sleep, and practice talking into her tape recorder at the same time.

"I... ddddon't ... know. He ... mmmet ... you ... at ... the ... bbbus ... didn't ... he?"

Lars shook his head. "I walked. It's snowing. You wouldn't notice, being nice and warm inside the house."

Switching off her tape recorder, Sarah got up. It was snowing all right, hard enough to blow snow horizontally past her window.

"It's a storm," Lars said. "Critter just went home. Where is Tage?"

Tage would never have forgotten to pick up Lars after school. Something must have happened. "Ssssstay up here with Emily, in case she wakes up."

She buttoned her warmest wool sweater and layered on two pairs of socks under her boots and went outside. Had Tage taken the dogsled?

The dome was empty of people. Lars said Critter had gone home, and the other trainer, Lisa, must have left, too. She checked where he stored the sleds. His touring sled was gone.

Outside, the training field was gray. The sky had darkened.

Sarah walked behind the stone kennel building, examining Tage's tracks. He'd taken the forest service road, but his tracks were already fading. The only way to follow him before the snow covered them entirely was by snowmobile.

The wind lifting her hair and sweeping it away, the snow collecting on her clothes, argued with her. Tage could take care of himself in bad weather. Tage was Saami. No one was stronger.

But if he was all right, why hadn't he met Lars at the bus?

There was only one answer. He hadn't been there because he couldn't be. He was in trouble.

LARS MET HER ON the stairs. "Emily has chicken pox."

"What?" Sarah gasped. Rushing past him, she asked, "Have...you...had...them?"

"Yes." Lars trailed after her. When he'd had chicken pox, his mother had given him oatmeal baths.

His mother was dead.

Wanting his mother and trying not to cry, he said quite steadily, "Where's Tage?"

Sarah bent over Emily's bed. Emily was whining and scratching at herself.

"If you scratch, you'll get scars," Lars told her. It was what his mother had told him. His father had gotten sick with chicken pox, too. Peter hadn't had them when he was little.

Sarah looked frantic. She pressed a hand to her face, as though thinking.

"It's no big deal," Lars said, "unless you're an adult. You've had them, haven't you?"

"Yes." Her head flicked nervously from side to side. "I need to go find Tage. He's gone...mmmushing. You need to take care of Emily, Lars. Can you do that? Will you call 911 if you have to? Do you know about that? Do you know this address?"

She must be really worried. She hadn't even stuttered. Lars didn't think he should point that out. "I should go find Tage," he said. "What if he's hurt? Who will drive the dogs back?"

"We'll tether them and come back for them. Emily, Lars ... will ... ttttake ... care ... of ... you. I'll ... cc-come ... bbback ... soon."

Lars followed Sarah out of the room.

"Mmmmake sure she drinks. Ginger ale."

Sarah owned a lot of outdoor gear. She dug through a mountaineering pack in her room. Lars was a little surprised that she'd have a headlamp and all of that, but Tage had once said they'd gone overnight camping together. He'd once said, *Sarah is the kind of woman who could run the Iditarod. She's very strong.*

Watching Sarah pack, it occurred to Lars that maybe she really was the right person to go find Tage. Except that no one should go. In weather like this, you counted on the lost person to build a snow cave and take care of himself.

But why hadn't he come back?

Lars's mother had made an oatmeal bath when he'd had chicken pox. She'd made him cups of rosehip tea. It was hard not to think about these things. Lars really missed her. He thought he missed her more than he ever had.

"Can ... you ... take ... good ... care ... of ... Emily? It's ... vvvery ... important. You'll ... call ... 911 ... That ... is ... the ... emergency ... nnnumber."

9-1-1. Lars knew that.

"I will make her rosehip tea," said Lars, "and oatmeal baths."

He felt his mother's love wash through him, as though she were right there, telling him he was a good boy, telling him she'd help take care of Emily.

But what about Tage?

Questions arose from nowhere and startled him, and he knew he would think about them the whole time Sarah was gone. How would he feel if Tage didn't come back? What would happen to his life without Frey, the Norse god of sunshine?

Maybe he should go instead of Sarah. Lars said, "I bet you can't drive a snowmobile."

"You're ... wrrrong. You ... ssssstay ... with ... Emily. If I'm not ... bbback ... by ... seven ... call ... 911. Mmmake ... sure ... Emily ... has ... ppplenty ... to ... dddrink."

"I should go," said Lars again.

Sarah just shook her head.

And Lars remembered his grandfather holding him while a strange man told him his parents were dead.

This couldn't be worse. It couldn't be worse, so he would take care of Emily and her chicken pox.

THE TRACKS WERE EASY to follow at first. Sarah drove slowly; having an accident wouldn't help anyone. As the color dwindled from the day, she half expected to see the dogs running toward her, Tage behind them. But the tracks went on and on. When she saw the entrance to the Boundary Waters Canoe Area Wilderness, she wondered how long her fuel would last. She couldn't remember what the gauge had read when she started.

Getting off the snowmobile, she signed in, then stared at the posted regulations. Symbols indicated activities that were allowed and those that were forbidden. No snowmobiles, of course, because it was a wilderness area.

Tough.

She was almost out of light, and she was cold. Her fingers would hardly work, and she hadn't found Tage. Something had happened to him.

Readjusting her mask, she climbed on again and drove

past the sign welcoming her to the wilderness area. Tage's trail veered so many times that under the dark skies, in the wind and snow, Sarah could no longer determine compass directions from the angle of the sun. Could he be lost?

He's hurt. He must be hurt.

Squinting at the gas gauge, she slowed the snowmobile. The snow had grown deep, fluffy. She'd never seen such snow in Colorado, snow that piled two feet high on tree limbs. The snowmobile bogged down in the powder. Sarah tried to turn the machine and slowly succeeded. She mustn't run out of gas, but if she did, she had her snow-shoes and an avalanche shovel for digging a snow cave.

Lars ... Emily ... For a moment, she had considered letting Lars come instead of her. Now she knew she'd made the right choice. Lars would take good care of Emily.

The light continued to leave the day.

The snowmobile refused to go farther. Too much snow. It skidded and stopped, and the snow was a wall on either side of her. She turned off the engine. Fear paralyzed her, fear of the volume of snow, fear that so much snow could fall on this hilly trail, that so much snow could fly on the wind, enough snow to suffocate a person.

Tage! If he was really hurt ...

If he'd hurt himself ...

If he couldn't get up, and it snowed on him...

Too much snow. Too much snow.

A familiar feeling, a familiar voice stirred through her. *Go on, Sarah.*

Arthur's voice. She used to like to think Arthur was with her, near her, giving her advice when things were hard. If she kept a void in her memory, he was only wise Arthur, not Arthur who had begun to look at her differently.

When someone loved you and no one ever had, you would give that person anything. When you knew what

would make him so happy and make him stay ...
never leave ... never leave ...

You're becoming a beautiful woman.

No one called her beautiful. She stuttered, and it was
ugly. She was a monster, a ghoul.

*You're becoming a beautiful woman. I understand how
Merlin must have felt about Nimue.*

Nimue had lured Merlin under a rock and buried him
alive. He'd wanted her maidenhead, and she had grown
weary of his attentions. She'd ensnared him by the arts
he'd taught her.

Sarah tightened the straps on her snowshoes. Her feet
were wooden, numb, her fingers stiff and painful. The
snow rose all around her. To straighten and stand alone
was to be weighed down by wind, a wind of quiet yearn-
ings. *I think you'll like this one, Sarah. This wine. I
thought of you when I picked it up. I bought a case....*

You're delectable, Sarah.

His hands guiding hers over clay. Pressing her hands on
the clay. She'd begun to know that it wasn't about clay at
all.

His voice, his face, his eyes, were with her in the snow.
It wasn't the Arthur who had wanted something, who had
wanted her maidenhead. It was the Arthur of wise advice.
Don't call them Lapps. They are Saami.

*Your mother loves you. She's just never seen her stutter
as a strength, only as a weakness.*

Arthur, Arthur, speaking in riddles.

He'd taught her to use the salt kiln. A piece of angle-
iron provided a tray for wet rock salt. When the kiln was
hot, the potter would shove the tray into the slot and twist
it, dropping the sodium chloride into the fire. Arthur had
told her to take a deep breath first. Then shove the angle-iron through the slot and twist it and dash inside the
studio.

But the kiln area was ventilated. And most of the chlorine gas went up the chimney.

Arthur had been an old man.

The snow was supernaturally deep. It wearied her legs to lift the snow-laden platforms, her snowshoes. Powder collected on her parka and gloves.

Look further, Sarah. He needs you.

Tage's tracks were gone, but a post, almost buried, marked the trail. A curve. She lugged her snow-packed legs and shoes along the trail. Trees. They blocked some of the deep snowfall. Beneath would be the loamy soil. A spruce bog. In summer, you couldn't walk here. Too wet. Mosquitoes so thick.

Arthur had taken her out in the canoe. They had gathered wild rice and caught fish.

Look at you, Sarah! You're quite the fisherman.

When she was a little girl, she was safe. She had a friend, and his name was Arthur, and when her mother didn't show up, Arthur sometimes did. Once, he yelled at her mother on the phone. Sarah wasn't supposed to hear. *You're not a mother at all. Someone should take her away from you. You have one treasure in your life, and if you stopped looking in the mirror you could see what it is. Sarah is exquisite. She is so beautiful....*

Her eyes watered, and the water became ice.

The black spruce were other beings. The Saami, Tage had told her, believed that every single thing in nature possessed a soul. These souls knew, as she could not, what was in a brilliant man's heart when he said she was exquisite, she was so beautiful, when he said she mustn't be ashamed and that some stories were old, very old....

There were bluer eyes. Arctic eyes. Tage was so good that he was sunshine. He was so strong....

He was never mortal until she saw him covered in snow.

He was just past the curve, and Sarah almost screamed.

She ran through the powder, snow dragging at her legs, pulling her down, pulling her back, making everything slow and white.

Tage's blood reddened the snow in front of his face, and Sarah knelt in the yielding sea of cold and grabbed clean snow to wipe his cheeks. *Oh!* A stick was embedded in one cheek, twisting his face oddly. His face was not moving, was so still. "Tage." She hugged his body. Snow on him. Snow on his eyelids when she'd arrived. His head felt too cold beneath hers.

She tore off her mitten, and the air burned her fingers. His skin bit her skin with cold, as insulting as death. He hadn't been wearing a mask. His hat lay in the snow beside his head. His skin was scraped and torn, his forehead gashed. And the stick... She was afraid to move it. It didn't matter without a pulse. No pulse.

She didn't know CPR.

She was all alone with him. "Tage." Her hands were in his hair. Magic hair. *You have to be alive.*

Where were his dogs?

Tage moved his head, and she almost vomited because *she'd* moved it, tricking herself, the way she'd once tricked Emily by making her stuffed reindeer appear to move. Playing with the dead. "Tage! Tage! Wake up! Wake up!"

If he was frozen, could she make him melt? The snow had blanketed him. He had died some time ago, perhaps.

What was the kiss of life? Some first-aid trick she'd never learned. These were the woods where the cycles of the season never died, even when Arthur had died.

These were the woods where a kiss could wake a northern prince.

Her tongue touched cold lips, and she remembered that irresistible urge to press one's tongue to cold metal. Wolves of a pack licked the face of their leader. Her tongue felt razor stubble. She remembered the dog smiles of mating, peace with something elemental, as simple and honest as natural desire. Her cheek knew his long eye-lashes, fluttering like insect wings waking in the spring.

Kissing lips, like tilling half-frozen ground. Making his lips warmer with hers. Licking him again. *Hurt leader, we need you. Wake up.*

The movement of his body beneath her didn't surprise her.

She continued her kisses. She kissed him for Lars and Emily. She kissed him for fifteen dogs he owned and for all the dogs that would ever be his. She kissed him for wolves and wolf dogs. She licked his chin.

He said, "Sarah."

Hold him, hold him, make him warm. Talk, because you can. Stutter if you must, because he loves you.

"You hit a tree. I'm here now. You're okay. Don't try to move."

Tage tried to touch his face, and Sarah made sure he didn't find the stick. "No. Keep your hands down. Does anything else hurt?"

His mouth moved, attempting speech. His eyes shut again. Beads of sweat appeared on his forehead. Red now. Faint white spots. Itchy. She knew he was itchy.

There would be fever.

Life. Life.

Sarah checked the back of his head for bleeding. He twitched, resisting. Itchy. She put his hat on him.

Where were the dogs? Where was his sled?

Snow tumbled from the sky.

It brought down night.

Sarah built a cave, and the wind carried fresh powder to thicken the walls. She dug out the door whenever it closed, and she warmed Tage. He itched, covered with chicken pox, and he never spoke after the one word he'd said, her name. When she turned from clearing the door, she switched on her headlamp, and his cheek had bled onto his hair. The stick was gone.

With drinking water and sterile gauze she cleaned the wound, drowning it in betadyne. He tossed restlessly as she held the gauze in place. The cold was all gone from him, replaced by a dry kiln heat that peeled his lips and scorched his sores. Bruises collected beneath the white blisters. When he drank, his eyes watered.

He didn't like to drink. There were chicken pox in his mouth; they reached down his throat as far as her light would show, and they were coated with a thin film of blood from the wound in his cheek.

He didn't make a sound.

She knew he could die without making a sound.

He liked snow against his skin, so she rubbed snow on him. When she lifted his shirt, there were more blisters. She melted snow with her camping stove for drinking water, and she began to hold him whenever he drank. He didn't have to cry for her to know what it was like, that there was fire eating up his insides.

It was rare that her thoughts left their den.

NO ONE COULD DRIVE in this weather, they told Lars.

We'll have an emergency vehicle out as soon as we can.

These people, thought Lars, did not have a clue. Tage was lost in the woods! Lars should have insisted on going himself, not trusted Sarah.

Upstairs, Emily said, "Lars!"

Angry, he hung up the phone and ran up the steps. "What?"

She was crying.

Oatmeal bath, like his mother had made for him. "I'll be back." Frantic, he ran downstairs and got the big box of Quaker Oats out of the cupboard. Should he cook them first? He didn't know. They were instant; he could just dump them in the bath with the hot water.

Where were Tage and Sarah? He was going to call someone else. He would call Becka. Or maybe he could find a number for Critter, Tage's assistant.

He took the big plastic bottle of Canada Dry upstairs for Emily. He might as well leave it up there, he had to refill her cup so often.

When he reached her bedroom, she had thrown up on her bed and her pajamas and was bawling.

"Go in the bathroom," he said. Good grief. He followed her with the oatmeal and dumped half the box in the tub and ran hot water on it. Better save more for later.

She shook her head and cried.

"It will make you stop itching!" If she could just understand. It was so frustrating. "Get in the bathtub," he ordered again and went out. He had to change her sheets. He had to find her clean pajamas.

How could his parents let this happen to him?

How come they died?

How come Tage was lost?

And as he stripped the sheets from Emily's bed, it occurred to him that maybe Tage and Sarah weren't just lost. That day, he'd made fun of Sarah at school to Becka. He'd imitated the way she read.

He felt bad.

He felt very bad.

Tage was his father. Tage really was his father, and he might be dead.

SARAH HEARD SNUFFLING outside the cave. What was it? All they needed was some rabid animal. Did she dare look outside?

What if it was a wolverine? Or even a wolf? Most wild animals were shy, but any rabid animal...

With a hand on Tage's skin, she watched the pocket of darkness beyond the door. Breath and an animal's footsteps. Only a rabid animal would explore in this wind, in this storm. Only a maddened animal.

A black nose sniffed the snow at the cave's window to the world.

Red-and-white fur. A racer's mask and blue eyes.

"Comet!" Sarah caught the lead dog's harness. A chewed-off tug line dragged wet beside him. "Tage, it's Comet."

Tage didn't answer.

She switched on her headlamp and shone it in his face. She saw blue and moved the beam. "Tage ... You ... have ... to ... stay ... awake. I'm ... going ... to ... look ... for ... the ... sled. I won't go far, but I can't be here to ... wwwwake ... you."

Comet wriggled inside the cave and licked Tage's face. "Can ... you ... sssit ... up?"

Gently, she helped him up. He was petting his dog and nodding, as though to say he was fine.

"Just ... sssstay ... awake. I'll ... take ... you ... home."

He drew up his knees, to rest his arms across them.

She kissed the side of his face and began securing her own clothing. Making sure she had her hat and gloves. As soon as she could, she crawled out into the snow. The wind had stopped. She opened her mouth to say Comet's name and blocked.

Comet, come! Horror overwhelmed her.

No, she could talk. Slowly. "CCComet...*come!*"

The dog emerged from the snow cave.

Sarah hesitated. What if she came back and Tage was dead?

In a nightmare, she shone her headlamp on the snow and saw nothing. No sign of tracks. But Comet bounded past her, showing her the way.

LARS BROUGHT SNUTTE into the house, then decided to
bring Anna in, too, from the whelping shed. She was used
to warm places. He would have liked to bring the wolf
inside, but it didn't seem smart. Anna looked pregnant to
him. Not her body—you just couldn't tell about that. But
she seemed...special. Snutte obviously thought so. He kept
sniffing her and wagging his tail.

Tage wouldn't be able to kill Anna's puppies. He just
couldn't.

Lars went to the dome and collected dog treats and toys
for both dogs, then thought to make sure all the sled dogs
had water. He was glad he'd looked because two bowls
were frozen. He fed all the dogs and put their water dishes
in the doghouses. Finally, he went back inside and found
Anna snapping at Snutte in the library.

He had a hard time taking Snutte back outside, but it
was necessary because he was being so obnoxious, both-
ering Anna that way, like a guy who wouldn't get a clue.

"She's having puppies with Moses. What do you expect?" Lars told Snutte as he put him in with the other
sled dogs. The wind howled. Without the lights, he
couldn't have found the Craftsman again. Sarah and Tage
were out in this weather. Tage's father had died on a migration.

It was best not to think of these things but to be very
strong.

In the house, Lars took Anna and the toys and treats
upstairs. Emily still had oatmeal stuck to her from the bath,
but at least she wasn't complaining. He had read to her
until she shut the book and seemed to want to sleep. Then
she'd kept talking about Sarah and *jultomten*, till Lars had
thought he would lose his mind. "Sarah, mo-ther. *Jultomten*, fa-ther. Lars, bro-ther. Emily, sis-ter."

She really didn't get it. Sarah and Tage weren't married,
and now they might even be dead. What would happen to

him and Emily if Tage died? Would they go live with his grandparents?

I don't want to live with them.

His grandfather didn't care about dogs, not the way Tage did. No one in Jokkmokk understood what an important thing it was that Tage had run the Iditarod five times. Lars fantasized about staying alone in the big house, taking over as dog trainer. Someday Tage would come back and say what a good job he'd done....

Petting Anna, Lars remembered.

Dead people never came back.

I shouldn't have been such a jerk about him not being my father. When he comes back, Lars decided, *I'm going to call him Dad and see what he does.*

"Dad" was American. An American way of saying "Father."

But maybe Tage didn't want to be called Dad. He'd never asked to be called that. He'd never wanted to be father to Lars.

Lars hugged Anna, and she kissed him and put her head on his knee.

Thinking of his father who was dead, Lars went to get Peter's troll drum. Maybe he could look for Sarah and Tage. Or maybe he could make magic by beating the drum.

It occurred to him that if he beat the drum until they came back, they would come back alive. And he felt his own father there with him, telling him that it was just the thing to do. To beat the drum and sit with Emily. And wait. *Don't go anywhere, Lars. Just wait. You're a good boy, Lars.*

SARAH HEARD THE DOGS long before she saw them.

They barked and howled, and Comet raced back and forth up the trail, as though saying, *Hurry! Hurry!*

She came upon them near the overturned sled. A few of

the dogs had chewed through their tuglines; and two of them, Boss and Oz, had bite marks on their ears. Comet must have kept them from running away or brought them back to the sled.

The sled was overturned against a tree and buried in a drift. She petted the dogs before she checked the sled. What could she do in the dark, in the terrible wind? What could she do now that she had the dogs and the sled?

What if I can't find the cave again?

She would find it. She had to find it.

With the dogs and the sled.

The dogs were used to running in the dark, but she wasn't used to driving that way. She wasn't used to running dogs without Tage running beside her, saying the commands with her.

Numb with cold and fear, only half able to make out things, she removed the snow hook from the sled and felt her way until she hooked it around a tree. *Now right the sled.* So much snow everywhere. With fumbling fingers, clumsy in gloves, with the wind freezing the feeling from her face, she began sorting out the dogs, untangling their lines.

The thought of not finding the cave kept her company as she lined up the dogs, stumbling in the holes they'd made in the snow. Afraid she wouldn't be able to give commands, she practiced speaking slowly to the dogs. "Hi...Jedi...you...fffurry...guy. Hello...Molinka."

Chicken pox was worse for adults. Why couldn't Tage have gone to bed like a sensible person?

The first time she tried to retie a broken line, it was too short, so she dug through the bag on the sled and found spare tuglines. By the time she was done, she was sure her hands were frostbitten.

When the dogs were ready and panting in the wind,

Sarah wondered if she shouldn't simply pull the sled back to Tage without the dogs, pull it herself.

But she couldn't pull him home. She wasn't as strong as the team.

She stood on the runners, heart pounding. Voice and speech. They'd never been hers to control.

No. They were always hers.

But Tage was the first person who'd ever told her so. If she spoke slowly, if she didn't force sounds, if she let herself stutter easily when she must, she could give the commands she had said so many times with Tage. She would try to hear his voice in the wind. He would say them, too. Their hearts were so close. They spoke at the same time.

And chicken pox was not enough to kill Tage.

She focused her headlamp so it would shine on the snow ahead. Then, she switched it off. The dogs didn't need a lamp.

Most were Iditarod veterans; two were leaders.

Practice talking.

"TTTage ... says ... you ... are ... the ... ssssssmartest ... dogs. ... in ... the ... wwwworld. This ... is ... your ... fffffinest ... hour." In their finest hour, they would choose the path. They had the instincts of wolves. They had the loyalty of dogs. Believing in their souls, in their dog hearts, she gave a sharp whistle, and Comet and Molinka, then all the others, pulled.

The sled lurched.

The dogs ran.

The path they took was fairly straight, but the sled began to creep up into the trees on the right. Knowing it might tip, knowing that the dogs alone couldn't do it, she called in a long slow way, "Hhhaaw over!"

The team moved at her command.

There was a slight left turn ahead, and as it neared, she called, "Hhhaw."

Comet turned. The others followed, and as the sled reached the corner Sarah moved her right foot behind the foot pad, pushing the runners slightly apart. She pulled up on the handle bow, lifting the sled away from the snow, and it cornered easily. Her breath became part of the wind and ice and the night. The trees did not frighten her, even as obstacles. She had stood on these same runners while Tage ran alongside, but it had never felt this fast. She had never trusted so much.

She no longer heard Arthur's voice, but sometimes she heard her own, a little late, the way a stutterer hears. She spoke slowly enough to cover each skip, each delay. "Gee!"

Then she saw a black hole in a hillock of snow.

The cave.

The den.

"Wh—" A block. She stuttered through it, speaking gently as she had been teaching herself. "Wh-whoooaa." Foot brake. Foot brake. *Please stop.* Shit, Comet was going right into that cave.

She stabbed the snow hook around a tree and ran to the hole in the snow, fighting Comet and Molinka and Oz for space.

Tage was still sitting up, reaching for the dogs.

"Are you okay?" Sarah touched him, felt his warmth.

He nodded, still trying to pet Comet.

"The sled's here. You can ride in the basket. Your dogs are going to take you home."

As he eased out of the cave, Molinka climbed over Oz to get to him, to lick him as Comet was licking him. Oz yelped and bit her, and the dogs snarled, erupting in a whirling tangle of lines and tails before Tage growled, *"Cut it out!"*

Sarah unhooked Molinka and hauled her around the others and back into line. As she hitched her to her tug, among the other excited, wriggling dogs, another night came to her. A campfire and sleeping dogs. A man saying softly, seriously, that he really wanted her, that he had wanted her for many years, since she was fourteen and fell through the ice. *If I had reindeer, I would drive them three times around your house.*

His wool pants were soaked, getting wetter in the deep snow from kneeling with his dogs, who were starting to paw the snow and quiver, to growl and snap at the air, getting ready to go berserk if they weren't allowed to run. "If I let you drive," he said, "what does it mean?"

Tage didn't talk to her that way. He always knew the answers. It was fever.

She knelt in the snow beside him. Beside the impatient team, they kissed, and she licked his face briefly, the way she'd awakened him, the way she'd brought him back. Not leaning on her, he stood and walked past his dogs and got in the sled.

While he drank more water from the bottle she held to his lips, he shook with silent agony. The pain sweated from him. He said, "You lost your chance to leave."

She knew it was a threat. That if she left again, he wouldn't have her back. He would find another. Easily.

He had called her his equal, and it felt very strange.

Molinka growled. Jedi began a high-pitched squeal. As she fought the wind back to the sled, the dogs' cries, their hunger to run, pushed her, and every decision was instantaneous.

Glove off, fingers in the pocket of her parka. The carving Tage had made for her was there. She'd always thought that someday she would burn it in her kiln.

But she couldn't burn up what had happened. What she

had done with Arthur would always be. It would always be part of her.

The wood carving was just another substitution. She tossed it away, and the wind caught it, and it disappeared in the night and sparkling ice. She gave it back to the darkness and the long nights. She never saw where it fell, where it vanished in winter.

The real thing, the thing it represented, stayed with her. It was. It just was. Forever.

It didn't change who she was or what was expected of her.

That was what Tage had said. You were expected to be loyal. You did not leave the pack. You cared for them and helped feed them. When they were hurt, you licked their wounds. When those you loved died, you mourned them. You kissed and played and worked.

You kept good rules.

You didn't inhale chlorine gas.

And when you had to be away, when it couldn't be helped, the pack waited for you to come home.

Because they needed you.

In the deep cold, she stepped on the runners of Tage's sled and released the snow hook from the trees and whistled to the dogs.

CHAPTER FOURTEEN

LARS ONLY STOPPED drumming when he heard the sled dogs in the kennel answering the sirens. Help was coming!

Emily sighed in her sleep, and he sprang up from the floor and hurried downstairs with Anna. He yanked open the door, and snow came in, but the wind had stopped blowing quite so much. He could see.

There was the sled and the team.

The emergency vehicles were pulling into the lot. "Tage," he said. Grabbing Anna so she wouldn't run out, he shut the door and shoved his feet into his boots. He left Anna in the house as he went out on the porch, into the snow.

Sarah said, "Lars, where's Emily?"

"Sleeping." He couldn't see Tage in the dark. Tage had been riding in the basket, and now people in uniforms were looking at him. They were all in the way, and Lars couldn't see Tage.

"Is he...dead?"

He hadn't meant to say it out loud.

Sarah was the one to answer. "He's—"

Whatever it was, she couldn't say it, and Lars pushed past her, past the people in uniforms, and there was Tage. All bashed up but obviously alive. He had chicken pox. Lars remembered when his father had gotten chicken pox. Tage seemed worse off, very sick.

He knew to stand back, to let the doctors or whoever they were work.

He thought he should go back to his drum, but Sarah was struggling with the dogs, struggling to put them away. Just as he offered to help, Critter came. She must have arrived with the search-and-rescue people, the people who had come to look for Tage and Sarah in the woods.

Helpless to move, Lars gazed through the snow at the spinning lights on the cars, bad lights, not like Christmas lights.

He felt that it was important to say something to Tage, but he didn't know what. He ran toward the front door. He ran, and inside with the door shut, he cried, remembering what his parents had looked like dead.

"OH... THANKS," Sarah said. She'd run up to see Emily sleeping, then come back down to find Critter taking care of the dogs she herself had hastily tethered.

Critter gathered the harnesses and coiled the gang line as Sarah led the sled dogs into their runs in the compound.

Sarah felt strong and shaky both. She had driven the dogs. She could talk. She would never again doubt that she could say what needed to be said.

Something needed to be said now.

Critter's long gray hair was turning the colors of the Christmas lights on the eaves.

"You found Arthur," said Sarah.

Tage's assistant blinked, then jerked away.

In the drifting flakes, Sarah came closer. Stutterers were good at waiting.

"What?" Critter asked.

"Was...there...a...nnnote? Or...anything?"

"A note?"

There was no note. Sarah felt stupid.

"All right," Critter said. "There was a drawing. It's dumb. I kept it. He was making a life-size representation of Odin, the god. I'm sorry."

He was making a life-size....

The mask was not the last piece he'd made, was not an end in itself. The mask was a Norse god. The mask was not Tragedy.

Everything blurred for Sarah. "I...wwwant...it. It...bbbelonged...to...this...estate. It...is...TTTage's." She'd never spoken to anyone this way. She'd never given opinions, never said the way things were.

"I threw it out. I'm sorry."

"Critter!" someone called. "Get Tage's girlfriend."

Tage's girlfriend. I'm not even a person.

She'd chosen not to be.

When she reached the paramedic standing beside the ambulance, she said, "I'm Sarah."

She thought of what Critter had said, and she was able to get in the ambulance to kiss Tage before they took him away.

Much later, as she wandered back to the house through the crunching snow, she realized that the drawing Critter had found and concealed and kept did not matter. If Arthur had killed himself with the salt kiln, the drawing would have been part of it. More theater. More sign of his cleverness.

I'll never know.

I'll never know.

The door latch of the house where he'd lived clicked under her fingers. Warmth rushed out to her. She stepped inside, greeting the wood. Reindeer fur boots in the corner. Emily's mistletoe over the library arch.

Lars crying at the foot of the steps and looking up, clearly not caring that she was there. Anna looked up, too, expecting her to do something, to make it better. She licked Lars's face as though to say, *Please comfort this boy.*

His tears must be about dead parents, and Sarah could not help.

She was the last person to have anything to say about this. Both of her parents were alive. Neither wanted her. The pain never went away. It never would. And it had nothing to do with Lars.

Sarah sat down beside him on the cool hardwood, the stately steps of what had become, somehow, a family house, very different from when Arthur had lived there. "You ... rrrreally ... helped ... by ... looking ... after ... Emily ... sssso ... well. You ... are ... a ... good ... person ... Lars. Very ... re-re-responsible. Tage . . . will . . . be . . . so . . . ppproud . . . when . . . he . . . learns . . . how . . . well . . . you've . . . done."

He didn't answer.

She asked, "Wwwwould . . . you . . . lllike . . . your . . . grandparents . . . to . . . come . . . for . . . CCChristmas?"

He nodded.

"We ... need ... to ... dddecorate ... the ... tree ... for ... Tage."

The tears stopped. The iron mask that followed was worse. The mask both hid anger and expressed it. Wearing his mask, Lars shrugged.

A pregnant silence was a silence before words. The silence gives birth to truth and real feelings that people usually don't say.

"He's not my father. Fathers are there. Fathers don't go away and pretend you're not their child."

She thought she gasped, but he didn't seem to hear. *Fathers are there.*

He was so right.

Arthur had been her father. Joel Calder was not.

What do you think it was, Sarah?

"Bbbut..." This time, it wasn't a block. The words

were there. She could utter them. She wasn't sure if she should.

Lars had suspicious eyes. His eyes said she would lie to him.

"Tage let his... bbbrother ... be ... your ... father. He knew you would *have* a father. You did have a father."

Does that make it all right, Sarah? What Tage had done wasn't okay. But it was done.

Her eyes hurt, as though the house was too hot, too dry. "I have a father and a ... mother. They ... don't ... care ... about ... mmmee. Yours ... loved ... you. It's ... okay ... if ... you ... love ... Tage. He's ... good. You ... can ... love ... him ... as ... mmuch as you like."

"He doesn't love me!"

The cry of her heart. Neither of her parents, as far as she knew, had ever loved her. Only Arthur had loved her.

She weighed Arthur's brand of love against Tage's supposed indifference to Lars. Lars could be right or wrong. She didn't know who Tage loved, except her. He loved her. But Lars and Emily? He would take care of them forever. He would give them his best.

He would teach them right from wrong and teach them by example.

She did not tell the lies grown-ups tell. She could not bring herself to say, *He loves you,* even if she thought it was true.

She said, "However ... he ... fffeels—you ... can ... live ... with ... it. As ... you ... grow ... you ... find ... it ... matters ... less ... who loves you ..." The slow rhythm of her speech faded into a comfortable naturalness. Calm, she finished, "Than who you love."

She didn't look at his face. He was quiet. And she felt that she'd been given the power of speech for that minute, to say those words.

"Remember that," she told him. "All right?"

"Is Tage going to die?"

She did smile then. "Probably not of chicken pox."

ON THURSDAY MORNING, Tage spoke with Sarah on the phone for the second time in his life. Her voice was different. Slow but smooth.

"I can't come see you till Lars comes home from school," she said. "He'll stay with Emily."

"Is he cooperating with you?"

"Oh, yes!"

"You make me suspicious."

"Everything's fine."

"*Very* suspicious," Tage murmured.

"Do you have more chicken pox?"

"Everywhere possible." The burning inside him was agony. With each breath, each drink of water. He had never been so sick in his life, but he didn't want to mention it. He just wanted her not to leave, not to run away to Sneffels, not to do what she'd done before. "I miss you," he said.

"I'll come after school."

When they hung up, he tried to sleep. There was just pain. The anti-itch cream worked where it could reach. A feverish fog surrounded him. Arthur and Sarah. Lars and Emily. A snow cave with Sarah. She drove dogs now.

She kissed him. He opened his eyes and found time had passed, and his arms reached up to hold her. Holding her, he remembered Nome.

He thought, *You won't leave?*

He never said such things, to anyone. He'd learned long ago that words, even promises, were meaningless in themselves. They could be broken. His wife could fall in love with his brother.

Sarah would not break promises. But she didn't make them, either.

He said, "I love you."

She kissed him for longer, and to him she tasted like a woman who planned to leave.

WHEN SARAH RETURNED home from the hospital, Lars asked her about the tree. "At home, we put it up on Lucia Day," he said. "Does Tage have ornaments?"

Sarah knew he must, somewhere. Emily was dozing, so she told Lars, "Let's ... check ... in ... the ... sssstorage ... in ... the ... dome."

They found the ornaments in the upstairs hall closet. There were not many, not enough for such a big tree.

"We'll ... have ... to ... make ... some," she said. "We ... can ... make ... them ... between ... now ... and ... Lucia ... Day ... and ... there ... will ... be ... plenty."

"Flags!" said Lars. "In Sweden, we hang flags on the tree. I'll make Swedish flags and the flag of the Saami nation."

"Good!" They checked on Emily and headed downstairs to the alcove, to find paper. Then Lars rushed back upstairs to retrieve felt pens from his own art supplies.

Sarah closed her eyes and prayed and planned. She could talk now. And maybe she could really help Tage, help make this Christmas the best it could be. Tomorrow, Emily could help string popcorn or cranberries. She would get Lars to help put up the decorations.

And maybe, just maybe, his grandparents' visit would help him through his grief. It wouldn't be the merriest Christmas of his life. In fact, it was a near certainty that it would be the worst. But she and Tage could make Lars know that there were people who loved him, that he wasn't alone.

Sometimes, Sarah knew, a person had to accept that the people he most wanted weren't available to him. Sometimes a person had to learn to live with great sadness.

But in those times, too, a person could find beauty and joy in unexpected places.

AT DINNERTIME, Sarah let Lars feed Moses. They went into the isolation kennel together, and Lars said, "The wolf dog cubs would make good sled dogs."

"How ... do ... you ... know?" asked Sarah.

Moses's yellow eyes haunted her. She wanted to go in his pen, to pet him. But she wouldn't without Tage there.

"Moses runs fast," Lars said. "And Anna's a gentle dog. Most of the cubs' nature will be determined by the mother."

"Hm," was all Sarah said. Tage was in charge of the dogs here. She wasn't sure Lars should be made responsible, even partly responsible, for a litter of wolf dogs. Like Tage, she wasn't sure the cubs should be born. She changed the subject. "Lars, could you please check on the reindeer, too? And exercise Anna for Tage."

Lars let Anna pull him on his skis, then saw to the reindeer. He hitched one of them, Dasher, to a sled and went for a ride on the lake. When he came back inside, Sarah was making dinner and asked him to look in on Emily. She was awake, and she wanted to be read to, and then she started babbling urgently about Christmas. "Sarah, mo-ther. Tage, fa-ther. Lars, bro-ther. Emily, sister. Christmas present!"

"Well, I'm your brother, and you're my sister, but the rest isn't true."

"Sarah, mo-ther. Christmas present!"

Lars got the picture. Emily sure was confused. He couldn't resist saying, "Did you, uh, ask *jultomten?*"

She nodded emphatically.

And Tage had said yes? Somehow, Lars doubted it. He just hoped Emily wouldn't be too disappointed on Christmas Eve. He hoped she didn't expect Sarah Calder wrapped up and tied with a bow. Sarah wasn't like any mother he'd ever seen. Except now that Tage was gone ... Well, obviously she was in charge. He knew he should do what she told him because it was what Tage would want. And she was interesting to talk with. She listened and—like Tage—she didn't tell lies.

Emily obviously couldn't remember her own mother if she wanted a new one for Christmas.

This Christmas was so different. Lars wasn't looking forward to it. Usually, he wanted *things*. This year, he just wished his parents weren't dead. He wished he had his old life.

Wolf dog puppies, though...

Even wanting Anna's cubs made him feel guilty. It was worse when things felt normal than when they felt bad.

It was bad that life went on and his parents weren't part of it.

At least, his grandparents were coming. Sarah had called them on the phone. Neither of them spoke English very well, so he'd talked to them and they'd promised to come right away. It had made him think about his parents more than ever. He knew that his parents being dead would seem worse when his grandparents were there, but he was still glad they were coming.

And Sarah had said that if his grandparents stayed with Tage and Emily on Saturday, she, Sarah, would take him to the dogsled races on Lake Gegoka.

He believed her.

He believed her because she hadn't said that Tage loved him.

Yes, one thing about Sarah and Tage both: they did not tell lies.

FRIDAY MORNING, CRITTER stayed with Emily while Sarah drove Tage home from the hospital. Karin and Nils-Isak

Nikkinen, his mother and stepfather, would arrive at about dinnertime. They were to be brought from the airport by limo. Sarah had spoken with the limo service herself and made sure they knew that the passengers didn't speak English well.

She told Tage nothing, except, "I feel great that I can talk on the phone."

He squinted at her from the passenger seat. "To me."

"I have talked to *everyone*."

He smiled. "That book worked very fast."

"I ... sssstill ... bbblock ... a ... lot."

He'd seen it happen, and he didn't argue. The blocks were inconsequential. They had lost their power over Sarah, a power to drive her into a shell of noncommunication. Of self-imposed isolation.

He imagined her like a new plant growing.

Her life was beginning anew, and he watched and admired and tried not to think very hard about their relationship. If he thought about it, he saw similarities...between him and Arthur.

IT DROVE SARAH crazy that Emily was awake that afternoon, refusing to nap. When he got home, Tage had gone right to sleep, but Emily was awake and itching and crying, just when Sarah wanted to be thinking, wanted to plan how to greet Tage's parents. He didn't know they were coming, so the only explanation she'd given for moving her things into his room was that she wanted to take care of him. He smiled and said, "Good."

She hid her fears, of making dinner and conversation, of answering the Nikkinens' polite remarks about their friend Arthur.

Tomorrow was Lucia Day, and she'd promised Lars she would make *lussekatter*, which she'd never baked. Every emotion she experienced felt like the fear of speech.

It was all fear of failure.

She wondered if that was why her mother had never taken care of her.

She decided, again, to stop making excuses for Poloma.

She drew an oatmeal bath for Emily and helped her get in and gave her bath toys to play with. For fifteen minutes, Emily would be happy. Then, it would be time to scrub the oatmeal off the tub.

Nervous... Nervous... When would they be here?

TAGE'S PARENTS WORE European clothes, not the Saami costumes so favored by Tage and Lars.

As the limo driver brought in their bags, Sarah hugged the Nikkinens. For half a year, when she was fourteen, she had seen them almost every day.

When Lars embraced them, he seemed to Sarah like a very small child. Every nervous thing she'd felt evaporated. Lars had needed his grandparents. She'd been right to ask them to come. Rather than alienating her, the burst of Swedish with which he spoke to them satisfied her. *Oh, please, help Lars feel better,* she thought. If she had a Christmas wish, it would be that.

"Where is Tage?" Karin asked.

"I'll show you," Lars offered and started up the stairs.

TAGE STARED IN DISBELIEF. His mother bent to embrace him, and he hugged her. He sensed Lars watching and knew how unfair it was that his own mother should be alive and his son's mother dead.

He felt other things, too.

There were things he'd never discussed with his mother and with Nils-Isak. Lars... That he'd let Peter call Lars his son. That he had denied his own biological connection to Lars. It was a conversation that had to happen tonight, despite a fever.

It was Nils-Isak he ended up telling, while his mother and Lars were downstairs with Sarah, seeing about dinner.

He spoke in Swedish, telling his stepfather the truth and hearing the desperation of the words, the confession of past error, of youthful thoughtlessness.

His stepfather smiled a little and said, "You've told Lars?"

"Yes."

Nils-Isak shrugged. "There is only one way to go in life. Forward. You do the best you can. And maybe, for reasons you can't know, this is the best time for him to find out."

It was a comforting thought. It didn't mean it had anything to do with the truth. Tage told his stepfather so.

Nils-Isak said, "Maybe you are more important to him than you know. And right now, however it feels, you are all he has."

In a haze of fever, Tage took the sentiment to his heart and made it a part of him, that he must be the best man he could be, that he must always have hope, because he was all Lars had.

SARAH WENT TO BED at two in the morning, knowing she wouldn't be allowed to sleep tonight. It was Lucia Day, and Lars had planned the festivities, and they did not involve anyone getting a good night's sleep.

It was not part of the plan that Tage would be awake, petting Comet and wanting to talk to her, when she came to bed. "You're sweet," he told Sarah. "I knew you would save my life sometime. My heart knew that sometime I would have chicken pox and you would make sure my parents came from Sweden in time for Lucia."

"Do you want something to drink?"

"I want candles," he said.

"You want ... too ... much. You're ... in the United ... SSStates, and there is no ... Lucia in this house."

"I want *lussekatter*. I want them so much that I smell them in the house."

The smell could not be disguised. Sugar and cinnamon. Fresh baking. *Glögg* simmering on the stove.

"You had no dinner. You have a fever."

"Will you make some *lussekatter?*"

"Maybe tomorrow, for Lucia Day. All right?"

"Read me a story."

In her sweatpants and long-sleeved shirt, pajamas, she went downstairs and found *A Christmas Carol*.

Lars emerged from the kitchen and hissed, "What are you doing?"

"He wants me to read to him."

"It will wreck everything, to have lights on." A moment later, Lars's eyes changed, became calculating. He wore his *gakti*, because, he said, it was a holiday. "After you read to him, ask him if we can keep the wolf dog cubs."

Sarah shook her head. "That is between you two."

She carried the book upstairs, and Tage lay with his eyes closed.

"Are you asleep?"

He didn't answer.

She knew he wasn't asleep.

She climbed back into bed, and he said, "I don't want you to read. Let's leave the lights off instead. It should be dark ... for the candles."

"There ... are ... no ... candles."

"You lie."

Minutes later, the door opened.

Lucia wore a crown of candles. But Lars was so blond he needed none on his head. They shone up from the tray of *lussekatter*, candles set in raku candleholders Sarah had made for Tage. Sugar and spice mingled with the scent of hot coffee and *glögg*.

When Tage sat up, Sarah placed the pillows behind him.

Lars set the tray in his father's lap, and Sarah suddenly recalled her conversation with Lars Wednesday night. Perhaps if they were left alone, things could be said. Maybe Tage would give Lars the reassurance he needed. She climbed from the bed. "I ... should ... check ... on ... Emily."

Lars shifted out of the way, into the shadows, as she went by. This was how he had always done Lucia Day at home, with his parents. He had brought them breakfast in bed. Usually, a girl was supposed to do that, but long ago his mother had said, *Oh, Lars, you're full of light. You make Lucia Day however you like, and your father and I will be so happy.*

What would Tage think? Sharing Lucia with Tage was strange, strange and awful. Lars didn't know what he'd hoped it would be. He knew only that it had frightened him to see Tage bashed up on the sled. He knew only that the people with whom he'd come to live were kind.

Tage said, "Thank you, Lars." He bit into a *lussekat* and told Comet he couldn't have one. Lars didn't mention the *lussekatter* he'd fed Comet and Snutte downstairs. Dogs liked *lussekatter*. Tage asked, "Did you make these?"

"Sarah helped."

Even with chicken pox, Tage looked like Frey, especially in the light.

Lars swallowed. Sarah had said it didn't matter so much if Tage loved him. It mattered whom he, Lars, loved. So, it really wouldn't matter if Tage hurt his feelings now.

And if he spoke in English, it wouldn't have anything to do with his parents. He felt his father the way he had the night he'd played the drum so Sarah and Tage would come home. He felt his father loving him and saying it was just fine, just fine to ask Tage this.

His eyes felt watery because his father, Peter, was there. Because his father thought it was all right to have a life.

To burn candles tonight. And feed *lussekatter* to all the dogs.

"Would it be okay," Lars began, and his voice did not squeak, "if I call you Dad?"

Tage had a coffee cup, one of Sarah's mugs, to his mouth, and he put it on the nightstand. His hand shook like an old person's, not like Frey's. But it was a strong hand. Lars remembered it grabbing him, remembered Tage telling him not to talk to him that way. *I am your father.*

Tage was staring at his own hand, too. He said, "If that...is what you'd like."

That was all.

Tage reached for the coffee cup again.

A strange hurt wrapped around Lars's heart, but he knew it wasn't Tage's fault.

"I feel very honored," said Tage. "By that. To be Dad."

Lars wasn't going to cry in front of Tage. Someday, maybe he'd win the Iditarod in front of Tage, but he wasn't going to cry in front of him. Lars said, "Would you like more coffee..." The last word came out with a crack. "Dad?"

A powerful hand passed him an empty mug. "Thank you."

"It's downstairs. I couldn't carry everything."

"I'll be here when you get back."

"Can I have the wolf dog cubs?"

Lars saw that familiar mouth open to say no. He saw Tage's head move in a way that meant *no.* He knew he'd blown it. "Forget it," he said quickly and rushed out of the room, almost colliding with Sarah.

She smiled at him.

It made him miss his mother and father.

But before he could go downstairs, the door of the sleeping porch opened, and his grandfather stood there. He had the sort of eyebrows that made him look fierce, but his eyes never looked that way.

In Swedish, he asked if Lars had forgotten his grand-parents.

Oh, yes, he had to take coffee and *lussekatter* to every-one.

He smiled at his grandfather and said he would be right back.

BY THREE-THIRTY, the house was quiet. His skin and sore throat kept Tage awake, though Sarah breathed softly beside him, asleep.

If he sat up, he could see the Christmas lights on the kennels.

Lars had strung them two weeks earlier.

This was the first time it had felt like Christmas.

Anna, don't be pregnant.

It was time for Moses to come out of quarantine. He would go into the new pen, and when Anna finished her heat Tage would let her share the place with Moses, if they continued to get along.

He tried to imagine Christmas presents for Sarah and Lars and Emily.

None of them were easy.

Lars wanted wolf dogs.

Emily wanted Sarah to be her mother.

Sarah...

He rolled onto his side to look at her. He'd given her everything she would take. He'd asked her to marry him... Well, in different ways, a few times. It was easy to tell himself she wasn't the same woman he'd known before.

But she was.

Most of all, she was the girl he'd pulled out of the cold lake, with broken ice around her. If he could go back, if he could protect her...

If he had done that, somehow, there would have been no Lars.

No boy to ask if he could call him Dad. No wonderful son who chopped down a maple tree because it blocked his view.

He contemplated the word "No."

He sat up and took the last *lussekat* from the plate on the nightstand. It was a very good dog who resisted such temptation, resisted stealing delicious things. Especially when that dog was usually a thief.

"Comet."

Before Tage could get the word out of his mouth, the *lussekat* was gone.

Comet sat down and smiled, saying, *Thanks. Can we go run now?*

LUCIA DAY PASSED in a blur. Sarah and Nils-Isak took Lars to the races in the morning, and he ran four dogs and came in third of four contenders in his class. When they got home, Nils-Isak and Lars brought in the tree and put it in Tage's tree stand, which was Arthur's old stand. Arthur's ornaments had been given away to his children when he died.

Sarah withstood the discussions of this and the Nikkinens' kind remarks about Arthur. She checked the lights, laid out in strings on the floor. She brought out the popcorn and cranberries she had strung with Emily—in other words, Sarah had strung most of them. Lars hung the paper flags and miniature paper airplanes he had made and colored.

When Sarah slipped into the kitchen to make coffee, she glanced at the window and glimpsed Tage outside. With Moses.

He was leading Moses from the isolation kennel, maybe taking him to his new pen. Was there anything to be said to someone who went out in the snow when he had chicken pox? She grabbed one of his coats from the utility room, put on a pair of his rubber boots, and hurried out onto the back porch.

He and the wolf gazed at her across the gray day.

"You're stupid," said Sarah.

He blushed. "I'll come back to bed soon."

"I'm embarrassed to...know anyone as...sssstupid as you."

The back door opened behind her.

It was Tage's mother, wearing *gakti*, for the holiday.

She began yelling at Tage in one of the languages they shared.

He blushed even more and made some apology and walked away, to take Moses to the wolf compound.

Sarah smiled at his mother, but her body felt tense.

Arthur, such a nice man, Karin had said that morning. *Oh, here is his book.*

Arthur had made a secret. Sarah wished, suddenly, that everyone knew. She wanted someone besides Tage to say that Arthur had violated her. At a minimum, she wanted to be known for herself. Sarah, who sometimes stuttered, who was trying to get over it. Sarah, who had done a dreadful thing. Sarah, who was exactly who she was.

Karin said, "You make sure he comes in." She shook her head in disapproval of Tage's walking around outside with chicken pox.

Sarah went to find him.

He was returning from the wolf compound, looking flushed, his eyes glazed. "I'm going. I'm going back to bed. After I see the tree."

"All right."

"Do you mind my parents?"

"I like them."

Tage kicked the stump of Lars's tree. "Nobody knows, Sarah."

"I ... wish ... they ... did."

He eyed her calmly, as though assessing if she meant it. He didn't look long. Twelve years must have taught him that she never spoke lightly. When he nodded, Sarah knew he would tell his parents the truth. And they would not talk to her about Arthur again.

"I'm … going … to … the … studio," she said. "You and Lars look after Emily. I … want … to … fire … the … salt … ware."

"Can't you wait?"

"You shouldn't be afraid," she said very slowly. "A person would have to deliberately inhale, I think."

The front door opened. Nils-Isak stared out, then shut the door.

Chicken pox made Tage hate touching people and hate to be touched. But he grabbed Sarah. "Please don't go," he said. And he wasn't talking about the salt kiln, and he knew she couldn't know that, which made it safe to say.

Her eyes hunted his, so that he wondered what he hadn't shown her, what she hoped to find. "Okay."

NILS-ISAK SAT BY Tage's window that night and talked about the reindeer. Reindeer were his passion. There were eight reindeer here at Tage's place, and he discussed them from their hooves to the tips of their antlers.

He ran a hand through his gray hair. He switched from Saami, the language for reindeer, to English. Tage knew it was a matter of courtesy. Nils-Isak spoke about Sarah, and Sarah was somewhere in the house, and this was her room, the room she shared with Tage. "Your mother thinks it would be nice if you and Sarah choose to be marry. She asked me to say this."

Tage enjoyed the words. *Be marry.*

He said nothing for a long time.

When he did speak, the words came slowly, like the way Sarah talked. "Arthur … wasn't … good."

Nils-Isak's head jerked in a half circle. His face crumpled strangely, into a mask of tragedy, an ancient face that said there were some human acts beyond explanation. It was a face that mourned finding evil in a friend. A face that wasn't shocked to find it there.

"You knew."

His stepfather resorted to Swedish, for the right words. He had not known. He had refused to wonder. He had liked Arthur.

"It happened later," said Tage. "She was twenty-three."

Nils-Isak's eyes were grave. "I see," he replied in English, being courteous again, "why you don't be marry. She wasn't good, either."

Tage closed his eyes.

No, he thought. *She wasn't. But she wanted very badly to be loved.*

CHAPTER FIFTEEN

SHE FIRED THE SALT kiln four days later. It was December seventeenth, and Tage's chicken pox had crusted over, and he felt better; he helped her stack the kiln. Karin and Nils-Isak were with the children in the house. Nils-Isak had said to him that morning, in Saami, that he hadn't meant to say Sarah wasn't good and he was sorry. He could not understand Arthur. Not at all.

Tage thought of this as he and Sarah worked beneath the lean-to. The ground nearby was thick with snow, yet the kiln gave off enough heat to make the day seem warm. His hands were steady as he held the piece of angle iron and Sarah distributed the sodium chloride inside.

He studied her skin up close. She had very small pores, like a much younger woman. Her mouth seduced him daily.

Without warning, she made a startled movement that spilled rock salt to the flagstone.

She tried to pick it up, then left it.

Helping her up, he said, "I know how to do this. You've told me. You go inside."

She stared and shook her head.

"Go inside," he repeated. "I want to do this. Alone."

She turned and slipped into the old building, the green clapboard in the snow. The door clicked behind her.

He enjoyed the clean air. He walked in the snow. He returned to the kiln and filled his lungs, and he shoved the angle iron through its hole and twisted it.

Now, he thought, *there's chlorine gas out here.*

Had Arthur deliberately inhaled it?

He reached for the studio doorknob and turned it, and went inside. He closed the door.

She was at the sink, crying. Her eyes were wide, her mouth stretched far. "I kissed him! It was my fault. He waited for me to make the first move. I didn't *have* to make it."

He understood her very well, then.

Like his own stepfather, he would never understand Arthur.

For Sarah, it had to be her fault. So that it wouldn't be Arthur's. He was the only parent who had ever loved her.

She didn't weigh very much. She hadn't weighed much with her winter clothes soaked through, when she was fourteen. He carried her into the other room, to the big chair.

"We should watch the clock," he said. "You'll have to check the glazes."

"Yes."

He kissed her hair. He hugged her more tightly. She made him feel desperate. There was nothing he could give her. Even if he could give wolf dogs to Lars and Sarah to Emily, what could he give Sarah?

The one thing he'd thought he'd given her, the truth, he had somehow failed to put securely in her hands.

What she chose to see now was up to her.

Silently, he let himself remember the first night in her room. How she'd told him not to move. How she'd cried.

She'd given *him* the truth. She'd let him see it that night. It didn't matter who had kissed whom first. Arthur could have demanded a kiss with his eyes. *She knows that. She has to know.* She'd certainly known the night she and Tage had made love, the night after she'd told him all about what happened by the lake. Tage had understood as well as he thought he could, because he had become Arthur for that short time. Arthur had wanted Sarah, and she had known. For a woman mortally afraid of even using the phone—let alone of spending her life in a frightening solitude—it had been enough.

Tage breathed the air of the studio. He surrendered the notion that he was anything like Arthur for Sarah. He had let her come and go from his life for twelve years. Now she had the power of language, and it changed things in exactly the way he wanted them to change.

She would argue with him now and tell him he was stupid if he went outside when he had chicken pox.

The thought made him smile. He said, "When we're done out here, let's go Christmas shopping. Lars and Emily want difficult things. I have to find substitutes."

Without knowing what either child wanted, Sarah said very seriously, in her slow way, "Oh, don't give...sssssubstitutes."

"Really?"

"Do you think it's true," she asked, "that it doesn't matter who loves you, that it matters who you love?"

"They both matter."

"You ... should ... tell ... Lars. I ... thought ... I ... was ... right."

But if she thought about Arthur, she must know she was wrong. Dead wrong. When had she said this to Lars—and why?

Before Tage could ask, she said, "It was his fault," and she wasn't talking about Lars. Her eyes watered. She dragged her words out, but they flowed smoothly. "I don't think he killed himself. He *was* that clever. And he wouldn't have had qualms about suicide. But you were right. He wouldn't have done it for regret for wwwhat we did. He..."

Tage waited.

She didn't finish, and it wasn't a block. Just words she would never say.

He wasn't that good.

He wasn't even that good.

THAT AFTERNOON, THEY drove to Bemidji, where the university was; for Christmas shopping. In the toy store in the mall, Sarah spoke to a sales clerk. Speaking to sales clerks was freedom. She said more than she had to. She said, "Oh ... I ... like ... your ... dress. Wwwee ... want ... one ... of ... those ... dolls." An American Girl doll. Immigrants to the United States, like Emily.

"Which one?"

Sarah consulted Tage.

He shrugged.

Sarah hesitated, then chose a doll with dark hair and braids and glasses. "She's so beautiful," she said when the box was in her hands.

"I think *you* want one for Christmas." If he'd believed it, he would have bought her one. Tomorrow, he should take the children out to buy presents for her and for their grandparents. He took the box from her hands and headed for the cash register.

The woman who had helped them with the doll batted her eyes after Tage and murmured, "Who gets *that* for Christmas?"

Grinning, Sarah pointed to herself. "Me ... me ... meeee."

They went to the music store next and bought compact discs for Lars, then a small CD player for his room. They hunted the mall for stocking stuffers.

Loading packages into the 4Runner, Tage said, "I guess it's enough."

"As long as they aren't substitutes."

He steered her to the passenger door and held her as he

unlocked it. His breath steamed close to her hair, whiter than the gray day. "What can I get you?" he said. "What wouldn't be a substitute?"

The smell of his coat was familiar. The feel of his arms, too.

"You."

"You know what you're saying." It was a question.

"Oh, yes."

"I don't mind if you hurt me," Tage claimed. "But there are other people..."

"I have been one of the other people," she said. "I didn't like it."

He kissed her in the cold before he let her in his car.

And when they went home, he walked out to the wolf compound to visit Moses. Thoughtfully, he returned to the whelping shed and brought Anna out and took her to the wolf compound.

She and Moses saw each other through the chain link.

Moses's golden eyes stared. He moved closer, and he seemed older than the creature Sarah had brought to Minnesota weeks before.

Tage let the bitch into the compound, and she and Moses wagged tails and licked faces. Tage went to bring them food and came back and wrestled with right and wrong. Moses had attacked Sarah when she'd tried to keep him away from a bitch in season. Moses wasn't to blame. But if Anna was pregnant and her cubs were born? *You can provide for these animals, Tage. And you will see that they're handled early and socialized properly, and you will never ask them to be what they can't be—house pets.*

Even if the cubs became a gift to Lars, Tage reserved the right to make the rules.

But would Lars follow the rules?

Tage hoped again that Anna wasn't pregnant. The vet had agreed to see her on the morning of Christmas Eve, for an ultrasound. Tage hoped to get her away from here unseen. This decision had to be his, unaffected by the wishes of a child he so wanted to make happy.

Footsteps broke the snow behind him, and when he looked through the chain link Lars stood outside the compound, peering in.

Tage left the compound, going through two gates. He secured two sets of locks. "Sarah said I must tell you that it matters who loves you and whom you love. That both matter." Lars had freckles on his nose. Acne, too.

He had grown taller since coming to Minnesota.

Just days.

"You're going to let Anna have the puppies," said Lars. "Aren't you?"

It wasn't a request. It was an observation. It meant, *I see what you plan.*

"I don't know. It won't mean anything whether I do or don't." He must say this. "When I say 'no,' it is for a reason. 'No' isn't for fun. You tell dogs 'no' sometimes so that they'll be happy." *You tell boys 'no' sometimes for the same reason. Because you don't want their hearts broken, the way Sarah's was broken just a little when Moses turned on her.*

It began to snow.

Lars lifted his chin. "It must be bad to suddenly have children when you never wanted them."

Lars had never asked about this coming Iditarod. If Tage had planned to run. Or if he had ever, for a moment, resented him and Lobsang.

No. This was about the first time, when Lars was born, and Tage had walked away.

A cold inside Tage turned to water, to slush, like ice breaking in springtime. "You're making many wrong assumptions." *Be careful, Tage. Let him have both of you, you and Peter. Let him have all his parents.* "I have never not wanted children," he said tensely. "And it isn't bad to suddenly have you and Emily. It's *good*. It is the single most important thing in my life. The single most important thing."

"More than Sarah?"

"There's room for everyone. But don't feel that I love you less than I do Sarah."

"Why didn't you want me?"

There were only trees to look at. The snow weighed on their branches. No wildlife in sight. *Why didn't you want me?*

"Because I was young and stupid." He felt himself smiling at Lars, but only with his mouth. He knew Lars didn't believe him and didn't understand, and that someday, in twenty years or so, he would figure it out for himself. Lars would say to himself that Peter and Marit had fallen in love while Tage was married to Marit and that it was an unhappy thing and maybe couldn't have been helped.

"You've never lied to me till now," Lars said.

Tage's mouth hurt from this smile. He let the smile die and met his son's eyes. Lars hadn't yet learned that some statements were more insulting than profanity. That some things one shouldn't say to one's father. Lars didn't know it was an insult to call a man a liar.

It didn't matter.

Tage hoped that if he lied, Lars would tell him so.

Fortunately... "I've never lied to you at all."

Christmas Eve

"WHAT, EMILY?" Lars suppressed a sigh. *Why is she following me everywhere today?* Now she'd followed him out to the reindeer corral. Probably, no one knew where she was. They'd all start worrying soon.

"Stomach hurt."

"Here comes Sarah."

Anxiously, Emily turned away.

In the frigid day, Lars waved to Sarah, to let her know Emily was with him. She nodded and went back into the house.

"What's wrong?" said Lars.

Emily lifted her eyes and they watered. "Tage not *jultomten*."

It was what he'd tried to tell her all along. He wanted to say, *So what?*

"You'll get presents anyhow."

She shook her head and burst into tears.

"You're being silly," Lars said, and his voice cracked, annoying him. "You'll get some presents! Tage will give you presents! Who told you he wasn't *jultomten*, anyway?"

"Sarah."

Sarah. Lars decided to deal with the question expediently. "She lied. Well, at least, she was wrong. Tage will be *jultomten* on Christmas Eve only. You'll see. He'll bring you what you want."

Then, suddenly, Lars remembered what Emily wanted. And maybe Sarah *didn't* want it. Or maybe she didn't know.

He knew he should tell Emily that she shouldn't ask for complicated things for Christmas. But if he were six, he knew what he'd be asking for. His parents. Peter and Marit. He would ask to be with them somehow.

Well, she'll find out Santa Claus isn't real.

Lars wondered if he should tell Tage what Emily wanted. Emily said she had told him herself, but with Emily you couldn't always be certain that she'd gotten the message across.

He picked up his little sister. She was really just like a

doll, and most of the time he wanted to give her whatever she asked for. He said, "Let's go have cookies. Sarah made cookies." Like a mother. "Everything will be all right."

Emily seemed to believe him, and he knew he'd better do something, so when she was eating cookies and being with Grandma, who was baking a pie, he went to find Tage.

Tage was leaving the wolf compound with Nils-Isak. And Anna was in the pen. Lars's pulse thrilled. Tage was going to say "yes" about keeping the cubs. He knew it. He knew it because Tage glared at him.

His grandfather put his hand on Tage's shoulder, then walked away, and Tage faced Lars as though to ask what he wanted now.

"Emily is upset about Christmas," said Lars. "She wants something difficult."

"I know all about this."

"Sarah?"

"I know all about this. I'll handle it."

"Are you going to marry Sarah?"

Tage, Lars thought, did not usually look at him quite this way.

"How would you feel if I did?"

"It doesn't matter."

"She would be your stepmother."

Another puzzle piece of Lars's future seemed to fit into place. A father and a stepmother. It hurt that his life had been changed like this. "It's okay," he said.

He was quite surprised. Tage hugged him, and Lars remembered the night the moose had almost trampled them, how hard Tage had held him. He knew why Tage had done that, why Tage had locked his arms around him that way. Because he was Tage's son.

"I love you very much," said Tage. "I will always do the best I can for you, Lars."

His arms were very strong. Lars's eyes started to water, to run like faucets, because here was someone so strong...who would take care of him. Who loved him.

Tage pressed his jaw against Lars's head. He remembered twelve years earlier—Peter offering that he could hold the baby. Lars. "I did tell a lie." The words came out of him, and they were love-inspired words, maybe shaman words. It was no crime against Peter and only justice to Lars to say them. As Sarah would say, no substitutes. For the truth. He pulled back to see Lars's eyes and his tears. "I always wanted you. I *always* wanted you."

Lars wished his father would hug him again, and Tage did. Tage hugged him while he cried and cried, and he knew his father would hug him again that night, that his grandparents would hug him, that there would be a circle of love this Christmas, with him inside.

"I don't care about the cubs!" he said. "You should do what you think is right. Dad."

His father had large hands to rub Lars's hair. His father said, "Oh, I will."

EMILY THREW A TANTRUM after dinner.

Tage had gone outside to check on the dogs, and Sarah had said Emily should put on her pajamas and brush her teeth.

Emily refused.

Lars said, "Santa Claus will come when you're dressed for bed."

That was when she burst into tears, when Nils-Isak said something about it being an exciting day, Christmas Eve, when Karin tried to pick her up and take her upstairs.

"Sarah, do something," Lars said. "Emily, stop it. You're hurting my ears."

Sarah, do something.

Emily had never thrown a tantrum before, and Sarah wasn't certain how to respond. She tried. ''Go ... pput ... on ... your ... pajamas.''

Wailing, Emily shook her head. Only when Sarah picked her up did she stop crying. Feeling strange, wishing she understood Emily better, Sarah carried her through the hall to take her upstairs.

She heard sleigh bells.

Emily stared toward the doorway.

Bad timing, Tage. Sarah carried Emily up the stairs.

Emily began to cry again.

''You can come downstairs after you put on your pajamas and—'' *Brush your teeth.* The block took longer than usual to correct. ''*Bbbbrush* ... your ... teeth.''

In Emily's room, Sarah switched on a lamp and took pajamas from the dresser drawer. More bells.

Curious, she stepped to the window and looked down.

Well, he wasn't driving all eight reindeer, but even three looked pretty good. He waved up at her and blew her a kiss.

Emily sat on the edge of her bed and glared at Sarah.

Sarah tossed the pajamas on the coverlet beside her. ''Ppput ... them ... on.'' She left the room and shut the door and hoped Emily would do as she was told. Sarah didn't know what to do next.

She sat down on the top step.

The bells jingled beneath the window in the upper hall. Where did he plan to stop? *Oh, come on, Emily, get dressed so we can go see Tage being Santa Claus.*

He hadn't looked like any Santa Claus she'd ever seen.

He wore his *gakti* and a hat with four points draping down the back. He looked like something out of *Snipp, Snapp, Snurr and the Reindeer.*

Emily's door opened. She had put on her pajamas.

Sarah pointed to the bathroom.

Emily went.

The bells seemed to go farther away, and Sarah stood and slipped into the center bedroom. She sat in the chair by the window and watched him drive by.

Tree branches creaked. It began to snow.

She could still hear the bells.

Emily came into the room, and Sarah sat her in her lap. Eventually he'd come by again, and they would look together. Then she would take Emily downstairs to meet him.

Emily sniffled.

"Wwwhat is it?" asked Sarah.

"Santa Claus." Emily began to cry.

Sarah winced. Earlier that day, she'd stumbled through the Santa Claus confusion. Emily had been frowning at the fat man in the red suit in one of her books, and Sarah had said one of the clumsy things adults say.

"Tage is coming," Sarah said now. "Santa Claus."

Emily shook her head. "No present."

"I happen to know he will ... bbbring ... you ... a ... pppresent. Or maybe ... ssseveral. And you have a ... pppresent ... for him." Emily had colored a picture, and Sarah had bought a frame for it. As for Lars, he had hand built a mug for Tage, and Sarah had fired it in the reduction kiln.

"No present," said Emily. "No Christmas present." She resumed sobbing.

The bells were coming back.

"Wwwhat ... do ... you ... wwwant ... for Christmas?"

The brown eyes gaped up at Sarah, then disappeared as Emily buried her face in Sarah's sweater.

"What?"

"*Mother*. Sarah mother."

The bells came closer.

Sarah was quiet, stunned to the silence of the winter night. Someone actually wanted her for a mother.

The things reserved for other people, the kind of life reserved for people who had not done what she and Arthur had, seemed within reach. "It's ... up ... to ... Tage. But it makes me feel good, Emily, that you ... wwwant ... mmee ... to ... be ... your ... mmother."

"Tage?" asked Emily. *"Jultomten?"*

"Yes. Look, we can see him."

Scooting Emily off her lap, Sarah stood and turned out the light to see him better. He waved up at them and blew them a kiss. Emily waved back. How many times was he going to drive around the house anyhow?

Sarah gasped.

She knew how many times. Three times. He was going to drive around this house—*her* house—*three* times!

"Oh, Emily!" She rushed to the door. "Come ... dddownstairs!"

Lars and his grandparents were in the living room. None of them got up. In the shadows of the vestibule, Sarah put on her boots. *He drives three times around her tent, and then, if she wants to marry him, she comes out and unhitches his reindeer.*

Lars said, "Emily, come here."

Emily shook her head and held her ground in the vestibule. *"Jultomten."*

Nils-Isak stood.

The bells rang in the night, outside the living-room windows. Then behind the house.

Sarah zipped her coat, glanced around. Everyone had come to the vestibule. They all smiled at her. Lars said, "You look, um, okay. You don't even have to say anything."

The bells came around again.

Outside the front door, they stopped.

Sarah opened the door.

Emily whispered, "Santa Claus."

Sarah turned to her, bent down and said, "I'll be right back. For always. I promise."

Nils-Isak picked up Emily. "Sarah and Tage will be back inside. Let's look at the lights on the tree."

Sarah stepped into the cold, and the door shut behind her.

The porch steps had a light frosting of new snow on them.

Tage waited, holding the first reindeer by a lead rope. "I thought you lived here," he said, smiling.

Sarah glanced at him in the lights from the house, in the Christmas lights from the nearest tree. She kept her distance and walked around the animals with their antlers and their thick fur. She stopped and petted one for a long time, till Tage joined her.

"That's Blitzen," he said. His lips grazed her cheek. Warm like innocence, like a teenager keeping her from freezing to death, a teenager who tried not to look when he took off her wet clothes. Like a man who would always treat her as though there had never been anyone else. For either of them.

The reindeer's fur was thick, soft under her hands.

Tage ducked his head around her and kissed her lips.

"Keep talking," she said.

The stars glimmered and shone among the trees.

He petted the reindeer, too, and then turned his back to the friendly beasts and surveyed the trees and the sky and the kennels.

"This place," he said. "This place is mine. Twenty-four dogs stay in that kennel building, and forty stay in that dome. And sled dogs outside. I've had as many as seventy-nine. I can buy you some, if you like. Those buildings are mine, too." His voice was uncertain, like that of

a young man who needed to make an impression. Sarah
thought it was an act.

"Oh," she said.

"Also, the house. There are four hundred acres here,
and I have a fine son. And a daughter named Emily. I
named her that—I let her name herself that—because it
started with a vowel."

His head turned, and Sarah bit her lip, feeling odd.

Feeling like no one had ever loved her until this moment, when a man admitted he'd allowed the child whose
guardian he was to change her name so the woman he
loved could say it more easily.

"You see," he said. "I love you very much. I've loved
you for a long time. All these things that are mine... If
you marry me, they will be yours, too. And you can wear
the clothes. You will be Saami, like me."

Sarah grinned. Edging away from him, she examined
the reindeer harnesses. They had a gang line, a bit like a
dog team, and they were attached to a sled with a sack on
it. Presents in the bag. There was one hook between the
gang line and the reindeer.

Drawing the sleeve of her parka over her fingers, to
protect her fingers from the metal, Sarah reached down and
unfastened the hook, then looked at Tage.

He held out the lead shank, and she came and took it
from him and tied it to a jagged prominence on a conve-
nient maple stump beside the porch.

His arms were there, grabbing her tight, and they kissed.
She said, slowly, without stuttering, "Mmmerry Christmas."

"Keep talking," he said.

"I love you."

"The Arctic Circle," he told her, "is an imaginary
line."

She kissed him again.

"You are *jultomten*, too, Sarah."

"Okay."

"It is your job to take care of the reindeer, now. I will tell you what to do...."

EMILY STARTED TO FRET.

"They're still out there," Lars said. "Don't worry, Emily. Everything's good." He had begun to regret telling Tage that it was all right to get rid of the wolf cubs. He didn't feel that way any more. It was more important, of course, to have Tage, but the wolf dogs would still make good sled dogs.

There was nothing under the tree that was a dog.

It will be okay, he thought. *That isn't what Christmas is about...getting things.*

The front door latch clicked, and Emily leaped up from the living-room chair where she'd been sitting and sprinted into the vestibule. Lars stayed where he was until he heard Tage speaking to Emily, saying, "Merry Christmas, Emily." Then he got up, too. His grandparents stayed where they were, in the inglenook, and Lars knew somehow that it was because this was a private thing.

His grandparents knew that the four of them, him and Tage and Sarah and Emily, were becoming a family, the way Emily wanted.

He was afraid he was going to cry again, because he remembered his family, his parents. Having a new family was strange. He walked into the vestibule as Tage was on one knee beside Emily, saying, "And here is your mother."

Emily hugged Tage as though he really was Santa Claus and had made all her dreams come true. Lars sat down at the bottom of the stairs. He leaned against the wainscot, and Sarah came and sat nearby, though Emily was already hurrying after her. Sarah, the new present.

Feeling okay, not happy but not awful at the moment either, Lars stretched back on the stairs. He really had never taken advantage of these stairs. There was a banister, for instance. He could race cars down it. The cars would crash very well on the steps....

He felt someone looking at him.

It was Frey, the god of sunshine, smiling.

"Finns det några snälla barn här?"

Words from forever. Words his father Peter had never really said. New words from old. *Jultomten* words. *Are there any nice children here?*

Lars felt hot and strange inside. He missed his parents but he was very glad for Tage. He was glad to go outside onto the porch with his father, and he was glad the tree was gone. Right away, he saw there were no reindeer here. There was another kind of caravan.

Jedi and Yul, who had been the best dogs in that first Saturday race.

And there was a lead dog, too. Anna, with a red bow on her harness. And his team of three was hitched to a gang line pulling Tage's Iditarod sled. And there was a bow on that, too, and bells.

He and Tage went down in the snow, and Lars knelt down so Anna could lick his face.

Tage said, "These are yours."

"Is she pregnant?" asked Lars.

Tage shook his head, hoping Lars wouldn't be too disappointed. "No. She wasn't pregnant, and she's not. But she is intact. Maybe you would like to breed her to Comet."

Crouching in the snow, Lars considered this plan.

His father wasn't a fool. "You would get the pick of the litter."

His father rubbed his head again, and Lars felt like the chosen one. Like Tage's pick.

SKIING WITH THE REINDEER and Emily and Lars in the sled, they went to Mary's Bonnet Lake to gaze at the field of white and the life-size nativity Tage's neighbor had erected. Lars had given Sarah a harmonica and a book entitled *Country and Blues Harmonica for the Musically Hopeless.*

Giving him a look, she rendered a sweet "Silent Night" on the harp, and Tage closed his eyes and let each beautiful note shiver over him. When he opened his eyes, the nativity scene filled his eyes, and there were miracles.

When Sarah had tucked the harmonica in her coat pocket, Nils-Isak lifted his voice in a Swedish carol and then a Saami *yoik.*

In the lights around the lean-to, Lars flattened himself on his back in the snow and spread his arms and legs to make an angel. He got up and showed it to Emily, and she wanted to make an angel, too.

Watching the children, Tage wrapped his arms around Sarah from behind. "There are angels," he said, "and angels."

The night softened to the sounds of runners on snow, of reindeer ankles clicking. Tage's road and the house and the trees around it glowed in Christmas colors, the shimmer made by colored bulbs against cold air and snow freezing to ice.

The house smelled like a place where pies and a Christmas ham had been baked, and wrapping paper littered the living-room floor. Emily's mistletoe dangled over the entrance to the library, where her doll, whom she had named Lucy, sat on a chair, awaiting her return.

The grandparents and the children went to bed.

Sarah kissed her daughter good-night.

Tage told his son to knock on his door if he ever needed to talk, no matter what the hour.

The house fell softly quiet, until only two creatures still

stirred, on the floor beside the fireplace. He gave her the ring he'd had for a long time, since before he'd won the halfway trophy.

"I wish," Sarah said, "you hadn't ... told ... your ... ppparents ... that it is ... fffor ... the clothes."

"My mother appreciated it. That you appreciate your new *gakti*."

"Did ... you ... ttttell ... them?" About Arthur?

"A while ago." It was impossible not to mention it, even on this night. Because Arthur had brought her to Lapland in the first place. And Arthur had brought him to the United States.

Tage stood and drew her to her feet.

He wanted to go to the summit, the place he'd planted a flag. Lars had done a better job of making clear to whom everything belonged, by cutting down the maple tree, but the mistletoe and a thumbtack were a start.

Arthur's raku pots flagged the entrance to the library.

Tage said, "You can change anything in this house that you like. Because it is yours, too. All those dogs, except the dogs that belong to Lars—yours."

"Guess what else," Sarah said. She did not whisper. Or stutter. Her only songs tonight had been carols.

Beneath the mistletoe, he combed her hair with his fingers. "What else, Sarah?"

"Guess what else is mine."

He teased her. You could tease a woman who could talk so well. "My car?"

"Yes. Guess what else."

"The wolf compound. And by the way, Moses is now mine, just as everything I have is now yours."

"Keep guessing," she said.

"You wouldn't mean... Oh, yes, well, that is yours,

too.'' His voice turned a little hoarse, doing a Lars thing. ''Me. That is. I am unquestionably yours, Sarah.''

She put her arms around his neck and kissed him, and Tage kissed her back, knowing who was whose. No one was afraid anymore.

HARLEQUIN WOMEN KNOW ROMANCE WHEN THEY SEE IT.

And they'll see it on **ROMANCE CLASSICS**, the new 24-hour TV channel devoted to romantic movies and original programs like the special **Romantically Speaking—Harlequin™ Goes Prime Time**.

Romantically Speaking—Harlequin™ Goes Prime Time introduces you to many of your favorite romance authors in a program developed exclusively for Harlequin® readers.

Watch for **Romantically Speaking—Harlequin™ Goes Prime Time** beginning in the summer of 1997.

If you're not receiving ROMANCE CLASSICS, call your local cable operator or satellite provider and ask for it today!

ROMANCE CLASSICS

Escape to the network of your dreams.

See Ingrid Bergman and Gregory Peck in *Spellbound* on Romance Classics.

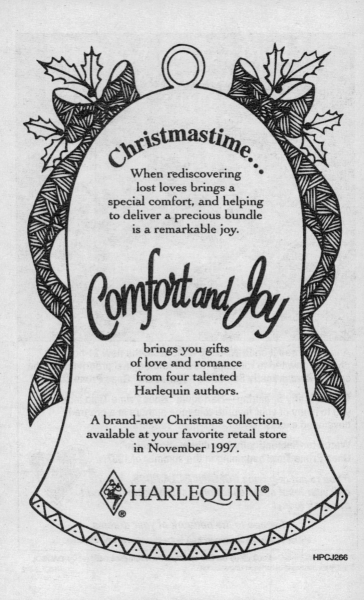

Three wonderful new books from
Judith Arnold

**Sometimes…a man needs help learning to be a dad.
That's what The Daddy School is all about.**

November 1997—*Father Found.* Cynical journalist
Jamie McCoy literally finds a baby on his doorstep. For
the first time in his life he needs help—in the form of
Allison Winslow, who runs The Daddy School. Soon he
simply needs Allison.

December 1997—*Father Christmas.* A hard-bitten cop is hot
on the trail of thieves—who turn out to be the precocious
children of a powerful lawyer. But neglecting his own son
wasn't part of the plan, and it takes the help of Allison's
partner, Molly, to teach him the true meaning of Christmas.

January 1998—*Father of Two* features the precocious
youngsters introduced in *Father Christmas.* Of course
there's romance as well as hijinks as two lawyers butt
heads over cases and kids.

THE DADDY SCHOOL
Don't skip it!

Available wherever Harlequin books are sold.

HARLEQUIN SUPERROMANCE®

9 MONTHS LATER

DECEPTION (#773)
by Morgan Hayes

Shelby Beaumont is madly in love with homicide detective
Johnny Spencer. They've been living together for the past
year, and they've just become engaged. And though Johnny
doesn't know it yet, Shelby's pregnant with his child.

But Johnny's been investigating a possible case of police
corruption. And someone on the force has found out....

Then a bomb is rigged on Johnny's boat. And Johnny's on it....

Find out what happens next in
Deception by Morgan Hayes.

Available January 1998 wherever Harlequin books
are sold.

Every month there's another title from one
of your favorite authors!

October 1997
Romeo in the Rain by Kasey Michaels
When Courtney Blackmun's daughter brought home Mr. Tall,
Dark and Handsome, Courtney wanted to send the young
matchmaker to her room! Of course, that meant the single
New Jersey mom would be left alone with the irresistibly
attractive Adam Richardson....

November 1997
Intrusive Man by Lass Small
Indiana's Hannah Calhoun had enough on her hands taking
care of her young son, and the last thing she needed was a
man complicating things—especially Max Simmons, the
gorgeous cop who had eased himself right into her little boy's
heart...and was making his way into hers.

December 1997
Crazy Like a Fox by Anne Stuart
Moving in with her deceased husband's—*eccentric*—family
in Louisiana meant a whole new life for Margaret Jaffrey and
her nine-year-old daughter. But the beautiful young widow
soon finds herself seduced by the slower pace and the much-
too-attractive cousin-in-law, Peter Andrew Jaffrey....

BORN IN THE USA: Love, marriage—
and the pursuit of family!

Available at your favorite retail outlet!

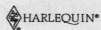 

Look us up on-line at: http://www.romance.net

BUSA3

WELCOME TO *Love Inspired* ™

A brand-new series of contemporary inspirational love stories.

Join men and women as they learn valuable lessons about facing the challenges of today's world and about life, love and faith.

Look for:

Christmas Rose
by Lacey Springer

A Matter of Trust
by Cheryl Wolverton

The Wedding Quilt
by Lenora Worth

Available in retail outlets
in November 1997.

LIFT YOUR SPIRITS AND GLADDEN YOUR HEART with *Love Inspired* ™!

Steeple
Hill™

LI1297